They're Calling You Home

They're Calling You Home

Doug Crandell

SWITCHGRASS BOOKS   NORTHERN ILLINOIS UNIVERSITY PRESS   DeKalb

Library of Congress Cataloging-in-Publication Data
Crandell, Doug.
They're calling you home / Doug Crandell.
p. cm.
ISBN 978-0-87580-676-1 (pbk. : alk. paper) —
ISBN 978-1-60909-032-6 (e-book)
I. Title.
PS3603.R377T47 2012
813'.6—dc23
2012001808

FOR MY MOTHER,

Doris May Crandell

May 5, 1940–October 20, 2011

Acknowledgments

This novel was written at strange times and in weird places. I'd like to thank the interior of my car where large sections of this book were hammered out. Also, airports, especially Hartsfield-Jackson in Atlanta, deserve some thanking. But maybe the most unconventional of all is the chicken coop. For some reason, during the spring, I went through a period of taking my MacBook into the coop and sitting on a bench. To this day, I'm not sure why it occurred to me to write there, but I'd like to thank the hens for their cooing and clucking, which sounded like encouragement.

On the human front, I'd like to acknowledge my agent, Robert Guinsler, for all of his patience and support. My family, Kennedy, Walker and Nancy always help to make me a better person, which I think translates into better writing. Thank you.

For the record, this is a work of fiction, and of course, doesn't represent anything about my family.

Lastly, my mother died the day we chose the cover for the book, and I can't help but think it means something, though I don't know what. Doris May Crandell was the first person I ever knew who actually wrote poems. She read them to me and I realize this may have had a great deal to do with my own writing. I'd like to thank her for my life.

They're Calling You Home

Part One

"Take me to your cinema."

—Mrs. Stephens from

Peeping Tom, 1960

Chapter One

The manila envelope lies on the desk, that damn clasp as gold as a capped incisor. I've picked it up over and over, sometimes shaking the contents, using my fingers to feel the stack of photos inside. I've smelled the envelope, touched it, stared at it, and even prayed over it, although I didn't know what to say, so I just kind of held the thing and meditated, then placed my rosary on top of it and climbed into bed.

Now, I take the envelope, and for the first time in the two weeks since it arrived from the Hartford County, Indiana, Prosecutor's Office, I actually open it some, slide my index finger under the seal and rip it partway open. I'd expected something cold and evil to come rushing out, but nothing happens, and I put it right back where it'd been when the phone rings. It's 2 p.m., and I know it's my agent, the man who will tell me how unlikely selling my novel now is; it's been to every editor who likes him, and some who don't, and this call is his sixth attempt to get me to write about the murders, to give up on being my generation's J. D. Salinger, at least for now. "Come on," he'll say, "true crime books aren't the kiss of death they once were. Your career's not dead yet. And it might help with your own family's . . ." He doesn't finish the thought, and I assume it's because he doesn't want to add, "criminal aspects." At least that's how I finish his sentence in my head.

I gaze at the caller ID and think about not answering, but he'll only hang up and call my cell phone. I grab for the cordless just as the last ring peters out, just before Michael Willet from Willet, Masching and Wallace Literary Reps gets the bland voice mail that only specifies my phone number with the 912 prefix of southern Georgia.

"You screening?" says Michael, his voice stuffy, as always, an allergy sufferer who hates spring even in New York.

"Always," I say, tense, waiting to hear why a certain editor liked *The Lost Children of the Tabernacle*, but couldn't figure out how to market it to the masses. Of all the rejections, every one of them has said something about the book being too dark, the violence and gore too much for a literary press, and the use of language too highbrow for a mass-market publisher.

"So what are you up to?" asks Michael, clearly trying to stifle a full-blown sneezing attack, his breath rapid and shallow, careful, as if he were working with nitroglycerin.

"I've been waiting like a Lab by the phone for your call. You're the master, I'm the dog."

Michael laughs and says, "Don't be so morose. I've got good news."

I know it's not what I'd call good news, but still, I'm eager to make him tell me that *Lost Children* has been blasted away once again. "Oh, you sold my dark and miserable novel?"

"Oh, now, come on. We both knew it would be a tough sell." Michael goes ahead and sneezes, then takes off on one of the common riffs we often explore in these abbreviated calls. "The publishing world is like a big balloon that's losing air, you know that. It's gotta be filled with the heat from best sellers, and then you get a chance, and hopefully one day you'll have the heat to replenish it."

"Okay, so what's the good news?"

"Well, I had lunch with a new editor who's really into true crime. I pitched the book to him, and he liked the part about one of the bodies never being found. Anyway, he wants to see the sample chapter and proposal." Michael pauses, and I can hear him suck on an inhaler, the phone lines ringing optimistically in the background; it's the one sound I like to hear on his end, because I imagine the calls are all good news, a novelist getting her debut scooped up for a cold million.

"What about the novel?" I say, staring again at the envelope, realizing I'm getting closer to having to look at the photos.

"Well, it can't all be good news. I'll e-mail you the feedback, but it's really about the same as the others, you know, they always think you're a great writer, but it's the market. Literary novels are like poetry now. If it was twenty years ago, and I've told you this before, buddy, it would be gobbled up, we'd have an auction on our hands. But people buy novels now that are happy, you know easy to look at, easier to read. Hell, in two more years the big-chain bookstores will only be selling java and iPods, and Kindles with preloaded teenage vampire crap. I'll be out of a job, and you'll have to put me up down there. I'll pick peaches during the day, and you'll kick me out because I won't put peanuts in my Coke."

"Right," I say, watching out the bedroom window as a small alligator creeps up the bank of the swamp, which is fenced off from the apartment complex's rear parking lot. The little ones have been swimming through the drainage culverts and trying to get to the foul-smelling bags of trash in the Dumpster. With six hundred residents, there are always plenty of empty meat packages that draw the young alligators.

"So, Mr. Burke," says Michael, who uses my last name when he wants to make me feel special. "Shall I send this over to the editor, then?"

"Sure," I say, standing up from the desk to get a better view of the alligator as it tries to scale the tall, razor-wired fence. They kill them with a .22, the maintenance crew, that is, three young guys who seem to enjoy it so much, I wonder if they are somehow baiting them.

"Great," says Michael, truly excited. "I'd pitch it by using your writing credentials, of course, the essays and your memoir, but also write up a couple lines about your work with the mentally retarded."

"Going for the sympathy jugular, then, huh?" I say, and add, "Remember, it's people with developmental disabilities, not mentally retarded."

"It's not the same thing?" asks Michael.

"They're not *its*, Mike," I say, taunting him some now. "Yes, sort of, but mentally retarded is an outdated term." I can hear the phone rustle and know I'm losing his interest; he's covered the mouthpiece, and a muffled version of his speech bumbles along in a series of abrupt questions to his assistant. He comes back to me, his voice in the courtesy mode.

"Okay," he says, and I always expect him to add, *our time's up.*

"Thanks, then," I say.

"So I'll send this over to him and add your day job stuff. I think since the killer's mentally . . . I mean, well, you know disabled, he'll see that as an extra credential for writing this book, not to mention your dad's involvement with the law. And since there's still a missing body, that'll be a good hook. One last quick thing, though, have you come up with a new title? This one's too literary. I was thinking about *A Midwest Massacre: The Murder of a Town.* What do you think?"

I can see the gap-toothed smile of the killer, Rodney Finch, in the newspaper articles. When he was arrested, he showed the cops how he shot the family.

"Boom, boom, boom," he said loudly, according to the story, pretending to hold a gun, blasting away. He smiled and acted proud. Rodney only made three boom sounds, not four. He was covered in blood they said, his white T-shirt appearing tie-dyed. He also talked about dinosaurs, and bones, which the police believed to be his hobby, a child's fascination.

I'm about to say the title makes me feel like a *National Enquirer* writer, but Michael has held off his other more important phone calls as long as he can, and he rushes through a good-bye and adds, "You'll see. It'll be an interesting book. Lots of potential. Much love."

Off the phone, I just sit for a while, staring at the photos of Wendy on the shelf above my desk. I've resisted putting up her new school pictures, the ones her mother sends from Indiana every year. Once my daughter started looking more and more like a young woman, I just couldn't stand replacing her fifth- and sixth-grade photos with the ones from ninth and tenth grade. I can't conceive of her now being a junior in high school. It's been almost two years since I've seen her, and while we talk on the phone, I sometimes wonder just how much it really matters to her if I call or not. I've sent her plane tickets, tried to entice her to visit with seats for rap concerts in Atlanta, and call every Sunday and Thursday nights. The idea of the true crime book intrigues me on just one front really; I'll be able to show up in Indiana, at the home Wendy's mother and stepfather live in, Cal is his name, with a fully vetted reason. Before, when I stayed at my mother's and spent the days with Wendy, it always felt like I was in town on work release, or some kind of probationary terms, watched and grilled for details: when, where, and why I was taking Wendy someplace.

She's also the reason I haven't been able to open the crime-scene photos; in addition to killing a fourteen-year-old boy and his two parents, the killer wiped out a girl of seventeen, and in the photos in the *Smallwood Gazette*, Lisa Riley had long, brown hair, just like Wendy's. For a guy whose novel is being rejected in New York because it's considered too dark, violence in the real world, with its mundane manila packaging, frightens me. My brother Ike, a court clerk in Hartford County, Indiana, tried to prepare me. "Have you ever seen crime-scene photos?" he asked, his kids talking in the background, a teenage boy and girl; his daughter looks a great deal like Wendy. I told him no, that I'd never even read a true crime book before. "Well, you should google some, but have a bottle nearby. It took me a couple of years to be able to really look at them."

Ike and the rest of my family didn't like my memoir, or what I wrote about my dad. When it was published, Ike said, "Nice book, asshole. You told the world about our father jacking off outside a tent. Or no, what did you call it, 'pleasing himself'? Nice literary technique. You're a chickenshit even in your choice of words. No one knows who you are in Georgia, but we've got to live this down up here. I've got children, Gabe. You do, too. . . ." It sounded as if his teeth were clenched. "Never mind. It's pointless talking to you about anything," he said, and hung up the phone, but it wasn't the last time he let me know how he felt about it.

I stand up from the desk, walk across the room, and get my bird-watching binoculars, drape them around my neck. The birds in southern Georgia are diverse and profuse. It's Sunday, and I have no place to be until almost midnight, when I'll work the late shift at the group home.

Through the apartment window, I spot a great egret, its long neck like a question mark, standing near the front entrance of the complex, one leg up, as stone-still as a statue. When I first arrived here, just twenty miles from the country's largest swamp, the Okefenokee, the pearly white egrets, with their stillness, tricked me more than once. I'd be out driving over the weekend, Pascal at my side, his long tongue dripping white spit, and notice an egret by the road and believe it was stuffed, put there by kids with nothing else to do.

Through the binoculars the egret finally moves, stepping mechanically toward a black gum tree, wire grass bunched at the base of the trunk. Behind the egret, an entire forest of shadowy cypress sits quietly, the Spanish moss dangling from the limbs, softly moving in the breeze; the edge of the swamp like old blood, clotted and claret, only a temporary stoppage. A car comes thumping into the complex, something from Chevy and the eighties, restored, jacked up, and blasting rap. The egret takes flight, slowly flapping its prehistoric wings as it climbs the cobalt sky, looking every bit the primordial harbinger as it disappears into the black gum forest. On any given day in and around the Okefenokee Swamp, I've watched wood storks, blue herons, and egrets probing for prey along the shoreline. But I admire the white ibises most, their deep russet faces looking as if someone had applied a clown's greasepaint.

I train the binoculars on the forest, but there's no trace of the egret, only the cypress trees, their skeletal limbs scratching the horizon, forming patchworks of arterial lace. I refocus and move the sighting toward the Dumpster, where the three maintenance guys with wispy goatees are laughing as they poke the small alligator with a tree pruner. It's snapping at them, teeth bared. One of the guys grabs the pruner from another, and through the binoculars, I can see he's trying to lop off a foot. I pound on the window, then lift it and make a whooping call to scare them. I'm pleased that the alligator, about the size of a small suitcase, snaps its head back and falls off the wire fencing, scrambling like a spider toward the edge of the lagoon. The maintenance guys punch each other in the arms and slap one another's backs. I quickly call the leasing office and report it, but the young woman on the phone acts as though she's been tranquilized, and I picture her looking through a *Cosmo* as I file my complaint.

I sit back down at the desk and reach for the envelope. Pascal trots into the room from the hall, yawning, his tail slowly wagging. A little shriek exits his tired throat. He licks my hands and then flops down at my feet, instantly asleep.

For some reason, I shake the photos onto the desktop, stalling the inevitability of actually touching them. They're 8 x 10 glossies, and I can't look at them straight on, so I partially cover one: a pair of bare feet sticking out from a doorframe, dark blood over the white toes; clearly the father's, Mr. Riley, a building foreman of forty-five. I slowly move my hand and lift the photo to expose the next one. Mrs. Riley is lying on her back, but most of her head is gone; only the left side is recognizable, the right side blasted off. I can't help thinking of raw hamburger. There's a large white knob sticking out from the base of her neck, and I realize it's most likely her spine. A cold, dark chill runs along my arms, and I feel the impulse to sprint down the stairs. Something gurgles in my stomach, and I try in vain to wake Pascal by lifting my feet. I can't turn the photo over, afraid I'll find one of Lisa Riley; I don't want to see her brown hair sticky with blood, or her pretty face obliterated. I've not taken my brother's advice, either about googling crime-scene photos, or having a bottle of whiskey nearby. The thought sprints into my mind about why Ike would send me these in the first place; after all, he'd told me when the memoir came out that if I ever wrote another book, he'd personally see fit to implant it sideways into my ass. I guess writing about another family's horror is okay with him, and maybe he's even hoping this book will forever obliterate *Leaving Smallwood*. I push back from the desk, and finally my movements wake Pascal. He nuzzles my thigh and whines as I stand and walk to the window. The maintenance workers are still there, and one has a pole with something tied to the end. I use the binoculars again, aware that the death photos are lying obscenely on the desktop; I can feel them there, cold and menacing. Pascal barks once, then again, as he too watches the scene out the window.

One of the skinny guys, wearing a cap with the bill squeezed into an arc, pulls a .22 rifle from the golf cart they ride around in. There's a two-liter of Mountain Dew on the seat, another empty one rolling off the floorboard, as they rig up the pole to fit through the fence, then prop it up to support the raw meat. Pascal growls, and I can make out a naked, taupe chicken hanging from the end of a broom handle, turning like a grotesque mobile in the salty breeze. The three guys skulk toward the Dumpster and light up smokes, puffing and stifling their laughter, hiding behind an open wooden door that surrounds the trash area. Pascal pops his head under my hand, wanting to be reassured. When he was a puppy six years ago, Pascal went through obedience training with a retired cop who lived near the swamp, a man named Pop Grassley. I'd drop Pascal off at Pop's fishing camp and pick him up before going into the group home for the late shift. At first, he seemed skittish after the sessions, but Pop assured me my dog was going to be the better for it. "They're always spooked with guns at first. He's getting used to the firing though."

Pascal and I see the alligator at the same time. It's a little bigger than the one before, and it seems less wary, too: strutting toward the dangling meat, bowlegged and army green, ready to swipe the chicken, swallow, and swim away with a full belly. The three maintenance guys don't spot it right off, as they are apparently engaged in some impromptu rap, bobbing their heads, making gang signs I'm sure they have wrong; they're pale, bony boys not much older than high school, probably working the only type of job they could find here. It's logging, or fast food, or group homes.

I pry the window up, hoping Pascal's steady barking will spook the alligator away before the guys shoot it. He peals off three deep gruff barks, but Pascal's barking only manages to steal the rappers from their rhyme in enough time for them to notice the alligator trying to reach for the bare chicken. The one with the rifle elbows the other two and takes aim. Pascal woofs, then snarls, as I put the binoculars down and yell at them through the screened window. All I can muster is, "Hey, leave it alone!" And my voice even sounds nasally and wimpy to me. If they heard me, they don't seem to care. The alligator can't reach the meat and takes no notice of the young men. The scent of blood and tasty flesh has all but blinded the creature from the danger around it. A dull report pops from the rifle, and an even duller thud echoes as the bullet hits the alligator right between the eyes. It twitches once, then lies still, as the maintenance boys hoot and holler. Pascal goes a little nuts, barking faster, turning circles, growling, his big weepy eyes cutting up at me, wounded, as if to question why I've allowed such a massacre to occur.

"Easy," I say to my dog, even though I'm pissed off and sickened. "It's okay." I dial the leasing office again and get the answering service. I leave a rambling, angry message, saying how I'll call the sheriff if the boys don't stop messing with the alligators. I'm sweaty when I hang up.

The sunlight outside is fading some, the late spring day preparing to close up. In less than an hour the area around the lagoon will be black. For now though, the azaleas in bloom along the chain link fence seem to glow with radiant colors: red and pink, white and deep orange. I walk away from the window and, without ever looking at them, feel for the photos and the envelope as if I'm lost in a haunted house; I shove them back inside by touch only. But the picture of Mrs. Riley's nearly decapitated head falls out, along with a photo of an empty bed. I bend to pick them up as Pascal sniffs the photos, then lays his ears back, looking like a huge yellow rabbit. I've read about the missing body, that of Wes Riley, fourteen, who some speculated was gay, and how he's never been found, but this photo of the empty bed, a poster of some boy band above the headboard, is scarier to me than the bloody ones. There's a soft elongated divot in the mattress, the shape of a thin teenager, and the pillow looks as if it had never come in contact with a sleepy head. I hold the photo, and my hand trembles a little. It's marked State's Exhibit 17. In the newspaper clippings, the ones I've pored over late at night, Rodney Finch was quoted by two Indiana Bureau of Investigation agents as saying, "The boy didn't get no boom," which they've interpreted as meaning Rodney killed him some other way. However, the prosecutor decided to leave Wes Riley's case open and only charge Rodney with the murders of Lisa Riley and Mr. and Mrs. Riley. On the yearly anniversary of the murders, October 31, a reporter from the newspaper usually does a story about how someone working on Indiana's death row overheard Rodney telling another killer where Wes's body is. One year he supposedly said, "We fed it to the pigs," and another year Wes was purportedly sealed in an oil barrel and driven to Lake Michigan, sunk into the cold deep blue waters.

It's gotten dark outside, and I can see flashlight beams bouncing around the Dumpster. A faint trill of laughter cuts through the murk. I shove the photo of poor Mrs. Riley back inside the envelope and decide to keep the picture of Wes's empty bed with me as I lie down. I have to be at the group home in four hours, and I need some rest. As I start to fall asleep, staring at the bed from which Wes Riley disappeared, I calculate he'd be twenty-one now.

Chapter Two

The drive to the Pleasant Hills group home is short but filled with flora. My headlights cut dirty ocher swaths down the country road, illuminating the edges of the long-leaf pine forests, reflecting little beady eyes of raccoons and possums clinging to the bases of massive cypress trunks; mounds of moss turn iridescent then fade to black as the truck rolls along. I coast over the spot that scares me the most, a weak guardrail of flimsy two-by-fours the only thing keeping my old Datsun from careening into a murky swamp, probably the same water that the alligators at my apartment complex were hatched in. Pascal senses my fear and laps the side of my face, then uses his tongue to lick all around his own muzzle. Once over the scary part of the trip, I apply more gas, and before I know it, we're sitting in front of the group home. I cut the headlights quickly so I don't disturb the six men living here. There will be one man awake though, a friend of mine named Ely, who prefers to be called Browder, his last name.

It's midnight on the dot as I try to quietly open the front door. Pascal is as careful as I am, sort of crouching, staying tight to my leg. Cindy—the person I'm relieving—comes out the door. We whisper on the stoop, a kind of rushed and hushed system of updates we've conjured after working together for the last year. Cindy rubs Pascal's ears and speaks softly, "Your man is waiting up for you. He's got a new movie for y'all to watch. Something about the Mafia." I nod, and Pascal licks Cindy's hand as she brushes past me and waves good-bye over her shoulder. She's married and has six kids, all of them boys, looking every bit like genetic stair steps. She's kind and religious, and we've only disagreed once, when she couldn't help herself from saying anybody who voted for a liberal needed to have their heads checked. But to her credit, she added, "Man, that was stupid. I shouldn't have said that here at work. Sorry."

The living room is lit by a floor lamp, and its yellow light gives the space a homey feel, the walls a warm honey glow. The television playing low reminds me of when my daughter was little, and her mother and I tried to keep from making any noise at all, lest Wendy wake up screaming, her little face red and round.

I put my book bag on the sofa just as Browder comes hoofing into the living room, one side of him lagging. He's got a huge grin on his face, his head turned to the side, as Pascal finds his usual spot near the fake fireplace, turning circles before lying down and nuzzling his own tail.

"I got one for you," says Browder, his mild lisp reminiscent of some kind of foreign accent, maybe British; I've never been able to describe it. He's holding a DVD, his slender thumb through the hole in the center to keep from smudging the surface. Browder has long fingers, big feet, and brown hair that seems to never get messed up. He's a movie buff, especially movies that have blood. Browder is referred to as mildly developmentally disabled, which sounds like how a meteorologist might describe a weakening storm front.

"What movie you got there, Browder?" He looks at me with his blinking doe eyes, kind of crab walking in my direction, a slue-footed sidle that gives him the air of a skittish performer.

"It's about the Mauve-e-uh. Capone and his gang."

"Great. Let's pop that baby in and eat some barbecue chips, Ely Browder."

Browder drags himself to the kitchen counter, then comes back with an extralarge bag of Laura Lynn–brand barbecue chips in his weak hand, the same side of his body where the leg tags along. He's smiling so much his missing molar is exposed, a dark empty space at the corner of his red mouth. His parents left him in the hospital shortly after he was born. They were poor pecan farmers with five kids already, and the news that he would need extra help learning didn't figure into their itinerant work; at least that's what his chart reads. The group home has a closet that's been converted into a records room, and before Browder came to live here, I'd sit for hours in there reading about the guys' pasts. There's no better drama than being unwanted.

"Big bag of barbecue," says Browder as he lugs himself to the couch. He flops down beside me and hands me the bag of chips and the DVD.

It's very late when I wake up. Browder has gone to his bedroom, and the TV is off, floor lamp, too. I crawl up from the sofa with a weak headache and start for the front door. My watch reads 4:40 a.m. Outside on the stoop, I take in a deep breath, shove my hands into my jacket pockets, sit down. The scent of a skunk spoor trails over the grassy pasture across the road, and a slightly floral whiff of cape jasmine tries to make it better. There are houses down the road, but the corner of the Pleasant Hills group home property sits on a lonely intersection, where Black Angus graze the hills during the day. At these times, when it's quiet and I'm alone, sitting out in front of a home where six men live who need my help, I try to imagine how strange this life might seem to Wendy. Once, when she visited as an eleven-year-old, she asked me why I was here, why I wasn't in Indiana, and for all my thinking on the subject, I didn't have an answer for her. Instead I said, "Because the fellas here need someone to take care of them." She nodded and was about to say something else, but Roy, one of the men who used to live here, handed her a balloon he'd filled with water, and she lost interest and squealed with delight as he offered his head to bust the water balloon on.

I stand up and stretch, a hoot owl calling in the woods, and a smile on my face. All I have to do is think of her, and it happens; sometimes in the grocery store I'll be doing it and spot my goofy face reflected in the glass doors in the frozen foods aisle. I miss Wendy all the time. The visitation schedule worked until she hit fourteen. So I ramped up our calls, the cards and packages I sent. I drove from Georgia to Indiana to be on her turf, but it was hard to find father-daughter time. I felt as if I were losing her to something I had no control over.

Back inside the house, I can't sleep and turn the television back on, but the infomercials dominate. I shut the TV off and sit down at the desk as Pascal snores. I open the book bag and retrieve the photos. I know I have to look at the photo of Lisa Riley. For a while though, I just stare some more at Wes's empty bed, the way his body indented the sheets; it's as if that's the only trace of him left, like a footprint on a beach, before the tide slowly, incrementally, washes it away.

I take the time to flip again to Mr. Riley's photo and then to Mrs. Riley's, hoping the savagery of her head wounds will brace me for Lisa's photo. I take a deep breath and shove the other photos behind the stack. I stare straight forward at the wall, where a small picture of a lamb nibbling green grass beside three crosses hangs on a nail. I pretend I'm playing Russian roulette and look down quickly at the stack of pictures, only to find a closeup of a gun shell casing with a copper top. It's so magnified that I can read the Winchester brand name on the metal cap.

I look back up at the wall and do it all again. The next photo is a different angle of Mrs. Riley's head, where her blond hair, only half of it, looks like a doll's, a large amount of blasted-away flesh lying next to her on the floor. I perform the game three more times before I look down and see Lisa's crime-scene photo, the picture of her death, before her body had been moved and sent to the morgue. She's lying on the kitchen floor on her back, a nightgown over most of her body, and a large bloodstain at her stomach. I look closer and determine the photo could easily be a fake, something taken by a giddy girlfriend who'd offer to upload it onto Lisa's Facebook page. Maybe it's the Halloween decorations, too; there's a paper skeleton on the refrigerator and several carved pumpkins on the kitchen counter above her head, some of the pulp on a newspaper. While I'm sickened by the images, there's a relief, too, a sense of accomplishment that I've actually made myself look at them. I pull out a notebook from the book bag and begin trying to write descriptions of the crime scene, but nothing sounds right. For more than an hour I fiddle with writing, drifting off at some point, only to be awakened by Browder. I open one squinted eye, my head still on the desktop, to see him standing next to me, a cup of coffee in his hand. He proffers it. "Here, sleepyhead. You were tired last night and in the morning, too."

I take the steaming cup from him. "Thanks so much, Browder," I say, sipping the hot stuff. He makes better coffee than I do, and in some ways it seems ridiculous that I'm the one paid to help him.

"Other guys are getting ready," he says, smelling like the shower: soap and shampoo, the scent of toothpaste. Browder used to work a job at a grocery store, but lost it because he patted a pregnant customer's belly. Now, he just helps the staff do their jobs. "Want me to make the eggs?" he asks. "The menu says eggs, orange juice, and toast."

"I'll help you," I tell Browder. As I stand up, he spots the crime-scene photos.

"That's bad if you ask me," he says, using his thumb to point at the picture of Lisa, but I can tell he's intrigued. I rush to cover them up and stuff the notebook, envelope, and photos in my book bag.

"Don't worry about that," I say, unable to come up with an excuse as to why I have graphic death-scene photos. "Come on. Let's get breakfast made." Browder actually pats me on the back.

After the van comes by to pick up the other five men, my shift is over. Browder can stay by himself, but I sometimes take him with me to run errands, and out to the swamp to bird-watch.

"Hey, you wanna come with me out to the swamp to watch the egrets?"

We're standing in the living room, the house still smelling like burnt toast. The kitchen is clean, and the dishwasher is running. I've checked off my duties and signed the time log.

"Okay," says Browder, smiling.

Out on the back roads, the spring sun is turning everything into a deeper green. There's been a drought for a couple of years in a row, but this spring the rains have filled the creeks and bogs, the rivulets and culverts gurgling with roiling waters, nearly orange from the red clay runoff. I turn the truck west onto the frontage road that runs past a small corner section of the Okefenokee. We park in a ditch and step out into tall wire grass and tangles of kudzu as Pascal leaps from the truck and sniffs in every direction. He's a good dog though, and keeps quiet, knowing if he's well-behaved he'll get a treat later. All around us the chatter of birds breaks the midmorning silence. I wonder if Browder thinks I'm some kind of murderous pervert, a guy with a strange infatuation with death, but then again, he's sort of the same way. Sometimes he says, "Blood and guts," when I ask him what kind of movie he's rented.

As we step down onto a verdant hummock, the last solid part of earth before the swamp waters make everything soggy and unsure, I can see Browder finally needs my help with something. "I'm stuck," he says, indicating that his pant leg is caught on a wild bramble. I walk back to him and slowly unwrap the vine from his leg as he stands still, looking afraid, as if it were a snake. I manage to set him free, and we trudge on, heading for the small back slope of the prominence, where the earth gives way to the briny water, and the dead stumps of the ancient cypress dot the swamp, dragonflies hovering over the surface like little helicopters. When we stop at the familiar spot, Pascal sits by my side at attention, almost as if he were commanded to do so.

I yank an old blanket out of the book bag and flap it into the air. Browder catches the edge and helps spread it out; he's a little breathless from having to drag his bad leg over soft ground. We sit down, and I hand the binoculars first to Browder, who on other trips like this usually ends up spying something dead in the grasses. There are several species of meat-eating plants, ones that snag insects and use them for protein. Browder likes to look through the binoculars at some of these, including the pretty yellow butterworts that use a series of microscopic suction cups to trap flies and gnats. I watch as Browder's mouth opens, teeth bared in a smile, his head moving from side to side like a professional hunter looking for prey.

"What do you see?" I ask, lighting a Salem Light.

"There's a dead something over there," he says, pulling the binoculars from his neck and handing them to me. My mind's so wired, so fully infiltrated by the Rileys' death photos, that I half expect to see a body at the spot where he is pointing. Through the lenses, I get an immediate up-close view of an emerged black gum tree, its old trunk turned up toward the blue sky, looking as if it had been recently charred by fire.

"Over there," says Browder, putting his finger in front of the left lens. I shift to get a better view, dial in some focus, and sure enough, he's spotted a dead deer, or what's left of it. I can see a hindquarter, and the head, but most of the middle is gone. Still, there's an arrow jutting out from under the shoulder. A hunter had shot it poorly, and it must've bounded away from the deep long-leaf pine forests nearby, finding its final resting place among an island of brush and fallen limbs, a patch of white phlox as its marker.

"It's a poor deer," I tell Browder, who squints in the direction of the carcass, his face sad.

"That's too bad," he says, shielding his eyes from the warm, bright sun. "Food for the gators I guess though," he adds, aware that he isn't convincing either one of us.

"Let's just look for some birds," I say, and begin scanning the space, the russet grasses and swaying pines, the limbs of the cypress. I spot a pied-billed grebe moving gracefully across the swamp water. It looks like a duck, but its beak is formed like a chicken's. I hand the binoculars to Browder, but he politely waves them off. The dead deer has quieted him.

Some enormous black vultures circle overhead, no doubt sharing the deer with the alligators. The air is crisp and earthy, as if the water could give sprout to a fabled beanstalk reaching to the sky. I let the binoculars fall to my sternum and sit with Browder quietly for what seems like an hour, as Pascal lies down and suns himself as if we're at the beach, his soft stomach falling and rising in slow, deep breaths, more than an ironic contrast to the rotting deer not fifty yards away. We breathe and watch, and I can feel my heart pounding softly in my ears. All around us, the water teems with buzzing insects, the darting movements of tadpoles and surface flies. Things plop and thud around the banks of the swamp, one after the other, followed by the throaty croaks of bullfrogs. Browder's cheeks redden in the sunlight as he hugs his long legs to his chest. After awhile, he says, "Why do you have them bad pictures, Mr. Gabe?"

"Remember, just call me Gabe," I say. It's a habit in this part of Georgia for people of supposed inferiority to refer to their superiors using the Mr. or Ms. prefix, adding it before a first name. It's always bugged me, but at the group home the woman in charge actually writes goals for the men that require them to talk this way.

"Why?" he asks again.

"It's kind of hard to explain," I say, realizing it's not hard to explain at all, but I don't want to have to hear myself do it. "It's for a book I might write."

"Oh," says Browder, sounding as skeptical as I do.

"You wanna go get some lunch?" I ask him, noticing it's nearly noon. He nods. As we walk back to the truck, Browder's bad leg leaves a fresh furrow in the soft earth.

After a hearty meal of greens and fried chicken, biscuits and black-eyed peas, all of it washed down with ice-cold sweet tea, I drive Browder back to the group home. It's well into midafternoon, and I'm tired, realizing I'll be back at Pleasant Hills in about eight hours. As he crawls out of the truck, Browder smiles and nods. He reaches through the open truck window and pats Pascal's big head. "See ya tonight, then. Got another movie." As he pulls himself up the front steps, I can't help but think of a wounded creature, maybe the deer from the swamp as it tried in vain to keep going after it'd been hurt.

It's dark again, and outside my bedroom window all I can see is the glow of a security light. My mouth is dry. I get out of bed and look at the clock; it's only eight but feels much later. I walk to the small kitchen and fill a glass from the cabinet with water, drink it all down.

My cell phone rings. I assume it'll be the manager at the group home calling me in for an early shift; somebody has probably called in sick. But the number is Michael's, the 212 area code blinking brightly in the dim light; the prefix gives me a brief rush of hope followed by an overwhelming pang of failure. Still, he is calling way past his office hours, which he's only done once before, when it looked like I might get an interview on a morning show in New York City to discuss memoirs with four other writers they called "young memoirists on the verge." It was canceled though after a high-profile memoir was outed as fiction, and everyone in the country tossed it in a donation box at Goodwill, then filed a class action lawsuit.

"Hello," I say, and stand still, not wanting to lose reception. The swamp messes with the cell phone tower signals, something about the high nitrogen content in the soil.

"Good evening, Mr. Burke." Michael sounds as though he's just a wee bit tipsy.

"Hey there, Mr. Agent. To what do I owe this call?"

He begins chuckling and then audibly sips from a drink. "Mmmm," he croons. "I just love a sweet cocktail after a long day of selling writers' souls." I can hear jazz hooting softly in the background. For a guy I've only spent a few hours with in person, I can't explain the closeness I feel for him; maybe it is because he has so much of my life in his hands.

"That's funny," I say. "It's been a great day here, too. The swamp is teeming with drowning agents." He stops laughing and is silent for a second.

"Now, now, now, let's not allow that dark side of yourself to rule. After all, I just got a call from our editor friend who likes true crime."

"Oh yeah?" I say, trying not to assume anything.

"Uh-huh, and as it turns out he acquires other kinds of books, too. He read your memoir. I had it couriered over to him at lunch a few days ago. He loves the book proposal for the Smallwood murders, but, get this," Michael takes his time sipping more of the cocktail, actually swallowing into the phone. "It seems our editor wants to try something different here. He was blown away by your honesty in the memoir."

I can feel my stomach tighten, and a flush of heat runs over my face. "He really liked the part of the book where you're so open about your dad's crimes, and his jail time, and well, you know, afterwards. Anyway, he wants to buy the true crime book, but he also wants to put out the memoir in paperback, to be released at the same time as the true crime book." Michael takes a deep breath. "Oh, man. I'm kinda dizzy. I sold a first novel and a short story collection today, too. Cha-ching," he says.

"Oh," I manage to grunt.

"Is that all you have to say?" whines Michael. "Come on, man. It's like selling two of your books at once. I thought you'd be effing thrilled! It's like the best of both worlds. You get to act literary but sell commercially. It's what you've been dreaming of."

"No, I am pleased, Michael. It's great news. I guess I'm just wondering what this means," I say, thinking primarily of Wendy, my brother Ike, and his kids, and my mother. But like any self-serving writer, I ask about the timeline. "When would he publish them?"

"Next spring, which means you'll need to write the true crime book and have it turned in by August 1. I know you can do it. And he's got some ideas about updating the memoir before it's published in paperback."

"Okay," I say, now leaning on the wall. "I suppose I should get busy."

"Hey, don't sound like you're the one that's been given a death sentence," says Michael, laughing again. "He's really a creative editor, Gabe. He wants readers to see your own family's struggle with crime, and kind of market the two books together. It's all about synchronicity. You know, a platform as the PR babblers say. They're dying up here, and it's the only way to keep books relevant, you know, make the stories play off of each other." I've never confided in Michael about my family's response to the memoir; he doesn't even know my uncle tried to sue me, my dad's brother that we only met once.

"Right, no I get it, Michael, and thank you. It's really good news. I better go. The dog needs to go out."

"Hey," hollers Michael as I'm about to say good-bye. "Don't you even want to know what the deal is?"

It's true, I've neglected to ask about the money. "Yes, right. What's the advance?" I say, making sure to give Michael his time in the spotlight; he's worked hard after all, submitting my novel over and over, even when the rejections kept pouring in. Now he's sold two books for me, and I should allow him some credit.

"Well, let's just say you won't have to keep working with the mentally disabled anymore, well, at least for a little bit anyway. The advance is okay. Twenty grand. It's enough to buy a new car and be broke, or put it in the bank and get to write for a year, if you live cheaply." Michael sounds tired now, the cocktail making his voice crackle some. I imagine him in a modern lounge chair, chrome armrests and soft brown leather. I'm tired now, too, my mind reeling.

"Thank you, Michael. I know you've worked hard for me," I say. "Really. This is going to be an interesting undertaking." He sort of snorts, then grunts, maybe sitting up straighter in the chair, the ice tinkling in his glass.

"You're a hopeless worrier, Mr. Burke," he says, and I detect an irritation in his voice, maybe even a nascent belligerent drunk, and wonder if he ever tells people around the office that I'm the kind of person who sees everything through the negative lens. "Call me if you have any questions. I'll push the contract through as fast as I can. And congratulations." Before I can return the sentiment, Michael hangs up, and all I can do is stare at the cell phone in my hand, my feet planted so solidly in place that it actually hurts to take the first step.

Chapter Three

I wake up often at night, and it's relatively the same each time. I sit straight up in my bed and stare at the wall, a kind of staticy drone inside my head. Now, a day after talking with Michael, I sit in the same position on my bed, legs out before me, and all I can see is my father's face, and what it must've looked like when women caught a glimpse of it through their windows. When I was a kid and he let me ride along on his sales route, hawking cheaply made housewares to farmers' wives, I'd love to look at his face, the way the sun had turned it a rich brown, so much unlike my skin. My mother is fair, but Dad, he was one-eighth Miami Indian, though he only gave my brother, Ike, his pigment. I turn pink near a sixty-watt bulb. On those rides that took us from Smallwood to all over northern Indiana, he seemed as innocent and polite as a man could be.

When I heard of his first arrest, I pretended I was completely confident he hadn't done a thing; in fact, I laughed out loud, but my neck and face felt hot; I tried hard to push back a specific memory of something private and soft shoved into his suit pocket at the Calhouns' house, a family that seemed intimately connected to ours. When he was first arrested, Wendy hadn't been born yet, and her mother and I hadn't been married very long, just a few months. My mom called and said it was all a silly misunderstanding, her voice monotone. Kate got on the line with her, too, and offered her brother as an attorney if it came to that. That night, I called my father up and teased him some, called him a real pervert, and Kate and I went to bed snickering. But then she said, "You look weird, Gabe. Your face looks like you've just run a 10-K. Are you all right?"

Looking back, I can hear the paltry denial in his voice, the sickly way he, too, tried to laugh the whole thing off. I remember when he hung up, and before I walked back into the bedroom where Kate lay in her bra and panties reading a Grisham book, how for a split second I realized the allegations would worsen, that we all stood now before some terrible cliff, things underfoot crumbling, the wind at our backs crowding us toward the edge. I stood in the living room with goose bumps on my arms. I recalled the times I'd been with him on the road in the summer, the way he'd tell me to sit tight, that he'd go see if anyone was home. I'd watch him on a front porch as he knocked, then knocked again, finally going to a window and peeping in. That night Kate told me as we drifted off to sleep, "I wonder what that woman thought he was doing outside her window. I mean, he was just trying to see if someone was home." I didn't say anything, but I could picture him twenty years earlier, cupping his hands around his face, leaning into a long, tall window, back slumped. Once the word spread, after more arrests, I started recalling kids in school snickering. Family secrets are known in your town sometimes before you know them yourself.

I crawl out of bed and whistle for Pascal, but he's dead to the world, snoring on the kitchen floor. I drink a glass of milk and look around the vacant place. I could leave here tomorrow, and all they'd have to do to rerent this apartment is vacuum Pascal's hair off the carpet. I have no table and use only one set of utensils. There are two dog bowls and a leash. I have a shaving kit and toothbrush in the bathroom, and two towels. My clothes are washed once a week, which means I have to wear the same jeans twice some weeks. I've kept it simple not out of some philosophical belief, but rather because I can't seem to muster the energy to buy anything more than some bread and tuna, a few beers.

There's a ratty love seat in the living room, and my desk in the bedroom. I could load everything I own in less than an hour. I walk back to the bedroom and sit down at the desk. The clock reads almost 10 p.m., which means I'll be in the truck soon, driving to Pleasant Hills. I pick up the phone and dial. Ike answers almost immediately, sounding wide-awake, which takes me off guard. I was afraid I'd get his wife, Susana, and she'd be as curt as always, not responding to me, just handing the phone to Ike and mumbling something like, "It's him." She, too, holds me responsible for exposing her kids to their grandfather's perversions.

"Hey, brother," says Ike, and for a moment it's easy to forget that we're no longer all that close. "Something wrong?" he asks, then blows his nose.

"No, not at all. I just thought I'd see what you were up to."

"That doesn't sound like you. If there's one thing I can count on from Gabe, it's that a phone call is never just a phone call." He's taken on the edge I know him for. I try to focus and get out the words. I want to tell him about the book deal, that as it turns out I'm coming home to write that book about the Smallwood Riley murders, but I don't want to mention that the memoir will come out in paperback.

"Really. I just wanted to hear your voice is all," I say.

"Don't be silly," says Ike. He breathes into the phone and surmises I'm calling about my daughter. "Wendy was here yesterday. She and the kids really had a fun time playing Monopoly. I don't know who she looks more like: her mother or my daughter," he adds, keeping things mild.

"Oh, good. I'm glad she gets to visit with her cousins." I can't seem to find a single thing to talk about. "I miss her," I say.

"Well, I'm sure she misses you, too," adds Ike, and he sounds as if he's trying to convince himself of that fact. He yawns, but tries to stifle it. "So, really. Are you okay? What's up, Gabe? Just spit it out."

"I thought I might come up for a visit soon. What do you think?" The other end of the phone is quiet, except for the sound of some muffled television. I imagine the rest of the house cloaked in darkness, silence surrounding their sturdy furniture and the heavy rugs, the brass bookends on the walnut mantel. They keep their home in Smallwood, Indiana, neat, furnished with investments.

"Why come up now?" asks Ike. "I mean, spring break is over. It's not like you'd get to see a lot of Wendy." He covers the mouthpiece, and I can't make out what he says to his wife.

"I know. I thought I'd just visit Mom, and you guys, and maybe Wendy would let me take her out to eat or something."

"You want to drive eleven hours to take your sixteen-year-old daughter out to Shoney's?"

"Hey, I was just telling you I was coming up. You don't have to treat me like you're the parent, Ike. I'll talk to you later," I say, and hang up.

I immediately feel guilty and think about calling him back, but Susana will have told him to ignore it, or maybe she'll pick up the phone herself and tell me off, just like she did when the memoir came out. Instead, I jump in the shower and blast the hot water, standing underneath the strong spray, allowing my skin to redden. In the shower, I can't help but mull things over. I can see myself leaving Smallwood nearly seven years ago. I had snuck into

Wendy's bedroom and kissed her warm little forehead. She'd had a cold, a small fever, and the smell of vapor rub and the two-day-old shampoo in her fine hair filled my nose. For a long time, I just sat there watching her, and for the briefest of moments I thought of taking her with me, but even I knew Kate would be the one to raise her, give her resilience, teach her about the effort it takes to make life positive, keep your heart open. Pushing back her bangs, covering her bare feet, making sure heat was coming out of her room vent, I hated myself so much, but nothing, not even my child's pain, could keep me there, and I closed her door and left. It's an image I'll never be able to forget, one I shouldn't be excused of. I'd told myself it was just a trip to clear my head, but by then Kate and I weren't even sleeping in the same bed anymore. It's hard to admit to cowardice.

Writing the memoir had made me solemn. Dad's crimes were the talk of Smallwood, and like a traitor I left them to deal with it alone. Early on when I'd first gotten to Georgia, I saw a Catholic priest in Waycross at Saint Joseph Church. He counseled me for nearly two months and urged me to return to my hometown. "Go now. See your daughter. Set up a visitation schedule and stick to it." Kate and I worked it out ourselves and submitted our own plan in the divorce. It all went better than I'd expected; I saw Wendy once a month, driving up to Indiana, or meeting Kate somewhere in between and spending the weekend in Nashville or Louisville. On school breaks Wendy was eager to visit, to see Atlanta. I flew up on the long breaks, too, and even kept her with me during Kate and Cal's honeymoon. It had all worked until she turned fourteen, and then I was lost again. She didn't want to come to Georgia anymore, and I allowed myself inaction, the stupid belief that time would work to soothe. I could feel the distance growing and started thinking of a reason to come back home. A new book seemed like an inroad, something that would provide an excuse to be in town without making my daughter feel as if I were there on some kind of mission to invade her life.

I towel off in the bedroom and watch Pascal as his internal clock wakes him. I've been working this shift for almost two years now, and he's always been by my side. When I left Smallwood, it was the first time I'd ever lived outside of Indiana, and I missed my dog Daisy, the old black Lab that poked her nose into Wendy's crib. I got Pascal when he was a year old, given up to a rescue group in Savannah. He might just be the only thing that loves me, and I can't forget that. He stretches now, yawns, a kind of sloppy smile on his goofy face. I pull on a fresh T-shirt and the same jeans from yesterday. He follows me to the kitchen where I find a piece of bologna for him. He gets a treat every night before we travel to the group home. "I guess we better get going, stinky," I tell him, because he's given in to the temptation to expel a little hot gas.

On the drive I'm distracted, my window rolled down a little bit, and the cool night air rushing in. I can't let go of the talk with Ike. Once inside the group home, Browder and I can't stay awake watching a movie, the sounds of gun blasts and screams lulling us deeper into sleep, until morning time, when he shakes me awake and the routine starts all over again.

Chapter Four

It's late afternoon, sunlight dappling the pavement, as I amble with Pascal along the sidewalk, the new green leaves fluttering in the breeze. All around me, it's as if spring will last forever, the white dogwood flowers bursting open, their petals as white as copy paper. Pascal stops every few feet and sniffs an azalea bush, hiking his meaty leg and pretending to pee. We walk until we run out of sidewalk and the ground beyond turns into a mucky mixture of swamp grass and black logs. The land stretches out before us flat and shimmering toward the horizon. It's as if the developers used the only decent piece of land to build the apartment complex and left the rest intact, a freshwater marsh that's dominated the landscape for centuries. Pascal pitches his nose and inhales the breeze rushing off the fen, the scent of decay strong and lively, the contradiction of life coming from death. For a while, we just stand and look out across the bog, until Pascal sits, looks up at me, and lolls his red tongue, thinking he's supposed to respond to a command I just won't give. I pat his head as the mailman takes a sharp turn into the back entrance of the complex; his wheels chirp, and he guns the motor toward the pool area where the metal mailboxes sit in the middle of a courtyard.

We turn and walk back toward the apartment, stopping off at the mailboxes. Thick pollen clings to everything, a yellow dust that looks more man-made than natural. I jimmy the key in the mailbox lock and fish out the envelopes. There's a slip inside, meaning I have to head to the office for a special package. Pascal tugs at his leash, grabbing it with his mouth and prancing sideways, much like a race-happy Thoroughbred, ready to get where we're going. In the office, a young woman takes my slip and smiles, so much gloss on her ample lips that her mouth looks fake, silvery and possibly shellacked. She's not the one who has taken my complaints about the maintenance punks and the alligators; this one seems as if she'd also care about such things. She hands me a priority envelope and smiles again. "It's from New York," she says, tilting her head to the side. "Aren't you a writer? It was in the apartment newsletter, right?" I'm ashamed of the newsletter piece, mainly because I submitted it myself. In a moment of loneliness and desperation, I offered to do a reading at one of the monthly resident get-togethers they call "Community Forums." Management provides bottled water and sodas, iced in a large plastic container, and residents are urged to bring their own finger foods, even share their recipes, but when I read at one, only four people were there.

"Yes," I answer the young woman. "I'm a writer." She nods, and the sheen of her lips looks mercurial, sunlight bouncing off the heart-shaped crystal paperweight on her desk.

"I thought so. I'm not much of a reader, but being a writer must be cool, right?" She picks up a ringing phone and suddenly is completely unaware of my presence. Pascal nudges my wrist as I hold the package in my hand, tapping it against my thigh. I wait a moment and think of telling her good-bye, but she's texting now, too, telling the person on the other end of the phone, "Wait till you see it. It's huge."

Back inside the apartment, I sit down on the bare floor in the small kitchen and open the mail. Michael's stationery, stiff and emblazoned with a seal—a plume pen and inkwell—is paper-clipped to a thick contract. In his demonstrative cursive, he's written: "Surprise! I rushed this through, seeing that you'll need to get to work right away. Sign all four copies and send them back using overnight mail. We should be able to get the advance for signing within a month. Good luck!"

I absentmindedly feed Pascal a slice of turkey lunch meat. His warm tongue licks at my fingertips even after I've heard him gulp down the treat. He puts his head on my knee as I read through the contract. I'm looking for some reference to the paperback version of the memoir, but can't find any mention of it. I feel relieved and secretly hope that part of the offer has been taken off the table, but there's a separate contract under the first one. I leaf through it, spotting the title here and there in the legalese. My stomach shifts, and now the smell of the lunch meat on my hand makes me woozy. In bold print, the agreement spells out that *Leaving Smallwood: A Memoir* will be published in trade paperback, as a reissue, complete with a new introduction. Selfishly, I decide I better get on my brother Ike's best side, so I dial his home number, which goes unanswered. It rings and rings, then Susana is on the voice mail, telling callers in her prim tone to leave a message and expect the call to be returned promptly. Ike doesn't pick up his cell phone either. Something inside me needs reassuring, so I swallow hard and dial my ex-wife's home. In two rings, Cal picks up, and for a moment it seems I'll chicken out. He says again in a baritone voice, "Hello. Can I help you?"

"Hey there, Cal. It's Gabe Burke. How are you?"

"Just fine, Gabe. How can I help you?" Calling to talk to my daughter is like a job interview over the phone; I'm nervous and slightly nauseous.

"Is Wendy in, Cal?" I say, sounding way too much like a salesman, like my dad.

"No. No, she isn't, Gabe. I believe she's with her mother shopping for prom shoes."

My stomach pitches, a queasy, fearful tightness at the center of my body. How could my little girl be going to a prom? "But she's just sixteen, a sophomore. Her first prom isn't until next year," I say, thinking Cal has miscalculated. "Do you mean they're shopping for homecoming shoes?"

Cal clears his throat; I can hear his sports news turned up loudly in the background. He's only about five years older than I am, but I feel as if he's a dad to both my ex-wife and my daughter, maybe even me. "No, Gabe. It's for the prom. Wendy has been dating a guy who's a senior. He's a track star. On a scholarship next year to Purdue. He's quite the pole vaulter, runs the 400, too."

Pascal nuzzles into my lap and rests his head on my thigh. "You still there?" asks Cal.

"Yes," I say, trying to think of some parental nugget about how fast they grow up or how you've got to let go if you love them, but nothing will come. "Just let her know I called, please."

"You bet," says Cal, followed by "Take care." All of a sudden, I can smell the Play-Doh Wendy used to love to sculpt into little balls, sticking her tongue to the surface of each one, knowing she wasn't allowed to eat them, looking at me from behind a big blue globe of the clay, her smile wide, eyes glittering.

I know I need to stand up, go to the desk in my room, and start sketching out an interview schedule for the true crime book, but I can't move. Instead, I gently extract Pascal's head from my lap, place it softly on the floor. I get up and go to the fridge, pluck a six-pack of Fat Tire from the crisper, sit back down again near my dog, watch his wet black nostrils expand and shrink, over and over. I drink one beer and then another; Pascal wakes up and wants a sip himself. The third and fourth beers quench my thirst, and the last two make me broody. My ass is numb as I stand up. I open a bottle of red wine left over from a date last fall, and wander into the bedroom. The woman was from the university in Columbus, an art historian who swore off alcohol after she destroyed two of her own paintings that she told me were valued at two thousand dollars apiece. I think we both realized the night was over after she told me the story; she didn't like that I didn't ask more questions, and I didn't like that she kept asking me if her actions were proof she had a subconscious fear of success.

The red wine is bitter, but I swallow it right from the bottle. Thumbing through the contracts, I'm drawn more to the reprint of my memoir than the book about the murders. Still, I toss both contracts on the desk and walk around my bedroom, inspecting the stacks of books, old copies of literary journals I used to read over long weekends in Smallwood, Indiana, as my wife, Kate, made a Crock-Pot of soup, and we were still young enough to think something great was heading for us.

On the floor next to my bed is the memoir. I snatch it up and flip the book open to the back, where even in the author photo I look scared. I toss it to the floor, lie back on the bed, ears buzzing.

My mind drifts to my dad, the images of him as crisp as his starched shirts. He was a thoughtful father, always prepared to spend time with us, my brother Ike and I fishing next to him, his white dress shirt and fat wide tie pressed and spotless even on the weekend. He wore his salesman clothes every day, as if he were never off from work, as if a sale were just around the corner. The old AMC Ambassador station wagon was always filled to the roof with the cooking items he hawked from door to door. An entire stainless steel cooking set was priced so high, the company used a monthly installment plan to make it affordable. The fancy pots were his featured item. He always kept sales goals neatly printed on a sheet of lined paper, taped to the dash and updated if it became dingy, or if he'd set new heights. On this day, a late autumn afternoon in 1978 we were fishing for bream off a dock near Whitesburg. The man and woman who lived there had bought from Dad for years, and they seemed more like family than anything else, as if they were our aunt and uncle. The Calhouns were always putting in orders for teakwood bowls, cast-iron pots and some camping gear, a coffee kettle and aluminum ice chests.

Inside the Calhoun house, Ike asked if Mrs. Calhoun could bring down the old board game called Whistle Stop Depot. He loved the miniature train set that came with it. Every time we called on the Calhouns Ike would request politely to see the board game. I liked going inside the house because the couple had a teenage daughter named Rebecca whose hair was the same color as the wheat field outside. She had large, green eyes and fingernails she painted a pretty pink. She smelled like bar soap, and her skin was pale like mine. I fell in love with her over and over each summer, but she was at band practice.

Ike and I played with the board game while Mrs. Calhoun and Dad talked about a test-tube baby that had been born in Manchester, England, which confused me because there was a town just north of Smallwood, Indiana, that was also called Manchester. While they chatted, I envisioned a very slender, strange-looking child flopping out of a beaker, spilling its writhing body onto a black granite countertop, crying and realizing its mother was made of glass. Then Mrs. Calhoun excused herself to answer the phone. She went deliberately to the wall and plucked a taupe receiver from its cradle. She said, "Fine. I'll come on down, then." She hung up, shucking off her apron, tossing it onto the table. She addressed us: "Mr. Calhoun has a flat just up the road. I need to take him a jack. I'll be right back, and we can all eat sandwiches." Dad nodded and smiled.

It was strange to be left in the house without one of the Calhouns. Dad stood up and walked around the kitchen, inspecting things. He picked up a *Prairie Farmer* magazine and flipped through it, tossed it back next to a stack of mail. He swiped a bill from the table and looked it over, whistling. Ike and I watched him, curious. I was uneasy, full of dread about being in their home without them. My stomach sort of gurgled as Ike snatched a locomotive the size of a school eraser from my hand. Dad disappeared into the living room, circled back, and announced, "You boys run the trunk out to the car. It's clear they're not going to buy today." He brushed lint from his suit jacket and added, "But just wait until I get out there to put it into the car. I don't need anything broken."

"What are you gonna do in here?" asked Ike as we each took hold of the trunk.

"If you have to know, nosy," said Dad with a quick smile, "I've got to use the toilet."

Ike rolled his eyes. The trunk was difficult to manage; on the way out to the car, we bumped our knees and complained about each other. It was so hot outside that the old station wagon was unbearable to lean against, the metal scalding us through our thin T-shirts. Ike usually took the lead on things.

He said, "I don't know why he'd want to poop in somebody else's bathroom. They're gonna smell it when they get back." Ike spit on the ground, rubbed his chin as if he had stubble. "This is stupid. Go in there and see if he's done."

"You go in," I said. "Besides, he told us to stay out here and wait."

"I'll stay here with the trunk. If you don't go in, I'll tell on you about the *Playboy*."

"Okay," I mumbled.

"Hurry," said Ike. "It's hot out here."

Inside the Calhoun house it was instantly cooler. I was sweaty but chilled, too. I tiptoed because I thought if I could stay inside awhile and not be detected by Dad, I could return to Ike and prove I'd done what he'd asked. But as I crept down the hallway, I spotted Rebecca's picture on the wall. She was dressed in her baton-twirling outfit, legs in shiny nylons, the silver and blue of her costume dazzling. I stared at the photo for a while, before I heard something in a room a few feet away. I crept farther down the hall to the entrance of Rebecca's room; her name was spelled out on the door in pop tabs, the little silver tongues glued to a piece of stained pine. My father stood with his back to me, hunched over Rebecca's dresser. He lifted a wad of fabric to his face, but I couldn't tell what he was doing. Then he shoved it into his suit pocket and quietly pushed the drawer back into place. I was confused about why he was stealing from Rebecca. He started to turn around. I darted back down the hallway and through the kitchen, outside and down to the car, where Ike sat on the trunk, fanning his face with a paper sack.

"Is he done stinking that whole house up, or what?" asked my brother, his face looking even more tanned in the sunlight, brown glistening with sweat, as he stood up and spit. My heart pounded, and my skin was clammy. Our father had been in the National Guard and was known to us to be a stickler for keeping our rooms clean and our hands off other people's property, especially his collection of rare rocks. He had an entire padlocked closet that we were forbidden to go near. I thought of that closet as Ike goaded me.

Dad walked out the front door of the Calhoun house, shielding his eyes from the bright sun. He smiled at us and waved. Something about him seemed forever changed, and I thought of our dad as being sneaky for the first time.

"Must be feeling better after his dump," said Ike. Dad approached us, his face flushed, a little wired-looking around his dark brown eyes.

"Let's get the trunk in the wagon and get outta here before they get back. If they're not going to buy anything, I don't want to eat their food. Then they'll have the upper hand. It'd been different if there'd been a sale."

Ike started to whine, but Dad shushed him.

In the car, I saw how tightly Dad had his hand clenched around his suit jacket pocket, as if he were trying to keep a small animal trapped. I stole looks at that hand clutching its prize while we listened to the radio. Dad hated pop music, preferred the Platters, but on this trip home, he steered with one hand and let us do whatever we wanted.

Chapter Five

Two days pass, and all I do is buy beer and wine and listen to classic rock stations. Tomorrow, I'm due back at the group home, but for now I crank up the stereo and smoke. The truth is I'm stuck. There were lots of nights like this one when I was working on *Leaving Smallwood*, nights when Kate was out late after her nursing classes. All I could do was sit numbly and think of all the stupid clues I'd missed, like how he kept that damn closet locked all the time in his study, or how he seemed to be able to lie about almost anything, even if it was of little consequence. Then, instead of writing, I'd be on the Internet, googling *voyeurism* and measuring him against the stated traits. He was a good dad, too, though, fun sometimes, taking Ike and me to King's Island to ride the Beast, surprising us one night with walkie-talkies or our own Walkmans.

Back before the book came out, Mom and Ike and Kate were mostly still in shock, and they thought I was simply working on a novel, which I was supposed to be doing, but then night after night, I'd get home from a management job at Hookum's Home Store and sit down at the computer and write as if my fingers were on fire, then just blank out, start getting drunk and listening to music. Kate thought I was clinically depressed, overwrought with anger and embarrassment at my father's crimes, but I could never agree with her. It was more like I was empty altogether, not a trace of anything; it was as if he'd also stolen my shame. I finally went to see him in prison in Pendleton, but even then all I could do was examine the lines on his face, the way he still kept his appearance neat and groomed. After I'd visit with him, it was as if his talking on and on behind the bulletproof glass put an electrical surge on my writing, and Kate would comment when I got home, "I'm glad to see you're happier, but how is that?" I couldn't tell her I was experiencing the high of a writer who's tapped into the theme of his work; it would've sounded awful, so I lied right to her face and just told her it was because I'd faced my fears by seeing him, which I could tell she knew was bullshit.

Pascal wants a walk, his long tongue dripping saliva onto the floor next to the front door. I click on his leash and rub his ears, talk to him. I call him "Lacsap." He barks once. It's his name spelled backwards, and I only say it to him before a walk or a treat. He loves it.

Outside, the sun is bright and hot, the trees filled with chattering starlings. As we walk, I picture the Riley boy's empty bed and wonder where his body is. Why did they only take him? I realize I'm already convincing myself that one man couldn't have done the crimes alone, which is not the point of the book I'm to be writing. After all, there's been a trial, reams of irrefutable DNA evidence, a confession, even an elderly social worker who had known Rodney Finch since he was a child and who testified that he'd told her all about the murders. Still, why wouldn't he also tell where the Riley boy's body was? He'd blabbed about everything, but not that, the most talked-about part of the murders.

I realize my hand is tense on the leash as Pascal trots along, sniffing and hiking, peeing little markers of his love for unknown mates. He's a good boy, and I find myself actually saying a prayer of thanks for having him. But going for walks has always made me anxious. It's taken me years to accept I'm not deviant, too, that my genes don't have some hidden, lascivious defect, an asp coiled around a chromosome, a stranglehold on my normalcy. Back in Smallwood, even before we all had to accept what Dad was, I had already been cautious about walking or running in the neighborhood, careful not to ever—even casually—glance at a house window. I'd stare straight ahead when we took walks, and sometimes Kate would laugh and say, "Jeez, loosen up, pal. We're on a walk, not a gauntlet." I'd smile and try to appear less tense, but somehow, way deep down, I suppose I'd known for a long time, and even though I put almost that exact sentence in my book about my father, Ike didn't believe me. He cussed me out on the phone after reading the memoir in one sitting. "Bullshit, Gabe," he said. "No one knew. Don't act like you're some kind of sage now that it's all out."

Pascal pulls on his leash, and I once again find myself trying to relax, tell myself I'm not my dad. The sunlight feels as if it might just make the pavement sprout. We turn toward the edge of the big swamp, and the familiar decay whips up into my face. When I ran away from Smallwood, I drove and drove, staying nights over in Louisville, then Chattanooga, and finally Atlanta. I met a guitar player in a twangy bar outside the city, not far from the Martin Luther King Jr. memorial. He was a native Georgian named Harry

Philster, and he drank with me between sets, telling me about how he grew up right next to a big ole swamp called the Okefenokee. That night I dug out my atlas and circled it. I got up and left early from a cheap Red Roof Inn next to the bypass and arrived at the swamp by midmorning. As I stood there next to its gigantic blackness, the smell of both death and birth swirling around me, I knew I'd stay. I found the apartment complex and paid my deposit, telling the manager I wanted to be as close as possible to the swamp.

Now, Pascal sniffs the air and whines, the scent of all that has come before pulling at his most basic instincts: to run, to roam, to find a spot that speaks only to him. It breaks my heart a little to see him this way, and I can't help but compare our lives. More than anything after Dad was exposed, I wanted to run away, yearning for something, maybe a kind of deep and solid anonymity, and I dreamed about fleeing into the wild, nothing but my notebooks and pens, a box of paperbacks to keep me company. But there were obligations and, if I'm honest with myself, a story. In that first year of his jail time, I was the only one who'd visit him, and I suppose part of that desire to see him, talk with him, was sheer selfishness. Ike had gone through two different stages with our dad, first a complete and utter denial, saying our dad was an upstanding guy, almost perfect, in fact, and he'd never do those things; it was all coincidence. Then, after the search warrants, and after the secret closet was opened, Ike went rabid, a state he has maintained, which is to say he now keeps everything about our dad buried. Other than facing my own daughter, thinking about going back to Smallwood gives me the most anxiety when I think of Ike.

Pascal and I begin to lightly jog, the strong afternoon sun shining hard in our faces, eyes squinted, the cool air rushing by as we traverse the hollows. It's a slow, steady pace, then I ratchet up the tempo, and Pascal follows. The sidewalk from the apartment complex dead-ends into a narrower road, a kind of bylane the power company uses to service the mammoth Erector set electrical towers. The ground is black, wet, and my feet slip some as Pascal glances over his shoulder at me, his smile big and goofy, the dangling tongue like a gag gift. Off to the east, a large flock of geese rises into the sky, only a small V from this distance, but the geese quickly accelerate, and before I know it, they are honking overhead, their fluid wing movements synchronized, slicing through the sharp air. They're black against the oceanic horizon, and I take in a deep breath as their honking drifts away with them, leaving only my labored breathing and the tinkling of Pascal's leash. My feet thump the ground, but the run seems cleansing, and we push on, up a small hill and down the other side. A power company truck barrels past us, the driver waving. Pinecones litter the clay road and make me think of how Ike and I used to pretend they were hand grenades, chucking them into the autumn air as Dad smoked by a pond, a slack line lying on the surface. He'd yell at us to take cover, that the enemy was about to blow our heads off.

As we hit about two miles out, I turn us around, heading home, which gives Pascal the energy he needs to set the pace now. I struggle to keep up with him, my thighs burning, lungs tingling; still, the running provides me with some mental distance. In my head, I begin to sort out the people I need to call and realize I should phone my mother when I get back to the apartment. She'll be mechanically thrilled, numb that is, just like she's always been, a kind of robotic optimism that could be shattered if just one more thing is piled on her. Unlike Ike, Mother never gave up her defense of our father. I suppose she's been depressed for decades, even when we were kids. She is monotone when she talks about everything, including truly good news, which she makes sound like a bland weather report. On the day he was arrested, she watched the police take him away in handcuffs, and she said, smiling, her lips sticking to her teeth, "Well, we better get some food put in Tupperware for him. He'll be back before you know it."

Pascal nearly drags me into the winding streets of the complex, slowing down some once our patio is in sight, the grill and his dingy tennis balls lying on the concrete like fuzzy creatures. He's panting as I use the key to enter, and before I can even close the door, I hear his sloshing laps at the water bowl. The kitchen floor will need mopping once he's done. I stand and watch him, smiling, realizing that the rush of optimistic energy will be short-lived, and I decide to use it wisely. I pull out a pad of paper from the drawer that sticks and then sit on the kitchen floor. The long yellow legal pages entice me as I scrawl interview questions for the DA, a man named Eric Wingel, who went to high school with Ike. I sit and suck on the end of the pencil eraser, remembering the guy some, how he played football and basketball, wearing his letterman's jacket even in the summer. I feel some of my buoyancy slipping, thinking of being in the DA's office. Even though Eric Wingel didn't get elected until after our father's prosecution, he'll know me, know of what happened. For a moment my heart sinks, thinking of my brother having to work within the same justice system. My throat tightens, and I'm aware of how likely it is that I might just run away from this, too. The long pad of paper now looks insurmountable, so I simply write the date at the top and the words "True Crime Interview–Rileys." But somehow it's a start, and I decide no matter what, even if he punches me in the face, I'm going to be good to Ike, try to understand his point of view.

To keep the momentum going, I flip the page and write down my itinerary. All told, I'll have just three months to complete the book, which means I can afford to use all of the first month doing research, interviewing cops, relatives on both sides, the attorneys, and the judge. Ike will be a great resource in terms of the official file. I sip from a beer bottle as Pascal lies sprawled out on the kitchen floor, his breathing slowing down more and more, until his soft stomach seems to stay inhaled for too long. I say his name and am relieved as his ears prick. He lifts his head as if it's made of lead and immediately goes back to sleep. For more than half an hour, I calculate everything from mileage to how long I can make the advance stretch out. I can't stay with Ike, his wife would rather a Sasquatch bunk with them; and if I'm going to make the money last, the only other option is my mother. I don't know if I can take it though, her pretend listening, as all the while she simply nods and smiles, petting her cat Freckles, who is completely black.

I down the rest of the beer and pound another one, feeling foolish in my forty-one years. Still, as I dial the number, the high-pitched beeps ringing in my ear, I'm glad to have a small buzz to help me out. Mom picks up on the third ring, and I swear it's a recording at first, the way she says, "Hello, Patricia here. How can I help you?"

"Mom?" I say, and the phone rustles against something. I can hear her pulling a chair out from the kitchen table.

"Hello, Ike," she says, sounding incrementally more tired with each syllable.

"No, Mom, it's Gabe. How are you?" She pauses, and I hear her trying to light a cigarette, the scratch of the thumbwheel three times before I imagine her bringing the Bic to her mouth, where she'll dip her head some, allow the flame to touch the tip of her Winston Ultra Light 100. She puffs then clears her throat politely.

"Oh, Gabe. Funny to hear from you. I'm fine."

"Really," I say, trying to add some levity, "and you sound fine, too, just like a recording." She makes a humph sound, then I can hear as she pushes the ashtray we made her toward the center of the table. Ike and I fashioned it out of clay at a summer camp near Fort Wayne, and it weighs as much as a stack of bricks. At her most depressed after Dad was in jail, she was uncharacteristically assertive. "I could just bash his head in with this," she told me shortly after his first suicide attempt, lifting the heavy ashtray a centimeter off the table. She laughed when I told her she'd need a forklift.

I imagine the smell of the cigarette smoke in her hair, that mixture of Aqua Net and menthol, the way it seemed to soothe me as a kid, burying my face in her shoulder, crying over some embarrassment, or a mean look from Ike. "What are you doing, Mom?" She seems confused by the question.

"What else, here. Just here at the house." Even with the beer buzz I can feel myself tightening.

"Well, what did you do today?" I ask, trying to get her to open up a little.

"Not much I suppose. Might need to go to the Quick-Mart."

"Oh, okay. I'll let you go, then. Take care." Mother begins chuckling some, then becomes softer, even a little sweet.

"Now, I know you too well, Gabriel," she says, exhaling a puff of smoke that I can imagine fills her tiny kitchen. My hand shakes some as I move the receiver to my other ear. It's strange to talk so nervously with someone who once carried me to bed, who held hands with me when Dad was gone long nights, whereabouts unknown, returning home late, a dark sock cap in his hand, hungry and barely talking. She adds, "I don't have to go to the store right now."

"Have you talked with Ike, Mom?" I ask.

"No, not lately," she says, now mashing out the cigarette; the wobbling of our massive ashtray sounds like thunder. She blows out one final elongated breath, and I hear the sound of her opening a can of Mott's apple juice, her favorite. "I saw him two weeks ago though. He said your baby girl stopped by his house with the boy she's dating. I guess they still call it that." Silence penetrates the very core of the phone now. I can see my mother, both of us in a small foyer, shortly after it all began, then again after the memoir came out. She reached for me as if my body were some shoddy, dangerous electrical contraption. She patted me abruptly, backed off, excited and relieved, no words at all.

"Hello," I say, my tongue suddenly thick in my mouth.

"Oh," Mom says. "Let's talk about your weather down there. Are the azaleas in bloom? Can you send me some more pictures? How's that funny old dog of yours?" She has to take a deep breath, and we both seem to realize the phone call is almost over.

"Mom," I say, really wanting to hug her, take her out to eat, and talk about things she can't. "I'm coming up for a visit. I'm doing another book; I mean, I'm writing a true crime book. . . ." I think I've heard her gasp, but in fact it's a yawn.

"Oh, that's nice," she says, and then adds through another yawn, "Gabe, I've got to go to bed, hon. I'm so tired, and I've still got to feed the cat. Good night, son." I think for a moment I've heard a man's voice, but the thought is so absurd it actually makes me smile.

"Night, Mom." I stand and hold the bleating phone in my hand, aware of an awful wave of guilt, a feeling as heavy as my post-run legs. As I crawl into bed, forgoing brushing my teeth, I picture my mother, how she's likely curled into a fetal position, too, waiting for that weighty curtain of sleep to descend, blanket our embarrassment, put us both into another world where words seem to matter much less.

Chapter Six

Almost three years had passed since that day at the Calhouns' house, where Dad had pocketed something private and clean, tucked it in his coat. We'd probably been back to the Calhoun house at least fifty times since he'd stolen from Rebecca, and with each visit, I could feel myself incrementally understanding what he'd done. This time, Ike wasn't with us.

Now, as we put the trunk down, Mr. Calhoun entered the room and shook Dad's hand; he was about ten years older than my father, and their handshake was violent and prolonged. They talked quickly and loudly about the weather, Reagan, and unemployment. I sat silently at the kitchen table, stiff, not wanting to appear anxious about the whereabouts of Rebecca. I imagined the photo in that hallway, the one of Rebecca dressed in her baton-twirling uniform, the glittering silver torso and tan stockings reflecting some of the shine, her fine strong legs planted on the green turf.

"Gabriel," said Mrs. Calhoun, "why don't you go visit with Becca. She's in the basement now. She just had to move her bedroom down there to get away from us." Mrs. Calhoun rolled her big brown eyes and pointed toward the basement door, soft skin wagging under her arm. I could feel myself tense at her suggestion. I nodded and walked toward the door, turned back toward Mrs. Calhoun, now needing her reassurance, but she'd sat down at the kitchen table and was laughing at a story Dad was telling about a man who wanted to order a still to make moonshine.

The basement door opened without a sound, and the carpeted stairs were equally as quiet. I stopped midway down and felt like running back to the Calhouns and Dad, sipping a Dr Pepper from a metal tumbler, the ice cubes freezer-bitten, bitter.

"I'm not hungry, Mom," said Rebecca from some spot beneath the stairs. Music played, something I'd never heard, the male voice repeatedly groaning long, strung-out *A* sounds, followed by the word "mon."

"It's . . ." I started and swallowed again, used more of my lungs, less of my throat. "It's Gabe Burke. Your mom told me to come down." I stood and listened to her rustling something, probably a blanket; the basement was finished, lit, and carpeted, like a little apartment at the end of the stairs, but it was colder.

"Oh, good. Come on down, Gabe. Gosh."

My feet brushed against the stairs, my limbs casting dark shadows on the wall. I stepped off the last stair into a dimly lit room of wood paneling and too many coffee tables. A mammoth television sat in the center, dried flowers on top, the sound turned down, the picture green. Rebecca was draped in a quilt, and I was surprised to see she'd gained weight, not a lot, but her face was round, pretty.

"Gosh," she said, smiling. "You've grown since last spring." I stood before her, embarrassed, my face red-hot, glaring at her soft beauty. "You should sit down," she added, shrugging the quilt tighter around her body. There were two beanbag chairs, and I plopped down in a crackled brown one. Rebecca flipped her hair and asked me if I liked the Rastafarian music.

I looked down. "I don't know what that is," I said, sounding sad and unworldly even to myself.

"Of course you do," said Rebecca, smiling. "It's this." She pointed to her towering boom box. "It's just a fancy way of saying that it's music from Africa and Jamaica. I didn't know about any of this either, until I started college. The Maroons, you know, escaped slaves, really took it with them from their homeland. We had to listen to snippets in my world music class and then identify them." I fidgeted, used one foot to fiddle with the loose sole of the other. Rebecca stood up and flashed her broad, glossy smile again, walked toward me. She stood there, then slowly knelt and sat right in the beanbag with me, edging me over with a push of her hips, the two of us about to fall off the thing and onto the floor. "It's cold," she said, snuggling up against me. My sternum seemed bonier, and I tried to tighten my arms as she clung to me through her thick quilt.

For more than fifteen minutes she told me about her classes at Midland University up north, near Chicago. Her warm body, even through the quilt, seemed to me a kind of secret world. "You're cold, too," she declared, and unwrapped herself, included me in the interior of the humid space under the quilt. My jeans felt cramped as she snuggled against me, the contact of our bodies so rich I felt guilty. "I'm just home for the weekend to get groceries and wash all my sweats." I sensed she was about to fall asleep. "I'm a little hung over from a kegger."

I spotted the chest of drawers from her bedroom upstairs; the same dresser Dad had invaded. I imagined helping Rebecca install little locks over all of her dresser drawers. She was fully relaxed now, asleep. I felt her warm breath tickling the hairs on my arm. I couldn't stop staring at the dresser, its drawers with golden handles, the walnut finish rubbed lighter in spots where she'd pushed her knees to close them. Rebecca squirmed briefly, then sighed. I had the urge to kiss the top of her head like our mother used to when Ike and I were little. My lips touched her reddish-brown hair, a little greasy, and I slowly and quietly puckered, lingered awhile.

"Did you just kiss my head?" she said, instantly alive. I could tell she was smiling even though I couldn't see her face. Blood filled my cheeks, and I confessed.

"Yes," I said, feeling embarrassed, scrawny and irritable all over again. "Sorry." Rebecca moved in the beanbag, the chair squeaking like a toy. She propped herself up and made me look at her.

"That's okay. It's sweet." She kissed me on the cheek, and we held hands, moist and grainy. She fell asleep again, and I was about to myself when the door opened at the top of the stairs, a wedge of shadow on the sidewall shaped like a magician's dark cape.

"Kids," said Mrs. Calhoun, "we're gonna eat ham soup and yeast rolls. Come on up now 'fore it goes cold." I couldn't move as Rebecca stirred; it was quiet in the basement, and I could tell Mrs. Calhoun was still up there, standing, waiting. "It'll go cold, now." We rose and Rebecca stretched, losing her quilt; it slipped off her shoulders and exposed her full, curvy body. She had put on weight, but I liked it all. Her eyes were sleepy, cheeks red, as she stooped, picked up the quilt, wrapped us into it, and gave me a tight, close hug. We ate, then I had to leave with Dad to go door to door.

That afternoon we hit eight more houses, all of them Dad's regulars. I could still feel Rebecca snuggled against me. At three of the houses, I stayed in the car and watched as men answered the doors. Dry leaves tumbled over the ocher yards and floated in front of the windshield. It was like watching a silent film, the way Dad gestured with his hands, plied the catalog from his dress pants pocket, and pointed to specific items. When he'd climb back into the car, he was somber and gripey. "You'd think I was asking them to buy the stomach flu, for Christ sakes." We called it a day.

The hotel was a motel, and it was named Macintosh Lodge, with little flimsy rooms and carpet that puffed dust. Dad opened a can of Budweiser and swished it around his mouth, turned on the television. There was only one single bed, but he'd called the front desk for a rollaway, which they didn't have. Instead, a skinny man with a pocked face brought us a sleeping bag. Dad tossed it at me. "It'll be like camping out at the Salamonie Reservoir."

Dad drank three beers and disappeared into the bathroom as I watched the grainy television. The shower steam escaped from beneath the door, and I turned over to watch it. My mind slipped easily into thinking of Rebecca. Still, I was tired, worn out. My eyes grew heavy, and I didn't wake up until the middle of the night, the motel room black. I had to pat the ground and crawl toward the bathroom. Once I felt my way to the bathroom door, the handle finally in my hand, I slipped inside and pawed at the wall for the light switch. I was thirsty after I peed, shoveling cupped hands of blasting water into my face. The hand towel smelled like Dad as I patted my mouth. I snuck back to see if I'd woken him up, light from the bathroom slanting across the floor. The bed wasn't touched; the pillow and shiny, thin comforter with mallards on it looked as if they were part of a theater set.

"Dad?" I said, and stood there barefoot, feeling weak and lost. My skin itched, and I could feel the topmost hair on my head quiver. "Dad?" I called again. For some reason, I felt the need to climb into the bed, and I did, pulling the covers up to my chin. I did it mainly to think about what to do next. Outside, wind blew something in front of our door, maybe a fast-food cup, tapping along the concrete, then slowly fading. The digital radio alarm clock burned a lusty red, showing 3:25 a.m. in block lettering. The room pulsed, and I thought I saw a shadow and for a moment believed Dad had been hiding all this time. But it was nothing, only a trick of the eyes; still, it made me angry, and before I knew it I was at the window, peeling back the scratchy drapes, the dusty thin liner. The blocky nose of our big Ambassador wasn't where we'd left it. I moved to the side table and switched on the lamp, pulling on my T-shirt and jeans, shoving my feet into sneakers with no socks. I yanked open the motel door and looked around. The parking lot was well lit by the stores nearby: a lumberyard, and a grocery store, plus a Quickie-24 convenience mart, its towering lights on the gas island. The air was cold, colder than it had been up until then. The buzzing from nearby transformers felt as if it might be doing me harm, stunting my growth. I was plugged into that rushing night, the energy coursing over my shivering skin. I stepped toward the office, then backtracked, looking around. I wanted to call for him, but thought better of it.

Slowly, embarrassingly, I began to understand something. I knew where he might be, what he might be doing. It had formed in my mind, rooted, but the words had not.

I stumbled back inside the motel and lay down again on the sleeping bag. The light from the bathroom made me feel better. I must've crossed into sleep and surged back out of it a hundred times before I heard the key in the door. I rolled over quickly, burying half my face in the thin pillow. He stopped abruptly, stood there, only his polished stiff brogues visible through my clenched left eye. Dad took a deep breath and stepped over me. He was tired, just like when he showed up late in our kitchen in Smallwood, thirsty at the sink, secretive. His shadow passed over me, and he peed a long time in the bathroom. He returned, sat on the edge of the bed. Dad smelled of cold wind and beers. He called to me quietly, as if he really didn't want me to hear him. "Gabe," he whispered, "it's cold out there. I had to start the old wagon or she would've been locked up in the morning. Wouldn't be able to use her." I listened to him lie like that, telling me a bedtime story I'm sure he believed just as much as I didn't.

We headed home in silence. The station wagon roared and jostled down the curvy back roads. At a deserted four-way stop outside of Bippus, three feral dogs, scraggly and thin, searched a deep weedy culvert for food. We stayed motionless at the stop sign. "That's just pitiful," said Dad. "Let's see if we can get them to come to us." He put on the blinkers and hopped out, but no sooner had his feet hit the cold pavement than the dogs bolted like deer out of the culvert, sprinting full blast across the stubbled, vast cornfield. In seconds, they were dots along the horizon. Dad flopped back inside the car, his mind still on the dogs running away from us, which is why he didn't notice the sheriff's cruiser slowly approaching from behind, flashers on, siren muted.

"There's a police car behind us," I said as I sat with my notebook splayed on my thighs. Dad cringed, licked his lips. In my side mirror I could see the deputy's breath as it puffed from his big head. Dad rolled down the window and began talking before the officer had even reached us.

"I'm sorry for sitting here, deputy. It's just that we spotted some wounded dogs and were trying to help." He handed over his license and registration, and the officer took them, stooping to peer in at me.

He returned to the patrol car as Dad mumbled on, "You can't block a four-way stop, Gabe, even out here. Rules are rules." We'd only been sitting there a minute or so though before the cop drove up. "They can't play favorites." He was antsy, rubbing his chin, talking in fast clips. "If you break a rule, then they've got no choice than to address it."

The deputy strode back to our car, some sunlight now peeking from behind a wall of gray, a dying glint that disappeared as quickly as it had arrived. The deputy handed Dad his items and then asked him to get out of the car. Dad looked at me as if I might know what to do. He shrugged and obeyed. The driver's side window was still rolled down, and I could catch snippets of the questioning. The officer said something about three complaints, and I could hear Dad saying things like, "Yes, we were in Wyant, but no sir, I wasn't out at that time of night," and "Well, no sir, he doesn't drive. He's only thirteen." I was ashamed, and the weight of a secret I knew I'd have to keep was lodged right in my gut. I drew spheres on my notebook page and felt my ears burn.

The officer said, "Three apartments called us after they saw your vehicle in their parking lot. One woman said she saw you with binoculars."

My dad said, "Can you please keep it down? I don't want to harm my boy." The officer ignored it. "Besides," said Dad, "I was only writing down addresses. I'm a household goods salesman for HomeBeam Wares out of Wisconsin." The officer was lecturing Dad. I leaned over to get closer to the open window; the cold air was a compress for my sickness.

"Sir, keep in mind these are considered serious complaints. Women need to feel safe in their own homes. Be sure not to let me find you in any Wyant parking lots in the future."

Dad got back in the car slowly, and he waited silently as the deputy pulled up beside us, stopped, then went on through the four-way, his cruiser disappearing down the long ribbon of road, growing faint on the horizon, just like the wild dogs. It was quiet in the car. I was pretending to scribble in my notebook. My dad took a deep breath; he seemed worn out. He said, "I guess people don't like door-to-door salesmen these days." He paused, plied his fingers, popped the joints, and latched his seat belt. "They just don't appreciate the service like they used to, but to call the police to tattle on a man's work, well, that's just un-American." We drove on toward Smallwood, and I was glad my father was nervous.

Chapter Seven

Ithink of my dad, the last time I saw him. He was behind a wall of bullet-proof glass, sitting in the lone chair, pressing the phone against his ear. We'd visited like this for months, and he was always glad to see me. His hair had turned almost completely white, and he'd put on some pounds, but other than that he looked more alert than I could remember. I think of how he asked for forgiveness and how I stupidly wouldn't give it. As Pascal and I drive to work, I can see my father's eyes full of tears as I hung up the receiver and theatrically left him there alone with his apology, believing there'd be another time to accept it.

The hidden crickets all along the ripe, black ditches sing as I drive the truck down the washboard road, the chassis jostling, Pascal's big frame under his yellow hide jiggling, too, as he sprawls out on the seat, head in my lap. The bouncing movement serves to wrest my thoughts free. This drive to work in the night, close enough to the swamp to feel its murky pull, smell the decay, and hear the faint hoot of owls and the splash of leggy things, is a little vacation each day.

Getting out of the truck, Pascal beating me to the door, I can see Ike reprimanding me through clenched teeth, "You wrote that piece of filth like you were the only one." He poked me hard in the chest and repeated, "The only damn one."

The group home is quiet, dark. The computer monitor on the staff desk swirls with a stupid geometric screen saver. I can smell baked beans and some sort of barbecue in the air, onions laced in, too. I put my book bag down gently on the desk and walk soft-footed to the kitchen, where a light over the oven casts a homey aura of yellow on the black burners below. The counters are scrubbed, and the dishwasher hums and clicks, the sound of muffled water spraying. Browder is in bed, and I'm sad not to have him to talk to.

It's 10:10 p.m. as I try to get up the courage to call my daughter. I tiptoe back to the living room and sit down at the desk, push the hulking book bag out of the way. It's late to be calling, but I know from Kate that our daughter stays up too late, and she gets it honestly; both of us are night owls. Back in Smallwood, Kate would purposely sign up for the night shift at ThriveStar Hospital.

The phone rings twice, then Kate answers. I can't talk for a moment, my cell phone damp against my ear. I clear my throat. "Gabe," she says, "you know almost all phones have caller ID now. How are you?"

"Kate," I stammer, "I didn't mean to get you. I mean, I was trying to talk with Wendy."

My ex-wife laughs. "Wow, you should be a writer, you're so good with words." Something about her voice sounds liquid, and I imagine Cal has just mixed her a smooth Scotch, ice cubes clear and solid, fake-looking, as if they're made from polyurethane.

"I didn't mean it that way, Kate." I can't think of how to move forward as the dishwasher kicks into a lower, more ominous-sounding cycle, groaning and swatting.

"Well, your daughter isn't here, Gabe. I know Cal told you she's seeing a boy who's a senior. They were out this evening looking at dresses for the prom."

"Why isn't she shopping for dresses with you?" I soften my approach, knowing I have no right here. "I mean, girls do that with their mothers, not their boyfriends, right?" I think for sure now I can hear her swirling ice in a glass, her hair over her shoulder, blue eyes inspecting the silver cubes of cold.

"Well, this may come as a surprise to you, Gabe, but things have changed since 1984. They don't wear fuzzy class rings anymore, or parachute pants, not to mention mullets." She laughs in a kind way and adds, "I'm just kidding."

One of the men in the group home, probably Fred, an elderly man with Down syndrome, is up and peeing with the door open; his fizzing stream of urine almost drowns out the dishwasher.

"Is there anything else, Gabe? I'll tell her you called."

"I'm coming up there soon. I'm writing another book." Fred stumbles back into his room and closes his door too hard.

"Oh, how wonderful," says Kate, using her most sarcastic inflection. I unzip my book bag, pull the photo of Mrs. Riley from the folder, and stare at the large, dark red clumps of thick blood matted into her hair, gleaming in the camera flash, reminding me of something from under the deep sea, wet and strange, dead and alive all at once. Kate continues, "So you're not coming home to visit your daughter. Perfect. Yes, let's have you write another book so that she'll be on course to want to see you when she's eligible for AARP."

"Okay," I say. "Just wait a minute, Kate. You wait a minute."

"Don't talk to me like that."

"Listen," I say, both of us still using our marriage rights. "Just listen for a fucking second, Kate." She sips from her glass and sighs, clams up. Peering at the photo of Mrs. Riley, I notice for the first time that a section of her hair has been completely yanked out, a hank of it lying like a squirrel tail near her half-exposed thigh. The sight of it makes me reconsider my tone, recognize my blessings.

"I'm not writing another memoir," I say, the last word almost whispered, as if it were something truly taboo. "It's a book about the Riley murders." Kate has lost interest, and I can hear Cal calling to her, a kind of gentle moan, followed by the sound of hooty jazz.

"I'll tell her you called, Gabe," she says, clinking the ice in her glass. "I've got to go. She has school tomorrow, and Friday nights are always unknowns. Maybe she can talk with you on Saturday, but don't count on it."

"Okay." There's a pause, and I don't hang up. "Kate, I really want to spend some time with her when I get up there. I'd like your help to make that happen."

"We'll see. Good-bye, Gabe."

As I sit at the desk, the house now sounds like I'm inside a large conch shell. The phone call with Kate has made it difficult to concentrate, but I force myself to research. I google the trial and print out newspaper articles on the group home printer, and remind myself to put a five-dollar bill in the petty cash drawer to pay for the ink. To get the events right in my mind, I draw my own timeline and fill in key dates: when the murders happened, the arrest of Rodney Finch, the search for the missing Riley boy's body. I stand up and go to the kitchen for a drink of water.

I sit down at the kitchen table and listen to the dishwasher now drying plates and bowls, the silverware and glasses. Steam escapes from the top of the GE, and I watch it, thinking of Wendy again, of how I used to tell her a dragon lived inside dishwashers, and when the steam came out, it was actually the dragon being extinguished by the water. He would float down the pipes and turn into a sweet and furry blue turtle. She loved it. It physically hurts to think about her, so I walk around the kitchen to soothe myself.

I slug back the remainder of the water, and notice a sealed envelope from Cindy on the table, my name blazoned across it. She's taken the time to also write the word *confidential*, underlined twice. Pascal trots into the kitchen. He falls down at my feet and curls up with a big sigh. I tap the envelope and tear open the end, pull out a folded paper, something on the letterhead of the corporate owners, a group called ComCare. The letter is addressed to Cindy and her boss, a woman from Atlanta who sometimes visits, stays a night in the spare bedroom, goes over the books with Cindy, and makes sure the charts are in order. Her name is Sandra Combs. The letter is short but sweet, saying that since Medicaid rates have fallen so drastically, the owners of ComCare can no longer afford to provide housing and support to the men living at Pleasant Hills. Next week, the letter reads, someone from the state of Georgia's Department of Disability Services will arrive to help make arrangements for all of the residents.

At the bottom of the letter, Cindy has written: "Call me. Kids are sick, but I'll be up late. This sucks!!"

She picks up on the first ring. "So what's up with this, huh?" I say.

"I know. Makes me mad," says Cindy, clearly in a rocking chair, its rhythmic squeaks almost a cartoon sound. "I hate it for the guys, but I don't know where I'll work now." We talk for a few minutes, griping some about short notices and the cruelty of the corporate office.

"What will happen to them?" I ask.

"Well," Cindy says, "you're not going to like this, but Sandra said they'll go back to the state hospital probably." The chair she's rocking in slows down, the rhythm like a very slow heartbeat now.

"But not Browder," I say. "I mean, he's smarter than I am. Won't he find another group home?"

"Probably, but not until he's spent a couple of months at the institution. Sandra says that's how it usually happens. But Browder is his own guardian, Gabe." She hangs on the line, waiting for me.

"Maybe he could go with me to Indiana until they find a group home for him," I say, knowing first off that I would love to spend more time with my friend, but also realizing I'm interested in having Browder along with me when I return to Smallwood. He's someone who will need me and, I shamefully think, might keep my family's anger at bay.

"Let me call Sandra tomorrow morning and see what she thinks," says Cindy. "But I think if Browder wants to go, he can." I can tell she's smiling.

"How's the book going, then?" she adds as Pascal lets out a couple of breath-taking poots of gas.

"Nowhere at this point. I guess you could say I've been putting it off like it's some kind of term paper." One of Cindy's children wakes up and begins to cry some. "Is he okay?" I ask.

"He's fine. Just a little feverish. I'll talk with you tomorrow," she says and hangs up.

Back at the desk, I feel invigorated; the thought of having Browder along for the trip gives me a kind of rush, something akin to having solved a puzzle. I'm actually energized as I read through one of the earliest newspaper reports of the Riley murders from the Fort Wayne *Journal Gazette*:

> Authorities outside of Smallwood, along with state police and personnel from the Indiana Bureau of Investigation, spent the morning processing the crime scene at the home of the Riley family. A neighbor out for her morning speed walking spotted something suspicious, an open garage door and what appeared to be oil in the concrete drive. Upon a closer look the neighbor noticed it was blood. She ran back to her home on Wilker Street and phoned the city police. At this point authorities are saying that at least four people were murdered with a shotgun, but one source close to the investigation claims that only three bodies were recovered, and that the fourth, that of the teenage Riley boy, has not been found. Smallwood, Indiana, is one hour directly south of Fort Wayne.

I put the article down on the desk and google Rodney Finch, then hit "images." A ton of photos tick onto the screen, one with him in silver shackles, another of him with his hair parted neatly as he sits at the defense table. He has a broad forehead and deep-set black eyes, but something about his cheeks gives him the look of a rotund child, even though he appears to be of average weight. In one photo, he's smiling as his defense attorney whispers in his ear. The caption states: "Rodney Finch, 23, who was just handed down a death penalty and is scheduled to die by lethal injection for the murders of the Riley family nearly two years ago."

I fall asleep with my head on the desk and dream intensely. Dark figures strap manacles to my feet, and I'm being pulled under an enormous, heavy fabric. I assume it's a parachute of some sort, until I awake. The sun comes warm and bright through the window, and I can remember as I open my eyes that what I thought was a parachute was actually a large pair of cotton panties, and that my father was trying to help me use them to leave Smallwood behind for good, but they wouldn't work because we were on the ground, not in a plane. I think I can recall telling him in the dream that a parachute only works if you're falling. When I sit up straight in the chair and rub at my eyes, yawn, Browder is there offering me a cup of coffee, his shirt neatly tucked into his pressed pants, and a friendly smile showing his gapped teeth. I take the coffee and thank him, hoping hard that he'll be allowed to be my travel companion.

Chapter Eight

Back at my apartment, the answering machine is blinking, and I think of all the bad news that comes from such a device: the arraignment and court-ordered psychotherapy, the bond and Mom putting up the house as collateral and the violation just four days after his release, the sound of Ike's voice as he tried to explain that Dad would be on the news, and that it would be best not to watch it. Lights—like the one that is winking at me now, mocking my presence, feigning an indication of good news but really holding all that is sickening, paralyzing—seem to follow me from place to place, a reminder that leaving is only a temporary solution.

I hit the Play button, and someone hangs up. The next call is from Cindy, trying to catch me before I went to work yesterday to tell me about Pleasant Hills closing. There's a pause before the third message, and Michael the agent takes the phone off speaker and talks directly into the mouthpiece. "Hey there, Truman Capote," he says, not a trace of irony in his approach. "This is your tried-and-true agent. Just checking in. I assume you're on your way to Indiana, then. Remember to make sure I have your contact details. Didn't know if you'd end up getting a local cell phone once you're up there. Give the corn and pigs kisses for me. Much love. Bye."

I erase all the messages and look around the place. Pascal whines to go for a walk, but I have to run to the leasing office to broker some sort of deal. I can feel the urgency now; last night's delving into the details of the Riley case, even if brief, has given me some energy. Dad was diagnosed with having an obsessive-compulsive personality, and maybe a tad bit of manic depression, although he only was treated with Paxil while in prison. I can't help but think about the highs and lows of my own life as I take a copy of my lease with me and head out into the crisp spring sunlight, feeling every bit the enthusiastic author, while just a few days ago all I could do was drink and smoke and listen to classic rock.

Blackbirds hop over a scattering of discarded French fries near the Dumpster, while several people are taking advantage of the nice weather to wash their cars, a sucking vacuum in use, pennies flying up the long tube, as a man hitches up his pants and looks at the end as if amazed by the force. I pass the pool where a black iron fence and security gate keep the blue water protected just for us residents. Up in the sky, turkey buzzards swirl in a gigantic swath, riding the wind shear and looping in slow, wide figure eights, slicing the electric atmosphere.

I jog up the steps to the office, and the little metal bell clinks against the glass door as I enter, its small tongue missing. No one is at the desk, and the door to the office at the side of the waiting area is closed. I stand in the center of the floor, holding the rental agreement in my hand as if ready to go to court. I turn around and look out the glass door in the direction I just came, but all that's visible is the sunlight on the pitted steps, and the brick facade of one of the buildings, the shadow of this one. I turn back and decide to knock on the office door. I rap lightly, then a little harder. Someone from behind the door utters something, which I take for permission to enter. I twist the knob, and a flurry of activity seems to bounce off the walls, the desk, and chairs. Two bodies whipping on shirts, a man stooping to yank up his jeans, and the young woman who is usually at the front desk, face red and eyes wide, trying to shimmy into her tight skirt, a bright green thong gone in a flash. "Jesus," says the manager, a man who lifts weights and is always in the complex's fitness center with his wife, spotting her, peering down at her, his legs spread. "I fucking said wait a minute!" He wipes his mouth with a sleeve as the young woman hurries past me, dangling her high heels from one French-manicured forefinger, her lovely brown pony switching like a horsetail.

"I'm so sorry," I say, embarrassed, feeling as if I'm the one who's done something wrong. The weight lifter shoves the tails of his shirt in and still grimaces, runs his hand through his hair. "What was so important that you had to barge in?" he asks, then seems to remember that he's been caught. He acts contrite now. "Please sit down," he says. "Is there something wrong with your apartment?" I don't sit but hand him the lease.

"I have to break it," I say as he looks over it and then tosses it on the desk.

"Usually we make people pay two months' rent to do that," he says, catching his breath, adjusting his crotch, before he sits down. "But seeing that you've been a really quiet tenant, I think we can make an exception." He licks his lips, and another thought dawns on him as the young woman out at the reception desk is printing something. "You've not been noisy like lots of our renters. I'll take care of this personally," he assures me. "Who knows, maybe someday I might need something from you." I nod and smile, leave the office quietly, the skies outside scarred with the ghostly contrails of jets.

I realize as I click the leash on Pascal that my busting in on the scene in the rental office has taken care of one of my major obstacles to leaving. We hop into the truck and head back toward the group home, where Browder will be waiting for me on the front steps to take him bird-watching in the swamp.

A stronger breeze riffles the leaves of the trees, exposing a lighter green on the underside. The Datsun truck bounces over the uneven road, and I try not to swerve as I dial Cindy. She sounds tired when she answers, but then perks up. "Sandra said all you have to do is meet with Browder's case manager. I've already called her, and she'll meet you at the group home in an hour." Cindy sounds utterly optimistic.

"But I'd need to ask Browder, too, right?"

"Oh, come on," says Cindy. "He'd go with you to watch paint dry." She laughs, then gets serious. "Listen, I've been meaning to tell you something, Gabe." Tall, spiky saw palmetto plants sit like sentries along the loblolly pine forest as sun shines silver off my windshield.

"What is it?"

"I want you to know, Gabe, that we're praying for you. My husband, too. I put you on our church prayer list last Sunday. I hope that's okay. Forgiveness is what I asked them to pray for."

I slow the truck as we pass the Black Angus grazing in a field of undulating fescue. A large bull swats his tail along his muscular gleaming hide as the herd inches forward. Pascal watches him as we slowly cruise by, careful not to bottom out in the spot we've driven over a thousand times.

"Thank you." I pause. "Just curious though. You think I need forgiveness?"

Cindy actually laughs out loud. "Hon, if you think I could get away with airing all my family's dirty laundry and not have H-E-double toothpicks to pay for it, you're crazy. Remember, I read your book!" Then Cindy gets serious. "But really, forgiveness, when you're willing to ask for it, and receive it, and when you're able to give it, well it's just a darn miracle is all. It works miracles in your life."

We chat a bit more about the approach to take with the case manager, and Cindy tells me to make sure I say the trip is educational, that it can count as one of Browder's goals, something called "travel training," which is a weird way to say that he will be practicing how to ride with me.

I turn into the drive of Pleasant Hills and notice a white sedan with the Georgia state emblem emblazoned on the sides. The letters GOVT. are printed on the license plate, and I nose the truck right up close. Several of the men are on the porch eating slices of blackberry pie. Fred hollers out to me, "They're getting rid of us, mister."

I don't see Browder, and I sort of shout back to the group, "Naw, they're just making sure y'all have what you need, is all." I hate the way I sound, and trying to make it seem more Southern doesn't help. I wave and slip inside the house, also hating that the men I've gotten to know will have to leave their home.

A rotund woman with wispy black hair sits at the kitchen table with Browder. She has his chart open, using a ballpoint to make notations, the metal binder pulled open.

"Hello," I say, and she holds up a finger as she scrawls on a form with the date printed in bold letters at the top. Browder smiles at me and folds his large hands together in his lap, then licks his lips and hangs his head. It seems as if the case manager is writing a whole page, pressing down so hard I can see the paper has torn in one place. I don't feel good about the chances of Browder coming along. I remind myself not to mention the Riley murders, and to focus on my family, their respective jobs and the opportunities Browder will have to meet new people. I think of telling her we'll also have the opportunity to eat dinner with family, but who? Surely not my ex-wife and my daughter, maybe not even Ike. I decide I'll tell her that my mother will be feeding us, a lie of course, but the thing Cindy told me was to focus on the trip's opportunities, and she didn't even mean it sarcastically.

"So," the case manager says, "have a seat." She points at the end of the table, and I instead pull out the chair next to Browder, but she says, "No, Mr. Burke. I'd prefer you to sit at the head." I freeze, hand on the chair back, and I can see the part in Browder's hair, the white scarlike line on the top of my friend's head. It seems I need to take my cues from Browder; after all, he's been through this kind of thing probably hundreds of times, situations where the only control you have is pretending you are okay with not having any control, acting as if it's just fine, even suitable and appropriate, to be treated as if you were unworthy of anything more than disregard. I think I see Browder kind of tilt his head toward the chair the case manager wants me to sit in.

"That's right," she says, "right there. My name is Marsha McLison. I'm the case manager assigned to Mr. Browder, and I'm the chair of the state's Learning and Training Subcommittee." I sit down and watch Browder as he sits so stock-still I think he might be catatonic.

"Hello," I say. "I'm Gabe Burke. I've worked here for—" She cuts me off.

"I know who you are, Mr. Burke," she says, and I can detect a tone of dislike for me. She wrinkles her nose as she flips through Browder's chart, and I see that she's stopped on a daily log with my handwriting. "But you sure couldn't tell it by your activity notes. Very vague, and certainly not connected to any of the men's goals." She tosses her pen onto the open chart and folds her arms over her droopy chest. She has a ripe pimple at the corner of her left eye, and her bracelets clink as she unfolds her arms. "Tell me why on earth I should let Mr. Browder go with you on a trip to Indiana instead of him getting used to his new environs at the state hospital in Savannah." Ire wrenches my throat, and I can feel the rapid thump of my pulse. I hate Marsha McLison.

"Well, I know it's not the norm. But I just thought Browder would benefit from a trip. We've become close over the years, and if he . . ." I stop because it feels wrong that I've not actually invited him along. "One moment, please," I say and turn to Browder, touch his arm, then retract my hand as quick as I can. "Browder," I say, "I'd like to invite you to come along with me to—"

"Whoa, whoa, whoa," says the case manager, standing up, almost yelling, as Browder slumps more into his chair. "We're not doing it this way. No sir. First, we'll see if this trip fits with Mr. Browder's goals." Marsha McLison slowly sits back down, and her face seems to register that she may have overdone it. She tucks a loose strand of hair behind her ear.

"What bothers me," she says, tilting her head, checking her iPhone as she talks, "is that this is just coming out of nowhere. There wasn't any discussion leading up to this, or any indication at all as to why you're so interested in taking Mr. Browder with you." The case manager sits up straighter and widens her eyes, looks at me with an expression that, if I'm honest, unnerves me, but then I'm pissed and trying hard to not let myself lose it on her.

"Yes, well," I say, "sometimes trips are planned, and at other times a trip may just form within a few days. As soon as I heard about the home closing, I thought it would be good to invite Browder along." She frowns and shakes her head, and I prattle on. "I mean, I thought it would be good to get permission to bring him along, then invite him." I'm tired and feeling bad for Browder.

For the next ten minutes Marsha McLison, state of Georgia case manager, moves from texting to grilling me about my trip. She scribbles notes and shakes her head over and over. The other men are starting to wander back inside, and there's chatter about leaving their house, and what will become of them, will they ever see one another again. My heart falls. Fred says, "*Que será, será*. Whatever will be, will be." Then he goes to the bathroom and pees without closing the door, which makes Marsha leap from her chair and scold him.

Slamming the door, she marches back to the table and sits down roughly, her unflattering, sagging bosom almost spreading over the tabletop. I feel guilty for noticing and look toward Browder. Marsha says, "That's a prime example of not providing them with solid behavioral feedback," and I want to tell her Fred's acting like any man who lives with a whole bunch of other men. The sunlight outside is bright and inviting, and I catch Browder looking at the green grass and birds flittering from the tree limbs and washing themselves in a little mud puddle. He loves the outdoors, even if he has an uncanny ability to spot dead things whenever we're in the swamp.

"So," I say, trying to sound chipper and fully reprimanded. "I realize I could do more to instruct. I've really heard your input, and you're dead on. I mean, I can take daily notes on our trip, even send them to you in the mail if you like."

"Oh, you will most certainly send the Instructional Therapy Progress notes," she says, "but it can be done online." She begins to gather her things, and I realize this has mostly been a formality, something that could have been done over the phone. Marsha McLison stands up and tosses her purse over her shoulder, looks down at the iPhone in her hand, makes us wait. "By the way," she says, "what is the nature of this trip?" I begin to answer, but she cuts me off. "I've heard you're a writer." She tucks her phone into a special holster at her ample hip. "I've heard about your book," she adds, saying the word *book* like it might be actual defecation. People I work with, or some college or high school friends I've bumped into, tell me they've heard of my book, meaning they've heard about my dad. Marsha McLison answers her phone and leaves Browder and me at the kitchen table as she walks out to her car. He finally looks up and smiles.

"So," I say, "would you like to come with me to Indiana? It might be a couple of months."

Browder stands up and so do I. He nods enthusiastically and gives me a quick, tight hug. "I'll be your co-captain," says Browder. Then he disappears to the back of the house to pack.

Chapter Nine

It's hard to pack for the trip. I can't get the image out of my head of the cops arresting my father during our family Thanksgiving meal in Smallwood. Ike was there with Susana and their firstborn, who was just a baby. Wendy was in diapers, too, but toddling around the house. It was a year after his two other arrests, all of us complicit, as if it were simply a man in the wrong place at the wrong time, but this was the third one, after a strange event that happened while he and Mom were camping near the Indiana Dunes. A woman had complained about him to the park ranger, who arranged his own stakeout, catching Dad in the alleged act at about 2 a.m.—on film, and compromised. He tried to run, but was apprehended in no time. Mom had called Ike, who'd called me, and I think it was the first time any of us started to silently figure out in our heads that he wasn't going to stop.

As I said, the arrest at the Thanksgiving meal was both a shock and an expectation; Dad stood up and went outside on the porch with the two deputies as Mom's face went white. She scooped out huge amounts of mashed potatoes onto our plates. She put so many potatoes on Ike's plate, it looked like a white beehive. I can remember my little Wendy at the living room window that looked out onto the porch; she knew her granddad was out there, and she pounded on the glass with her chubby hand, squealing with delight. Mom screamed a tiny bit, then ran into the bathroom and puked, while Ike and our wives and I watched them cart Dad away in a shiny cruiser, the autumn sun gleaming off the hood and loose leaves somersaulting over the dead lawn. Wendy started to wail, her grandfather gone. We'd find out later he'd been the focus of surveillance: pictures of him, some video, and three women willing to testify that he was the one they'd seen taking pictures of them from the parking lot at some apartments in town.

I actually have to shake my head to get focused, pack up the little bit I own. There's a photo of Wendy and me in a black frame; she has on her winter coat, zipped up to that vulnerable little neck. Her hair is in a French braid, one that I had done, poorly, off center, but she was little and thought I was the best dad ever because I could give her a braid. I tuck the photo into my large rucksack, along with tablets of paper, four or five pairs of jeans, a wad of T-shirts and underwear. There's not much else in the apartment, a few cooking items, some of Dad's beloved HomeBeam Wares pots, a few cans of soup, and boxes of dried noodles. The muscleman in the leasing office assured me my mattress and kitchen items could be stored until I return.

I drag the big duffel bag toward the door. Pascal tries to attack it, almost riding the thing as he paws and chews on the top. I look back into the empty apartment that has been my home for almost five years. I'm about to close the door behind me when the phone rings, and I realize it's something I've failed to disconnect. It rings and rings, and I'm reminded of how much the memoir pissed off Ike. He kept calling one night, until finally, drunk and surly, he said to me, "Hey there, tattletale." I thought I could hear him almost vomit. "I've been reading your little book of horrors, asshole. Nice work, I mean, I'm sure our kids will be so proud of their genealogy." I could hear Susana telling him to get off the phone. He told her, in a high-pitched sarcastic tone, "Shh, honey, I'm talking with the greatest writer of our generation. He's gonna be on *Oprah* next week. There'll be a parade thrown in Gabe fucking Burke's honor right here in Smallwood. He's a regular Jack fucking Kerouac." I tried to say something to him but knew it was useless.

"Shut the fuck up," Ike said. "Listen," he continued in a whispered, conspiratorial tone, "let me make one thing clear, asshole." He burped, and I pictured him swaying in neatly pressed pants, his tie still knotted in a double Windsor. "I'm gonna sew your ass to your face." Ike hung up then, and I couldn't sleep that night. He wouldn't take my calls for months, then ironically enough, on Thanksgiving he left me a message, and we talked about Wendy and the weather and the Riley murders, which had just happened, and from then on the memoir was just another of our family's ugly secrets.

Pascal and I climb into the truck after I've thrown my rucksack into the bed and jogged back to the apartment for his bowls and half bag of food. As we drive by the Dumpster, I see the maintenance guys huddled there; Pascal growls at them when he spots the .22 rifle. As we pass them and head out of the complex and onto the frontage road, I realize it's the last time we'll make this drive to the group home, and I can't help but feel nostalgic. Pascal lies down and puts his cowlike head in my lap, the swamp slowly eddying in the tree line that stretches out like a horizon of black ice, the spring sunshine bobbling off the surface, giving the whole expanse the look of gray and orange, the only two colors the artist had to work with. I steer half aware, and before I can even think about what I'm doing, we're at the group home, as if time had warped and dropped the idling truck right next to the house.

Browder has a lunch box in his hand and a vinyl-shell suitcase the color of a yolk sitting at his big feet on the front porch. I'm shocked to see him there alone. As we get out of the truck, he holds up a piece of lined paper, folded into thirds. He says, "They all went to eat at the buffet." He looks disappointed but happy, too, as he lugs the suitcase toward the truck and throws it into the bed.

"Did you eat?" I ask, and Browder shrugs.

"Not much. Just some cereal." I tell him once we're on the road, we'll eat even better food than at the buffet.

"Hard to beat it," says Browder, and he's right. The browned sweet potatoes with pumpkin butter alone are enough to make my mouth water. I open the note, which essentially lists the Web site I'm to access to update Browder's chart, report on our activities together. The case manager has written at the bottom: "Make sure to notify me if *anything* changes."

Browder doesn't even look back as we pull from the driveway. He pets Pascal's neck and rubs his ears. Once we're nearly at the bylane we use to access the massive swamp, I ask Browder if we should stop one last time. "We won't be back here for a couple of months. Should we stop and tell it goodbye?" He nods yes, smiling, his white, square teeth reminiscent of someone from a milk commercial.

As we tread along the worn path that weaves through swaths of sedges and ferns and rushes, I'm aware that we'll soon be on the road toward Smallwood. I put one foot in front of the other as Pascal bounds over soggy furrows of muck. Browder manages well enough, his bad leg sort of flopping over the terrain. Lily pads dot the expansive landscape, and I can see I truly have been hiding out. I ran away and chose a life where being a caretaker was a job, not a familial role.

Browder and I stand side by side on a ledge of semisolid peat, the air around us ripe with the earth folding in upon itself. My stomach hurts, and chills pimple my arms and legs. We don't talk, and I wonder what's going through Browder's mind. I think of Wendy, and Kate and Ike and Mother. The images of the Rileys' bloody bodies seem to pop up on the horizon, and the tangle of Spanish moss dangling from a tree reminds me of Mrs. Riley's wet, bloody hair. The tea-colored water in front of us, glinting from time to time with patches of sunlit vegetation, seems so still it could be a pane of glass. This giant bog was once part of the ocean floor, something I've told Browder so many times I've started to believe he thinks of me as some kind of grandfatherly crackpot, telling the same stories over and over. In my head, I try to imagine actually arriving in Smallwood, showing up at their houses and hugging them with the truck doors still open, Pascal chasing a squirrel, but all that comes to me are those faces of disappointment and betrayal. I can picture Dad's gravestone, the simple boxy marble marker that holds his dates: Born January 28, 1940. Died August 22, 1994. At the funeral, Ike had worn black shades and finally started to accept what our father was. I can see him now fixing us pancakes, sledding with us on a massive hill near the Michigan border, having driven hours to get there, sundown almost turning everything to black, the snow packed and hard and cold against our wet butts. I hear our dad singing a song from some 1950s crooner, something about the white sands of Arabia and a woman whose mane was torturous to look at, it was so beautiful.

Browder slowly sits down next to Pascal, and we look out over the swamp waters. I know he'll ask shortly to use the binoculars that dangle around my neck. Instead though, he just reaches up and peers over his shoulder at me, holding out his hand, squinting into the sunlight. I hand them to him, and he begins to survey the area with precision, moving his head in minute increments to take in the swamp line, the hundreds of islets that sit like little countries in the calm waters. Browder spots a turtle climbing a log and shows me, and then an osprey feeding its young in a high, bulky nest. He stands up, and Pascal barks, knowing it's about time to go, and then Browder, as usual, spots something dead on one of the lonesome isles where a rookery of wading birds chatters and breeds. He hands me the binoculars and points, and when I look through the glasses and focus the lenses, I can make out a mound of black-brown fur, some white bones, maybe a hip, like chalk in the bright sun. It's a bear, or what's left of it, and I hate to see turkey vultures flapping lazily over the hump, pecking greedily, and pulling away bits of flesh just for themselves.

Part Two

"Happy families are all alike;

every unhappy family is

unhappy in its own way."

—Leo Tolstoy from *Anna Karenina*

Chapter Ten

The interstate stretches out before us like a foreign land, elongated and crammed, littered with rubber, our fellow citizens erect or slouched in their vehicles, SUVs thumping rap, pumping pollution, and hybrids decaled with self-important pledges and mottoes. In America, the highways are like the rest of the nation, angry and diverse, wild and numb, with only the occasional human being, someone willing to let you over, make way for you in their travels. I wave now as a man with a long, black beard driving a Malibu sedan slows down and allows us to switch lanes. He toots his horn and gives me a thumbs-up. Browder smiles and rolls down his window and waves. Pascal's tail thumps against my leg as we glide toward the off-ramp and head for some food.

"Bet you're really hungry now," I say to Browder, who is fiddling with his satchel, digging around in it. He nods yes, but is preoccupied. He pulls out a pair of pajama pants with red-hot chilies on them, and an assortment of Mafia DVDs, banded into a stack with a thin strip of torn cloth. His eyes are intense, the skin above his nose crinkled into a pinkish ridge. Finally, he pulls from the satchel another type of bag, a black, shiny leather pouch. We trundle off the ramp and into the parking lot of a Cracker Barrel, its homey front porch adorned in all manner of down-home flair, rocking chairs and old Coca-Cola machines, rusty plowshares and antique motor-oil signs made of tin, the paint peeling. All of it manufactured to look authentic, regionally rustic. The windows are like massive mirrors, reflecting the cars in the parking lot. Browder unzips the black pouch as I shut off the truck and leash up Pascal. He has a Nikon camera, and a nice one, too.

"Wow," I tell him, "you've got quite a camera there." Pascal licks my face, and I can't wait to stretch my legs. We've just crossed the state line, and I figure we're nearly on top of Lookout Mountain, Tennessee.

"Cindy gave it to me," says Browder. "She brought it by last night. Her husband got a new one, so . . ." As we load Pascal into the back of the truck bed, Browder snaps a picture. When I open a can of dog food and mix it with some water, he takes another one.

"Don't waste all your film," I tell Browder, who just laughs and points to the digital counter at the corner of the camera. "It doesn't take film," he says, and I think two things: one, that Cindy really is a good person, and she practices what she's preached, and two, that Browder has once again shown me that the idea of disability is all relative.

The sight of Browder snapping photos of the faux old-timey checkers table at the entrance to the Cracker Barrel reminds me of a Christmas with Mom and Dad. Dad had bought Mom a big, fancy camera and a long, almost vulgar telescopic lens. It was an expensive purchase, one that mystified us all, not just because our parents usually didn't give each other anything more than trivial gifts for Christmas—a box of Salems tied with a red bow, and for Mom a set of dish towels she knew Dad gave out as freebies to his HomeBeam Wares customers—but because our mother had never once shown any interest in photography whatsoever. Even before New Year's rolled around that year in 1987, Dad had taken over the camera, leaving the house for hours, the thing around his neck, and coming back with vague answers to Mom's questions about where he'd been, what he'd been photographing.

Browder and I sit down at a table so we can keep an eye on Pascal through the windows. I can't keep from thinking how I'd used Dad's camera to take pictures of Becca, and how I couldn't for the life of me figure out where the film had gone, how I had fretted over it, afraid to tell her about it.

"You boys want to start with something cold to sip on?" asks the waitress, but Browder orders everything at once. "Chicken fingers, fries, baked potato, and a big Coke, please." The woman smiles as if I'm traveling with Rain Man, and really for the first time, I realize my friend's differences must show more than I think.

"And for you, sir?"

I order catfish and coleslaw, to which Browder adds, "I'll take that, too." There's some confusion over whether he wants both or just a change in his order, and I'm amazed to watch him polish the two meals off in less than twenty minutes. At this rate, the trip is going to get expensive quickly, but I'm glad to be watching him get a chance at freedom.

"I didn't even ask you," I say, "when's the last time you went on a trip?"

"We went to Six Flags last year," answers Browder, and he flashes that charming smile.

"But where else? Like what other states have you been to?"

"None," he says. "This is my first time to go away from Georgia." I like the way he's phrased it. If none of this works out, if Ike and my daughter and the rest of my family turn me away at the state line, refuse to let me enter Hoosier Land, it will all be worth it just to see Browder so hopeful, so optimistic that he snaps a photo of me drinking coffee, and then another of a pear-shaped woman with pinkish hair returning from the bathroom and heading toward her table near us, where a boatload of grandchildren are fidgety and a little testy, at least one of them saying how hungry they all are. The woman stops, poses now for Browder, and he laughs, snaps two photos in quick succession. I'm glad when she tells him he's precious and goes to her own booth.

"Well, we're gonna have a good time, Browder. I mean, I'll have to work, and there'll be lots of visits and people to meet," I say, purposely not using the word interviews, but he picks up on my restraint.

"You gonna write that book about those murders? Those pictures you have?" he asks, kind of taking his cue from me, tucking his head and whispering. "Those bloody ones?"

"Yes. That's it. But we'll also see my family. You remember the times Wendy came down for a visit, my daughter?"

"Uh-huh. She liked playing Uno with that thing that spits out the cards," says Browder, and I can see the two of them now, although I'd forgotten it, lying on the living room floor for hours, Wendy telling Browder to play one more game. She drank glass upon glass of watermelon Kool-Aid, so much that she threw up that night. It had been humid and hot, a Georgia June, and Kate had allowed her to stay with me for three weeks. When I drove her back to her mother, meeting in Tennessee, I thought my chest would always feel heavy and sickly.

"She's sixteen now," I say, and Browder raises his eyebrows, shakes his head, a little overly dramatic.

The dining room of the Cracker Barrel starts to empty, the entire space growing more quiet with each five-minute set, and it's nice to just sit and let the human activity hum around our lingering. It seems everything reminds me of Dad lately, the way we also took our time at the little restaurants around Smallwood, and all those other Indiana towns. The little cafés always smelled of cold wind, gasoline, and hot grease, cigarette smoke, and burnt coffee.

When Browder tells the waitress he'd like a to-go cup for his next glass of Coke, I figure we better get on the road. I've not really called anyone to let them know we're on our way, and I have to admit to myself that I'm putting it off. It feels right to drive toward Louisville, maybe stop around Bowling Green.

At the cash register, I start to pay, but see Browder shopping the cluttered "country store" part of the Barrel. He picks up a little stuffed pig then puts it down, and then finds a trucker's hat that says: "Real Men Eat Grits!" It occurs to me he hasn't a cent on him. I fish out three twenty-dollar bills from my wallet and walk toward Browder. He's now looking at a harmonica in a blue velvet case, his eyes wide. "Listen," I say to him, trying to sound casual. "I forgot to tell you I'll be needing a photographer for this project." I hand him the money and say, "This is an advance on your pay. If you work with me, I can pay you a hundred dollars a week."

Browder says loudly, "What? Oh man! I'd be the picture man!" He's so excited he gives me a bear hug, almost knocking over a tree tower of round lollipops.

"So it's a deal?" I ask him, holding out my hand. He shakes it in quick pumps.

"Sure." He takes the money and shoves it into his pocket. "I'm gonna buy this," he tells me, holding up the harmonica, and I watch as he marches up to the cashier. As we leave the restaurant, Browder is already putting the thing to his lips, and I pray I can take the awful whinnying all the way to Smallwood.

I can't help but think of Becca; we had taken road trips together, and the pavement rhythmically thumping beneath my truck brings back her memory so clearly that I can almost smell her menthol cigarettes and the spicy perfume she wore on her neck. It was late summer, and she'd been to college twice by then and dropped out, while I was just about to start in the fall. By that time, Dad had become withdrawn and sometimes negative, a look of pain on his face. HomeBeam Wares had closed for good a year earlier, and now he took temp jobs all over the northern part of Indiana. Sometimes he'd be selling vacuums by phone, something called a Swedish Double Cyclonic that he told people could suck up softballs. If he wasn't telemarketing, there were the little repair jobs he did for people, patching roofs or fixing a front step. I tried hard not to think about those houses, who might live in them. Like my mother and Ike, I started to ignore all of him just to forget the part that terrified me. He vanished not only into the countryside, that damn camera around his neck, but he was starting to fade from our lives, too, becoming more and more a phantom father, a man who, when he did appear, was red-eyed and as white as copy paper, but he never stopped wearing a tie, or carrying a handkerchief in the back pocket of his suit pants. I had chosen not to write about Becca in the memoir, mostly because no one else knew about us, not Kate nor the man Becca eventually ended up marrying, then divorcing.

Now, as I flip my blinker to move over so a nut in a behemoth Hummer can surge ahead, I think about how sad she'd seemed that summer. Becca had told me that our six-year age difference would make our time together short. "You'll make it through college," she had told me. "I just couldn't. I can't figure out what I'll ever do with my life." Then we'd drive to the Salamonie Reservoir, the drought having sucked away almost all of the russet water, and walk down to what had been the beach. There were shanks of driftwood and brittle cans, pieces of lumber and old tires washed into a scrum of maple saplings, all of it so depressing and desolate that we would reach for each other's hand at the same time. Becca would strip off her clothes as she talked, unhooking her shiny taupe bra and shucking off her cotton panties as if she were simply getting ready for a bath, oblivious to me or her surroundings, talking on and on, telling me things about her fiancé and how he irritated her sometimes. It went on like that all summer, sex outdoors and little drives that turned into full-blown road trips, as we ended up in Chicago or the Indiana Sand Dunes, drunk on tallboy Buds, and smoking. Only once had Becca said anything about my father. "You know," she said, lying on a blanket in the sand, brown hair black-wet, pulling on her jeans, sucking in her stomach to fasten them. "He stares at me sometimes when he comes over to visit. I don't want to offend you, Gabe, but your dad kind of freaks me out." At the time, I acted as if she hadn't said a thing, and wrestled her to the ground, tickled her until she screamed and kicked and laughed, the sand stuck on our damp bodies.

I slow the truck to merge into another lane as Pascal snores lightly and Browder snoozes into a rolled-up sweatshirt. The skyline of Nashville looms erect to my left, the Batman Building on Commerce Street dominating it all, masked and foreboding against the sky, a perfect pinwheel of orange starting to slide toward the bottle-green horizon. I can't shake the idea of Becca, how she'd been right about it all; we'd see each other a few more times when I was back home from college, and even once after she had married that guy, what was his name? Roy? Rod? As the traffic clears and I can maneuver better, I say his name out loud, as if I've solved a trivia question, "Rich!" After that though, it was as if all the time we'd spent together was just part of some alternate universe. The radio plays softly. I sing along a little and actually feel my state of mind buoy some as the traffic thins and I feel the open road expand. I speed up. My cell phone rings. The area code from New York appears as if on an electronic billboard, 212 spiraling around in tangerine digits, and a mixture of sullen dread and edgy hope makes me reach for the volume on the radio.

"Hello?" I say, and the agent just begins laughing.

"Ah," he says, "you're on the road. Capote out on life's highway, about to crack things wide open, am I right?"

"Not quite," I say, and like the good agent he is, Michael switches immediately into the counselor role.

"Hey, listen," he says, "this is an important story. Yes, it's got all the elements of a true crime book, but you can really make a difference here. The community and the extended family of the . . ." He's forgotten the Riley name.

"Riley," I insert as Pascal wakes and looks around, tail like a metronome on the split seat of the truck.

"Right, the Rileys. You can do this, Gabe. And with the reprint of the memoir, maybe we can get some traction for other projects." There's a pause, and then he adds, "Listen, tiger," and for some reason I think I should pull over, prepare myself for what he's about to say. Half of me would like nothing more than for my New York agent to tell me the deal's off, that on second thought, the editor has changed his mind. "Hey," says Michael. "You there, Gabe? Gabe?"

"No, I'm here," I say. "We must've hit a patch of weak signals."

"Anyway, the editor would like for you to write a new foreword, but he also wants an epilogue, you know, something about his death." Even Michael finds the last part hard to say, and isn't willing to specify whose death.

"I can't write about my dad's suicide, Michael. My family already hates me."

"Hate is a strong word, Gabe. What I mean is, I don't think they will get any madder about it. Sometimes these things are freeing, you know, like therapy."

"You always tell me writing isn't therapy, Michael."

"Damn, Gabe, don't you forget anything? I'm talking about bringing you to a larger audience. We might be able to finally get some real traction here."

"The problem though, Michael, is that my family isn't made up of characters. They're real. And I'll be lucky if they don't beat me around the head and neck when I see them."

The agent lets out a little squeal of laughter and adds to the banter. "Or they might just throw a parade in your honor, let you ride a boar through town as people pelt you with roasted maize and a jug band plays a Crystal Gayle tune." The conversation is starting to make my ear hot, and I'm now more aware of how little I've been paying attention to the traffic. Out of the corner of my eye, I can see that Browder is stirring, sitting up some, stretching his long arms, petting Pascal. Just as I look in my side mirror, I hear the first flat, dread-inducing note from the harmonica, followed by something new, a small but undeniable howl by Pascal. Browder allows a longer note to grate and scratch, and my dog again plays his own instrument.

"What the hell is that?" asks Michael.

"Just some of my wayward kin we've picked up along the highway. They are buck-toothed and shirtless, feet as dirty as their sin. One of them has a banjo on his knee. Two of them are eating from one drumstick." Michael laughs again at this, but I can hear he's also getting another call—an assistant who seems to always interrupt at the same intervals. I assume it's part of their office workings, like a signal friends work out before a party so they won't get stuck with a raging conspiracy theorist.

"I've got to go, Gabe. So remember, the editor needs the prologue and epilogue in a month. They want to print review copies and have the memoir all ready to go when you turn in the true crime manuscript. Bye-bye." I don't get the chance to object, and knowing Michael, he'll call in a couple of weeks to see how far I've gotten on something I said I wouldn't do in the first place.

I put the cell phone in the cup holder and listen while Pascal and Browder, my road trip partners in crime, make their awful music together, while the sun begins to disappear from the sky. As we rush down the highway toward our destiny, I can't for the life of me say which one is the worse musician.

Chapter Eleven

We've been in the hotel room for almost two hours, and Browder is totally engrossed in a movie called *Gomorrah*, an Italian film about the mob in the south of Italy. The description on the Internet said the writer of the novel the movie was based on had to leave the country for his own protection, afraid of an assassination plot from the Neapolitan branch of the Mafia. It sounded like a film I'd like to watch, but since we ordered it on the plasma in the hotel room, I've only been able to glance up every now and again, forcing myself to read and take notes, complete the interview schedule, plan things out. Pascal is at my feet, taking deep, syncopated breaths, his hot air soothing my bare soles. I shelled out an extra thirty-five bucks to have him with us. It's nice to partake in this little out camp before we make it to Smallwood tomorrow. The television's turned almost all the way down, and while I asked Browder if he needed me to sit and read the subtitles, he just waved me off, sitting impossibly cross-legged on his bed, back straight. We've ordered room service: Angus burgers and onion rings, two slices of chocolate cheesecake, and a can of Sprite each, but we're still waiting.

I put my pen down and stretch my back, reading what I've written down in bold letters: "Call Ike to get a time to look at the courthouse files!" I pop my back and twist my neck, a movement Pascal thinks means we're going for a walk, which is something I suppose I should do before it gets much later.

"Hey," I say to Browder, who isn't moving a muscle as the movie plays. His lips are moving though, and his brow is furrowed in intense concentration. It's a view that touches me, kind of breaks my heart. "Browder," I say as Pascal yawns and yelps, "I'm gonna take him out, okay? Answer the door if the food comes, all right?" He quickly turns toward me, pops a fake smile, and nods, getting back to the movie and its maddening, unending subtitles, his lips instantly moving again.

I slip on my shoes and click the leash, leave the room, slowly letting the door shut on its own. I test the handle to make sure it's locked as Pascal pulls and pants.

Outside, the smell of spring is damp and cool; a scent of something sweetly floral permeates the side yard where Pascal hikes his leg. The dark sky is clear, pricks of silver stars dotted in the spaces beyond the glare of the hotel lights. A crescent moon hangs lopsided halfway up the blackness. There's a bench in a little garden area, surrounded by an entrance to a golf course. Little topiary lights twinkle, and I sit down, pull out the cell phone, and dial Ike's house. On the second ring, Susana picks up, and I tentatively say hello.

"Hey there, Gabe," she says, and I'm taken aback by her chipper tone. "Ike said you were coming up. When is it?" Something also sounds strained in her voice, as if she wants someone to talk to, anyone, even her disloyal brother-in-law, the guy she once said only wanted attention, that he was just pretending to be a writer, and although she pointed her finger at me and said as much outside the courthouse, over the years I've heard her in my head a million times and can see where maybe she was right.

"Oh, I'm actually on my way now. I mean, we're on our way." I feel winded, and my face has reddened. If this is any indication of how I'll do in my hometown of Smallwood, I might as well turn around and head back to the swamp.

"Good, good," says my sister-in-law, and I can picture her with a hand on her hip, hair tossed over a shoulder. Back when we still did things as couples, before we all had kids, before Dad was arrested the first time, Susana liked to smoke some pot, and drink a shot or two of Stoli.

Pascal lies down at my feet, and the spring air gives me the chills; I try to make sure I'm not chattering into the cell phone. Susana and I talk about the kids, and she asks if Wendy knows I'm coming up. I tell her how I can't seem to reach her, but that Kate and I've talked. Then Susana lowers her voice, almost whispering. "Ike, um, he's been sort of drinking a lot lately. Last night he was telling me how he was looking forward to your visit. I think having you around will help him, you know, give him something else to do at night than pour Scotch over ice and watch CNN." I think of asking if she's been hitting the bottle a little, too, what with the way she seems to have buried the hatchet with me, but I just try and sign off, thinking of Browder in the hotel room alone.

"Well, Susana. I'll call you when we're almost there. I guess it would be around midafternoon, depending on what time we get up."

"Hey," she says, interrupting me. "You keep saying 'we.' Are you involved with someone, Gabe? Is it serious?" She actually sounds excited for me. The dark, cool night envelops me, and I tilt my head back and peer up at the sky.

"No," I struggle to say. "I just mean my dog and me is all. I also . . . Well, good night, Susana. See you tomorrow."

Walking back inside the hotel, with its shiny plant leaves in gold boxes, and the damn mauve color scheme that seems to consume all lobbies, I feel bad for not mentioning Browder. The doors to the elevator ease open, and for the first time I think of actually trying to contact Becca when I get into town. Not right away, but sometime soon. She may be married again, but that's not the point; I'd just like to see an old friend, someone who somehow always knew my father was broken, but didn't make me feel bad about it. When he was arrested the last time and finally pleaded guilty, I got a letter from Becca, a sympathy card of all things. In it she'd been careful, maybe not sure if I'd ever told Kate about our summer of love. She had written something about how sorry she was that things had gone poorly for our family, and that she knew deep down my dad was a good man who was simply, in the end, addicted. When he killed himself, Becca sent flowers, and when her father died during my first year in Georgia, I failed to return the favor, something that makes me feel unworthy.

Inside the room, Browder has eaten his cheeseburger and half of mine, a perfect knife cut along the portion he's left me. He grins and dips an onion ring into a pool of ketchup. "I thought you weren't coming back," he says, an even more mischievous smile beaming from his face.

"Yeah, right," I say, lifting the silver pan with a hole in the center from a plate that I assume holds the dessert. "Good, at least you left me this." I can see his cheesecake hasn't been touched either. I lift the pan from his to make sure the order is right, only to find the other half of my cheeseburger there on the plate.

"I got you," says Browder, smiling, food in his white teeth. "I'm just playing," he says and pats my arm. He scoots over, and we sit on the bed. "Can you read the movie to me?" he asks, and I can tell after all these years working the night shift at the group home that he's about to conk out.

I read and read as the words flash onto the screen, my eyes scanning the bottom of the television. Browder now slides up his bed to the pillows and leans back, sighs. Pascal has climbed onto my bed and is lolling his tongue, eyes heavy. If I could, I'd conduct all the interviews from here. Like the swamp in Georgia, this is a safe outpost, a place where I can make things ordered and plain. Browder is now under the covers, scrunched into a fetal ball, slightly snoring, a little tick, tick, tick in his chest, as if there's been some type of counter placed there.

I crawl into my bed with Pascal, thinking of what Susana said about Ike, his drinking and that he was looking forward to my visit. Sleep won't come now that the room is dark, but all I can do is make it through until morning when the trip will really begin.

Chapter Twelve

Forty-five miles outside of Smallwood my intestines begin to rumble. The potholes on the Indiana state highway don't help, and I'm regretting having a big breakfast buffet at the hotel. It's almost 1 p.m., and we'll be in Smallwood in less than an hour, but a burp makes me slow down. My stomach roils, and I'm embarrassed that a series of uncontrollable flatulence seems to rumble the inside of the truck. Browder waves his hand in front of his face, but doesn't look at me or say anything; he simply appears to be wholly irritated with my uncouthness as he shines his harmonica. I can't help it, and another round of wind escapes me. Finally he says, still working a tube sock over the silver mouth harp, "Gross. You're rotten."

"Excuse me," I say. "Sorry." We drive on as flat fields stretch out toward the cirrus horizon, and large tractors creep over black earth, plowing under last year's corn stubble, while smaller John Deeres pull discs over the furrows, and others drag harrow rakes, the clumps of fertile topsoil splitting into perfect loam, the land ready for seed. It's windy, and gray, the newly green fescue in the ditches bending parallel to the ground. There's an old gas station along State Road 13, just outside of Swayzee, where in 1996 workers at the limestone quarry discovered the Pipe Creek Sinkhole, with fossils dating back five million years. White dust settles on the hood of the truck as I unbuckle and hurry into the station, clinching, taking the key and rushing to the rest rooms outside. After ten minutes I step back into the fresh air. I'm feeling no better, chilled, sweaty, and hollow, as if I could simply blow away in the strong wind.

Across the street, in a chain-link fenced yard, a little chubby boy in a knit cap and seed corn company parka tries to hold on to a kite that is lifting at an alarming rate into the drab atmosphere. I walk back toward the pickup and don't see Browder anywhere. Pascal is asleep on the seat when I jog up to the truck and peer inside. I look around, heart starting to pound some. I haven't even gotten him to our trip's destination, and already I've lost him.

I quickly move back inside the station, but a man with a short-cropped goatee, grease on his hands, holding them up as if he's a surgeon, hasn't seen Browder. I run back out to the parking lot and holler for him. The cold air feels more like winter than spring, and I can hear the howl of it in my ears, taste its clean, frosty breath on my tongue as I call out for Browder again. I turn toward the truck in time to hear Pascal barking, sitting up in the seat now, back to me, his attention across the street, where I can see Browder inside the fenced-in yard, helping the little boy with his kite, the unfurled tail tangled in the maple tree.

I jog across the street and try to smile as Browder methodically removes a long plastic strip from the tree that has ripped off the kite's tail, and the runny-nosed boy winds the string around a miniature rolling pin, his chubby hands red and chapped. I feel a freezing rain droplet bounce off my nose as I put my hand on the gate, but decide to stay on this side. "Hey," I say to the little guy, who smiles and then sucks in the snot under his pink nose, swallowing and breathing through his mouth, sounding like Pascal panting. "That's nice of you, Browder, but we better go now." He nods, and from the kitchen window a woman waves, and while the glass is glared, reflecting the dull sky, I think I can see her smile broadly. The little boy finishes rolling up the kite string, then takes the tail and kite from Browder, who is patiently standing over the kid, holding the whole plastic tangle in one hand.

"You got it okay?" asks Browder, and the boy nods, sniffles, licks that shiny lip.

"There's bones in that big hole down there," says the little boy. "They found all kinds of 'em, and once I saw them pull a big elephant head out of there. It was before Easter service." The boy is nodding his head, looking at both of us, eyes cutting back and forth.

"Wow," I say, my stomach, and the idea of arriving in Smallwood, still the two things most prominently on my mind. "I bet you could be an explorer one day." The boy looks at me as if I've mentioned he has twelve arms.

"Nope," he says, heading toward the leaning concrete steps that lead into the back of the shotgun house. "I'm gonna help little kids ride ponies at the fair." With that, he waves and runs awkwardly up the steps, his rubber boots flapping, kite crammed under his arm.

Browder and I walk back across the street and climb into the truck; Pascal greets us with watery eyes and foam on his snout. I start the truck and give a little lecture to Browder. "Don't leave if you haven't told me about it, okay?" He buckles up, saying he's sorry. "Browder, it's just that sometimes people think you're up to something when you're not, okay? They might think you're hanging around to do something wrong to someone." He looks at me just like the little boy did, as if I hadn't the foggiest idea about people at all. I think I see a little smirk ease onto his face, then disappear. He pats my leg and sort of gives me a look of pity.

As we pass the Smallwood high school, I realize how close I am to Wendy. The rain has turned to sleet; Indiana has not let me down in terms of weather, the streetlights clicking on, even though it's midafternoon. Gusts of wind send old leaves tumbling over the road. I flip on the radio as we sit at a light, the courthouse and library squat and gray on a slope off the Wabashiki River, the bulky slabs of drab limestone blocks giving them the look of something impervious, as if they still might be standing here in five hundred years. The man on the 1510 AM station says the weather overnight might be dangerous, a half inch to an inch of frozen rain accumulation. The power lines could come down, roads could turn to utter panes of glass, and the county schools might be closed. I feel butterflies in my stomach replacing the sourness from before; it's as if we've arrived at some kind of optimal catastrophic moment. Wendy might be home tomorrow, and a winter storm in spring might just be what I need to make my coming back feel extraordinary, magical, rather than desperate and needy.

For a while, I just drive us around, pointing out things to Browder I'm sure he has no interest in: the Millford Park where I broke my pinkie; a fire hydrant that I backed into when I put the old AMC in gear while Dad was in the Burger Dairy; the "cut," which is the massive hull of limestone that had to be blasted with dynamite over and over to make way for the main drag. After we've circled the town center, and there's nothing else to do, I pull into a gas station and fill up, top off really, and think maybe I'll recognize someone, but the cashier behind the thick glass doesn't even look at me when I pay.

Back in the truck, I ask Browder if he wants to hit the park. "You already told me about your pinkie," he says gently, as if I might be an elderly Alzheimer's patient.

"No," I say, not able to keep from laughing, which gets him going, too. "I mean to walk around, let Pascal do his thing." Browder seems uninterested until I add, "You can play your harmonica for the squirrels."

It takes all of two minutes to double back across town to Millford Park, where workers are already applying salt to the sidewalks. The freezing rain is superfine, like sand granules. It tapers off, then picks back up, bouncing over the thick green grass like minuscule Ping-Pong balls. A man stops and tells us the forecast has changed, and that it could be up to 1.5 inches by morning. He's walking a little Schnauzer, and the little pooch and Pascal sniff butts and become best of pals in ten seconds, nibbling on each other's ears and trying to get the other to start a chase. The man laughs and tells Browder, "You can play one mean mouth harp, son." He winks at me. Before he moves on with his feisty pooch, he adds, "They're letting school out early." His words give me an exciting idea, and I can't wait to say good-bye to the man so I can try and reach Kate, ask her if I can pick up Wendy from school.

As soon as his back is to us, I'm dialing without thinking about it, and when Kate picks up, I assume my breathing has alarmed her. "What's wrong?" she asks, just like the nurse that she is, and I picture her as I always do, as if she's in one of those emergency shows on television, where all the medical personnel are cool-headed and attractive, even the ones with flaws, their big hearts the only thing keeping them from having normal lives.

"Nothing," I say, trying to regulate my breathing. "Listen, we're in town and this guy just said that school is letting out early and I thought I'd go by and pick up Wendy as a surprise." The tension in my neck makes me shrug, and it seems as though the freezing rain stops and starts five or six times before Kate answers.

"Gabe," she says, apparently walking and talking on her cell. "Wendy either drives herself or Todd drives them both. She rode with him today. I'm sure they're probably already on their way home." I start to tell her I'll just call Wendy later, but Kate continues, "Listen, you need to take it slowly with her, Gabe. I told her you were coming up, but she's not seen you in two years. I know that may not seem like a lot to an adult, but for a kid, for her, I mean, it's . . ."

"Okay," I say as little piles of the white sleet begin to form at my feet. "What did she say when you told her I was coming?"

"I've got to go, Gabe; my shift is just starting. I'll talk to you later."

In a matter of ten minutes I've gone from excitement to exhausted disappointment, but Browder and Pascal couldn't be happier as they play in the cold weather, their breath escaping them in white puffs, the crystallized air hazy, damp. I lean back on the park bench and listen to the soft drone of the icy drizzle. I don't even realize I've drifted off for a quick minute until Browder nudges me and says, "Somebody's coming at us."

Pascal barks, turns a wide circle, and kicks out his back legs, spreading his fierce scent. A man walks toward us in short sleeves and a pair of dark shades like bug eyes. The man is thin, and his fancy shoes tap the concrete sidewalk, and the sound is even more pronounced because of the tempered rustling of the icy pellets sifting through the trees. When he stops and points in our direction, smiles, I realize it's my brother. Ike walks faster toward us, then begins a minor jog, his tie bouncing from his chest. His dark hair is combed back, and his face looks deflated, as if he's sucking in his cheeks. I stand up and can't help but be a little disoriented, even though I now realize the back of the courthouse is adjacent to the bench we've been sitting on.

"You picked a fine time to visit, brother," bellows Ike as he shoves out his hand and we shake. He looks up at the sky, and I can see the freezing rain falling into his hair, then melting instantly. "My God, would you look at this," he says, taking his hand from mine, spreading his arms wide, then looking back at me. "You'd think it was December, not Easter." He smiles a crooked kind of waning grin, and I can see he's sad, sadder than I can ever remember him being. Something about his cleft chin and red lips makes me think of the little boy back in Swayzee, the way he told us about all the bones in the quarry.

"How'd you know we were here?"

"Really?" says Ike, amused. "Who else but Gabe Burke drives a 1984 Datsun the color of Mylanta?"

"Ike, I want you to meet a friend of mine." Browder steps forward and bows his head some, afraid that someone new might not like him. "This is Browder. He's come along with me to take photos. He's real good."

"Good to meet you, Browder. Welcome," says Ike, and I feel awful for not having been a better brother to him. For a while, we just stand and look at one another, while Ike tells me how much Pascal reminds him of our childhood dog, but then he catches himself and wants badly to make this interaction, this day, have nothing to do with the Smallwood of our past. "Listen, I figured we'd go down to Smitty's Wings and get some grub. Sound good?"

"I love wings," says Browder. The weather is making the cars on the streets spin tires at the green lights.

"Well, good. But we better get down there before this blizzard snows us in."

"This is a blizzard?" asks Browder, his voice cloaked in dismay. "Like in

A Simple Plan starring Billy Bob Thornton and Bill Paxton?"

Ike nearly giggles, and when he puts his arm around Browder and sort of hugs him, his mouth wide open, head thrown back, that's when I can smell the booze, the sweet liquorish spoor of a daytime drunk.

We make our way down the street as Ike tells me all about the files he's pulled, the court records and the other crime-scene photos he didn't send me because they were too "corporeally devastated," a term he pronounces like he does the names of the expensive cigars he smokes, the words annunciated succinctly, as if he's counting the syllables.

Inside the wings restaurant, the people, mostly men, wear the Indiana University sports logo on their hats and sweatshirts, a little tribe donning IU as if it were some sort of cultural tattoo. Ike is like a celebrity; his elected office gets us an enormous booth by the window, and no one seems to care that Pascal is now slobbering into a bowl the waitress has brought and set at the entry to the booth. The manager comes out and greets Ike with a gregarious handshake, telling me this city would be nowhere without a man like Ike Burke. "Hell, we'll get him to run for mayor, just you see."

Browder is smiling broadly, snapping photos and giving men the thumbs-up, his lanky body straight and erect, paying attention to all the people around us. Ike hams it up some for Browder, who is taking so many pictures, I figure the camera will start smoking. Ike is as excited as when we were kids. His face flushed, he looks up every moment or two as people stop by our table to shake his hand; more than a few mention the possible bid for mayor.

"Are you really going to run for mayor?" I ask, more sarcastically than I intended, and my brother stops in mid-motion as he hands us menus; it's as if someone has hit the Pause button. He looks at me with a smile pulled to the left side of his face. I can smell his pungent cologne as our eyes lock. For a moment, I think this is as far as we'll get. My homecoming will be short-lived, but Ike allows the comment to roll off him.

"I don't know yet, brother," he says, now letting go of the menus. Browder holds one up in front of his camera and snaps a photo. "But, Gabe," Ike says, "you'll be the second or third person I let know of my decision. Besides," he adds, now almost giggling, "I might need you to write my speeches."

"I could be the photo man," says Browder, and Ike lets out a bellowing cackle.

"I sure like the way you think!" says Ike as the waitress approaches, asking politely what Mr. Burke would like to order.

"Give us three dozen wings, one spicy, one tame, and the other sweet-honey." Ike slaps the menu down on the table, and as the waitress scrawls on her pad, he says, "And bring us three beer mugs and a large pitcher of New Belgium, the Sunshine Wheat." He pauses and looks back at Browder then me. "Orange slices? Like real Austrians drink it?" Browder shakes his head yes so fast, it looks sped up on film. I just shrug.

"We probably shouldn't . . ." I start, then direct myself to Browder. "Have you ever had beer before?" I ask.

"Grandpa man next to the home used to give me sips when I mowed his yard," says Browder, his finger poised on the camera button. He's talking about Mr. Wise, who up until he died a few years ago used to pay the men at the group home to do yard work; this is the first time I've heard about the beer though. Browder adds, "He gave me Bud Light."

"Well, then," says Ike, "you'll like this a lot better. The orange slice makes the hoppy trait really pop."

As we wait on our food, Ike goes over the Riley case in breathtaking detail, describing the order of events, who was murdered first, and the theory on how each of the other Rileys died. My brother's nonchalance is disturbing, and while I realize this is his job, part of his daily work, I would feel better if the other parts excited him this much; say the plats of farmland the clerk's office has to legally describe or the millage rates he must track in some convoluted database. His dark eyes shine like a seal's as he pulls out a tabbed folder so organized it looks like a NASA chart. "All of these," he says, "are the names of the jurors. There's phone numbers and addresses. I've got you scheduled to meet with the prosecutor, not the new one but the guy who argued this case, and the defense attorney. Tomorrow morning. Later in the day we're going to meet with the sheriff's deputy who arrived first on the scene. They'll be able to show you all of the forensic evidence, but let me just say this, brother," and Ike dips his head toward us, another whiff of liquor warming our faces, as Browder revels in this Mafioso-style sit down. "You've got to promise me to stick to the facts of the case as it was pursued and brought to closure. The missing Riley boy's body has already stirred up so much conjecture and folklore, I'm surprised that bleached-haired bigmouth Nancy Grace hasn't sniffed out a story to milk and exploit." Ike eases back into the booth seat, the red vinyl giving him the look of sitting on a throne, the King of Smallwood, Indiana, holding court in a wing joint, as the weather outside turns the town to an ice-coated hinterland.

When the waitress sets a cold pitcher of beer on the table, Ike first tries to make himself pour the beers for us, but something deep inside him overrides his politeness, and in a kind of shaky, frenetic gesture, wobbly yet precise, he tilts his mug and the amber liquid trails along the inside of the glass and Browder and I both watch him closely, as if he might be doing some kind of complex crime-scene work. It's like we're not there as Ike plucks a fragrant slice of pulpy orange from a blue saucer and lets it fall into the head of the beer. He tilts his head back and takes a long, sustained guzzle, and when he finally places the mug back on the table, he seems to have snapped out of his daze. He pats his mouth with a maroon cloth napkin and sits up straighter, looks around, nodding three times to men at the bar, waving, mouthing, and winking at someone. Then he turns back to us. "Anyway, can you give me your word you'll just use the information in the records, no traipsing around the county like a sleuth?"

"Of course," I say, "but what is the story about the boy's body? Why wasn't it ever found? I mean, I can't imagine that a guy with . . ." and I stop.

Ike rolls his eyes. "Look," he says, still trying to keep his composure. "I understand that a missing body might be tempting to a writer," and he says *writer* with a slight clench to his teeth, "but if you want my help, you'll follow my rules. And just in case you think somehow that your own brother is part of some deeply forged small-town cover-up job, I'd remind you of your old high school hero Geraldo. You don't want to be an ass like that and have the whole world watching when you find nothing but more dirt in the tomb." Ike seems pleased with his rant and finally pours our mugs full of beer, using tiny tongs to drop orange slices into the heads.

Browder smiles wickedly, a grin I haven't seen before, and I'm touched when Ike tells him, "Just sip it now. I don't want you getting sick. Try to focus on the hops and the citrus tang, the notes of coriander." Browder nods his head, eyes bright over the rim of the mug, and it's easy to see he's starting to like Ike, maybe even look up to him.

As they chat, I look out the large plate glass window to the street. I would swear it was January the way the town has turned glassy and gray, the sleet now slanting in the wind. A half-barrel planted with tulips sits at the center of the sidewalk, and the flowers' yellow and pink heads grow heavier by the second, the ice accumulating on the petals like hard fructose. I think I can see them edge farther down, the progression like watching a kitchen timer; your eyes see movement, then they don't, and you're left wondering why you're looking this closely in the first place.

The bar grows louder as four musicians tune up and test sound levels. Ike says, "Oh man, you guys are in for a treat. These guys are regulars here, but they live in Indy. They're called the Straightbacks. They've got a song I love called 'Which Way Home.' It's kind of like Dylan a little, but they really rock this place."

No fewer than ten other people drop by our booth, and each time Ike gets the manager's attention and points at our visitors, and I assume he's indicating he'll buy their next round. A young couple approaches, no older than drinking age. The girl looks familiar, something about her eyes and the way her mouth sits full and slightly smirked. The boy has dark hair, and he's wearing tight black jeans that make his legs look like sticks. Ike introduces us.

"This is my brother Gabe, the writer, and his friend Browder." Ike gives me a quick glance, smiling, almost teasing me, indicating I should know these kids. The couple stands at the end of the booth, holding hands, hip and slender. Ike turns in the booth to address me. "Does Candace look like anyone you know?" I open my mouth to say no, but then look back at her as she tilts her head and furrows her brow, her small nose crinkling, and then it hits me.

Ike sees how it's now dawned on me. "Candace," he says, talking to the girl directly, "my brother and your mother knew each other back in the day, in the eighties." She smiles and nods politely, then her boyfriend whispers something in her ear, hidden behind a long brown-red strand of shiny hair. She nods and tries to talk over the music that's starting, but then just smiles and waves as they turn and leave.

"Does that make you feel like one old bastard, or what?" says Ike. He drains the mug of beer and orders another pitcher, snagging the waitress as she zooms by. I'm out of sorts, a little disoriented. The homecoming has snuck up on me, and I realize I haven't thought much about actually living in Smallwood for a couple of months. The idea settles into my lightly buzzed brain, and a spreading darkness works its way into my mood.

Browder has gone easy on his beer, and when our food comes, he leans toward me and asks if he can order a Coke. He looks sheepishly at Ike and apologizes. "I like Coke with my dinners."

Ike pats Browder's hand and talks loud enough to be heard over the band. "That's a good choice, Browder." He holds up his mug of beer and adds, "This stuff will kill you for sure." He smiles and says louder, "But just about everything will these days."

I can't get over Becca's daughter. I catch glimpses of her and her boyfriend as they mingle and dance.

Time seems to ebb and flow around us. The smell of stale beer is infused with cold wind and cigarette smoke each time someone walks through the door. They shake off ice from their heads and jacket sleeves. "Should we get going?" I ask Ike. "It looks like the ice storm is just getting worse."

Ike puts down a wing, wipes his hands, uses a Wet One, too. He's done eating, but Browder is still maneuvering a wing back and forth in his mouth, working it so he can get every bit. "You didn't eat much," says Ike, his lips a little redder from the hot wings. "Why should we leave now? The whole town will be closed down tomorrow."

"I need to go by Mom's. I haven't even told her I'm in town. She'll lock the place up and go to bed, and we won't have anywhere to stay."

Ike orders two shots of something and tips the waitress with a ten. "Nonsense. You guys are staying with me. Mom will have you going to bed by eight if you stay there, and she's been quite busy socially these last couple of months. Besides, I want my name on the front of this book, too." He winks at me. "I got you guys all set up in the attic. Plenty of room up there. I even found a writing table for you." I start to ask him what our mother could possibly be doing socially, but I'm tired and I'm perplexed at Ike's seemingly sincere efforts to welcome us to Smallwood.

The night ends at 10 p.m., but only because Browder says he's sleepier than Sleepy. We can't drive the car on the ice, and so the three of us start out on foot, which revives Browder, and before long he is snapping more photos. His bad leg seems less of an impediment in the ice storm, because now all three of us fight to stay upright. Browder takes a picture of me and my brother sliding on the ice in the dark, the twinkling street making us kids again. Ike helps Browder by offering his arm for support as we walk and talk through the quiet streets. We laugh and take our time, careful not to slip, and I think this is the best the trip will get. It's all downhill from here.

Chapter Thirteen

It's very early morning, just after 3 a.m., and I can't sleep. The attic is so nicely furnished, I feel guilty about Ike putting so much effort into preparing us a place to stay. When we dragged in from the icy April night, Susana fixed all three of us decaf. I tried not to look too intensely at the photos of Wendy on the mantel or the ones plastered to the refrigerator, her hair fine and shining, glossy lips and big brown eyes looking into the camera with a fixed determination. The photo of Wendy with Cal and Kate was the hardest not to stare at where it sat in a black frame on an end table in the plush living room. We talked, and Browder ate almost an entire box of Tagalongs bought from Susana's niece's troop. Susana had said, as we marched up the stairs to the attic, "He's got it as nice up there as down here. He worked on it for three weekends." She smiled at him, and Ike acted aloof, saying something about the attic needing cleaning anyway.

Now hours later, I can see Browder's shiny hair across the open attic space, a low-watt bulb highlighting his head, hanging in an alcove where Susana's wedding dress is sheathed in plastic. A single dormer window at the front of the attic is too high to look out of without a stool. We each have a single sleigh bed, beds their kids have given up for pillow-topped queens. A writing desk, just as Ike said, is all set up, a printer full of paper, the chair comfortable, looking almost new, but I can't think of it long, can't imagine Ike out buying a chair for me at Staples, maybe buzzed, taking shots in the car, as he drove around town looking for a suitable chair for his brother.

The floor of the attic is smooth, made of resilient cork, and there's a throw rug in the center of it, along with two leather recliners and a footstool. And to Browder's astonishment, Ike had put a dorm refrigerator in a corner of the attic, along with a little bar of sorts: whiskey and vermouth, some gin and a case of beer. Somewhere along the way, alcohol has become to Ike what writing is to me; it soothes him, makes him feel prepared, an escape route for when nights like these come along. He told Browder, "I'll make sure to get you some Cokes up here, Brow." Then, maybe because he was tipsy, he hugged Browder good night and kissed me on the cheek, but a little too hard, as if he sort of wanted to open his mouth and bite me, his front teeth cold and quick against my skin.

Wide-awake, my mind drifts to the medication they gave Dad. I can still see its strange name printed out before me in block letters: PAROXETINE. I can remember the generic name so well because the publisher's legal department wouldn't allow me to use the trade name in the memoir. So all through the last section of *Leaving Smallwood*, I had to type *paroxetine* several times, and at night the name would swim around in my head, the letters gobbled up in a dream about my father, his mouth relishing each vowel, as I tossed and turned, only to wake up saying the letters out loud as if the word had been given to me in a spelling bee. After he killed himself, the prison psychiatrist reported in his notes: "No realized episodes of suicidal ideation." We had to explain it to Mom, along with how Dad had hung himself with strips of bedsheets. His fingertips were raw. "Industrious to the end," Ike said, for which Susana slapped him. I spell the antidepressant again in my head as if I'm counting sheep, the word hovering before me when I close my eyes.

The attic is so quiet I can hear the streetlight hum to life, then flicker with strain, then brighten, and flicker more as it tries to turn off again, the weak flashes like dry lightning through the dormer window. My nose detects the sweet decay of a dead mouse, probably already tossed out by Ike during his cleaning. I actually feel like I'm growing more and more awake rather than being able to return to sleep. I miss Pascal, who is downstairs in the living room with Ike and Susana's chocolate Lab, a female named Ruby, who took to Pascal so quickly I thought they might be long-lost littermates. I hear ice falling off the roofline, and as I try to find a chair to look out the window, a limb creaks, then thuds to the ground. Finally, I find a small stepladder and arrange it quietly by the window, step onto the rungs in my bare feet, the cold aluminum ridges a little painful. Once up, I hold on to a bare pine truss and look out the window. There's a tree down in the street, and one solitary car turned sideways at the bottom of the hill, the entire vehicle coated in ice, as if adhered there by epoxy.

For a while, after I have gotten down off the ladder, all I can do is stand in the darkness of the attic, the house breathing, the furnace like some single lung, slowly struggling. It's strange to be here, stowed away in the attic like Algernon, on the precipice of something I cannot name. Coming back to your hometown is one big, untamable memory, meandering recollections of the grooves on your second-grade desktop; of the smell of your brother's soap; of the way streets have reduced, shrunken; of the look of off-kilter fences and misplaced trees; of the sound of distant mowing in the park; of how even now Smallwood is not just a place, but a character, a living entity, something that grows and changes and has the capacity to bring joy or sorrow, or just a simple, sad observation, that you actually can come home again, but your town will pretend not to notice.

I tiptoe back to my bed, careful not to wake Browder, or Ike and Susana in the room below. I have to make myself not think of how creepily peeping-tomish this arrangement is. Under the covers, I begin to spell out Dad's medication, and the letters are at first hard-edged and prickly, but soon, after I've spelled it maybe fifty times, the cadence inside my head starts to bring me down some. In jail, Dad had complained that the medication made him lethargic in every way. "It's like I've been darted by Jim from a *Wild Kingdom* helicopter."

I resented him at the time for the comment, because Sunday nights home with Mom and Dad and Ike had been one of those memories where things seem to expand, colors enhanced, the room cozy, and your family at its best, normal and sound. I had said back to my father that day in the ugly green prison, walls taupe and worn white at hip level, "Maybe Jim should've just used a regular gun on you. Marlin Perkins, too. Put you out of our misery. We'd want to get you insured first by Mutual of Omaha though."

Dad had smiled sadly then and run his hand over his hair, and I could see those eyes fill with tears, and I thought my chest would pull me down to the center of the earth. "I'm sorry," I said, and he was already getting up from the chair, a guard moving toward him. Dad stood before me, swallowing hard, giving me a smile. I was trembling by then, thinking I might vomit. I had hurt him just to feel better myself, but all that family shame played trump and I was left with the knowledge that parents sooner or later turn into children.

"I wish we could've had more time together, Gabe. I wish you all didn't blame yourselves. Like it or not, I don't know why I am the way I am. It's not comforting, I know, but it's likely the only truth we've got." I tried to go to him then, but the guard waved me off. Then my father did the strangest thing. He blew me a kiss, or rather puckered his lips and kissed the air in my direction, and I let out a bawl and said how sorry I was. After that day, I decided

I'd make the memoir true and hard, a testament to his flawed, unfixable life, to our broken, weird, and diluted family. Even now, I wonder on nights like these if I got it right. Probably not.

In the morning, I'm woken by the sound of Browder's harmonica, the moaning in and out, low then high, squealing then blubbering. The attic is filled with light from the dormer, and even up here I can smell coffee, Ike's woodsy aromatic cigar smoke. It's early, maybe 7 a.m., and I must be the only one who wants to sleep in. The scent of damp cedar trunks and pine cleaner hits me full on as I climb out of bed and pull on jeans. Browder lifts the harmonica from his lips and smiles. "I like it up here," he says, and goes back to blowing fragged notes.

It sounds like Geppetto's workshop as we make our way down the narrow attic stairs, the creak of the wood and the groan of joists. For a moment, Browder won't take another step. "I'm gonna fall," he says, and I tell him even if he did, I'd help him up. Finally, only after Ike comes quickly up the stairs, holding a cup of coffee, which he hands to me so he can help Browder, does Browder fully descend, escorted by my brother. Browder laughs and slaps Ike on the back, who in turn does the same to Browder.

In the kitchen, Ike pours a steaming cup of coffee for me from his Jura-Capresso, a silver contraption that really does look like it costs thousands, a gift from Susana's father, an attorney specializing in defending Eli Lilly in Indy. "And here you go, Brow," says Ike, offering a cold Coke can from the refrigerator. Browder actually claps and then pops the can immediately, slurping, before moving his lips to the harmonica. I tell him that he'll wake the kids, but Ike snorts a laugh. "No, they've been gone since six. They both have practice. Softball and track." I start to mention the weather and ask how they'd be at school now, but I'm still a little sleepy and can't form the words. Ike sips his coffee, and I can hear Susana from somewhere in the house, talking to the dogs, her voice much more subtle than I remember. "You know," says Ike, "Wendy usually cheers at some of their games, their track meets. The Cousins Burke!" Ike sort of jumps up from his seat, and I remember how he uses action, energy, movement, as a method to run away from the downtime, the thoughts, the phenomenon of just sitting and staring and drifting backwards, mulling over the stories we've told ourselves.

Ike now moves around the kitchen, stacking and restacking things—a pile of *Dog Fancy* magazines, a bundle of bills, the saucers he's put out by the coffeemaker, all the while the lazy smoke from his cigar soothing me.

"Do you know Wendy's schedule?" I ask, and I can see my hand shaking as I bring the cup to my lips.

"No, not really. She has cheerleading practice after school sometimes, but her boyfriend or Cal usually drives her home. Kate is working more of the late shifts now at the hospital. I think." Ike shrugs his shoulders, and then turns to look as Susana enters the kitchen, Pascal and Ruby panting, bumping into each other as they rumble toward the pantry to the water bowls. I'm bothered that I can't ask more about my daughter, but I'm determined to tell Ike I want to make sure to see her today.

"How was Pascal?" I ask, and Susana smiles, pink cheeks aglow.

"Oh fine. They are like two peas in a pod." For a moment it occurs to me that Susana may be on antidepressants, her voice and view of the world so different from before, a placid almost serene look on her face, not gentle, not resigned, more as if she's in a mild trance. But I could be wrong; maybe like the rest of us she's given up on being angry, melted into that middle-aged state of numb acceptance, a kind of strength in letting most things go. She holds out a cup as Ike pours her some rich coffee that she blows on momentarily and drinks straight black. She steps toward my brother and plants a kiss on his cheek, then lets her free hand rest on her hip. "I was thinking maybe today Browder and I could go out to the reservoir and shoot some pictures. Give the Burke Boys time to work together." At first, Browder comes off less than enthused. He shifts in his seat and looks to me, then back at the camera around his neck, fiddling some with the lens, touching and retouching the strap.

"That'll be fun, Browder," I tell him. "Susana has a big camera like yours. You two can get shots of the spillway, and there's a huge redwood tree down by the docks that's petrified. No one knows how it got there. People have carved their names into it." It doesn't seem to budge him though.

"What about the police photos you need me to take?" he asks.

"Oh, well, we won't even be doing those today. We're just talking with people in an office. You can be outdoors, maybe take the dogs with you, right, Susana?" She nods and then puts her coffee down on the counter, walks to Browder, and places her hand on his shoulder.

"There's a great pizza place out there, and it has an ice-cream parlor attached to it. They have bubblegum ice cream." At this, Browder perks up and even stands, gives Susana a light hug.

"Okay," says Browder, and just like that he and Susana are talking about the pizza toppings and what kind of camera he has. She explains, as they gather their gear and coats, that the reservoir is empty now but will be filled soon. Their talk reminds me of the weather outside.

"Is it still icy out there?" I ask. Ike takes me by the arm and escorts me to the window.

"It warmed up sometime in the wee hours," he says as we stand side by side at the window. "Schools were already closed though. Looks like the kids get a freebie today. Evan and Katherine wanted to go to practice though. They're probably lifting weights. Sports before classes, I always say."

We look at the cold spring morning through the large window as Browder and the dogs and Susana make a stampeding sound out the front door. She yells, "Bye" and "Good luck" and says, "Love you." And Ike calls back to her like a crow, his eyes smiling, and I can feel to my core everything I've pretended I wouldn't miss.

We watch the Saab station wagon back out of the drive, the streets still patchy in some places, the rest of the ice now dripping off eaves and running down the streets. Some limbs lie in the yard, tusks of oak and maple, the antlers of spruce and sycamores. The sun is glinting over the houses across the street, an orange ball radiating out along the horizon, giving the sky a Pepto-Bismol tint. Smallwood, Indiana, so versatile and defiant in its weather, not caring about the time of year, and I think of the Halloween when Dad and I and Ike used snowshoes to go from house to house as Mom drove alongside in the car, window rolled down, laughing at our Eskimo outfits. Six inches of snow on the ground, covering all the pumpkins and making people do stupid things like give out last year's candy canes as treats.

"We better get going," says Ike. He looks me up and down. "Did you bring a jacket and tie?" He smiles at me as he fingers my T-shirt sleeve, then removes his hand as if I might combust.

"No, I mean, I really didn't think I'd . . ." I shrug my shoulders and follow Ike out of the kitchen when he motions for me to follow. We climb the stairs and stand in the master bedroom; the intimacy of their marital slumber lulls me some—the heat, the scent of laundry softener—as Ike rummages through his closet. He shoves a suit jacket, shirt, and striped necktie at me and taps his watch. "Meet you in the driveway."

In Ike's Range Rover, I sit in the passenger's seat and use the visor mirror to adjust the clothes he's loaned me. I can't breathe. I'm preoccupied as we pass house after house, some kids out playing in the melting patches. "Hey, could we drop by Kate's real quick? I'd like to let Wendy know I'm here."

"It's only a little after eight, brother. Your daughter is probably sleeping in." Ike glances over at me, then back at the street as the SUV grinds to a slow halt at a red light. I want to be with my daughter by myself. He doesn't seem hung over, but I can smell the mouthwash trying to hide the booze. We pull into a parking space labeled especially for him: Mr. Burke, Clerk of the Superior Court of Hartford County. The official seal of Indiana is emblazoned under the text.

Ike shuts off the engine and just sits behind the wheel staring at his nameplate. I look over at him as I arrange my things: the tape recorder, pens and notebooks, the list of questions I've outlined. I do a double take after another long moment of him not moving, and for a second I believe he's had a stroke or a heart attack. "Hey, Ike," I say, leaning forward to look in his eyes. "Hey, you okay, man?" He finally shows some life, sucks on his bottom lip, then takes a deep breath, turns in the seat toward me.

"Listen, I don't want to be a prick here, Gabe, but let me ask the questions, okay?" I'm stunned by the suggestion, a little confused, too.

"What do you mean, like kind of open things up? What?"

"No, I mean let me handle these two interviews. You can take notes, but I ask the questions. That way you can get the information you need, and I can make sure things don't get off track." Ike raises his eyebrows and unhitches his seat belt.

"Jesus, Ike. I can't write a book about these murders if my brother is the mouthpiece. Besides, I've already written down the questions. I think I can handle it."

Ike's right eye flickers with stress, something he probably thinks I don't notice. I can tell he's trying with every fiber of his being not to escalate the situation.

"I know you can handle it, that's not what I'm implying. I just think it's better if I do the talking." He starts to open the door to get out. A ray of sun glints off the hood, and several people, women in long black skirts with boots and men in charcoal-gray suits, three buttons, seem to all arrive at once as the court doors open and the day's legal business commences.

"No way," I say. "I should've known you'd be controlling like this, Ike." I shove my items into my satchel and start to get out, too.

He grabs me by the arm, and at first his fingers dig deep into my biceps like incisors, then he realizes it and loosens up, but not all the way. "Close the door," says Ike, providing a little more pressure on my arm. I do as I'm told.

"Gabe, I'm not trying to be an asshole, okay? It's my job here, and I don't want things to get out of hand. I mean, I did go to the trouble of setting up these interviews; the least you could do is let me play it my way."

I'm tired of his spiel. "What are you afraid of, huh? That I'll ask about the missing Riley boy's body? I mean, God forbid someone ask the most obvious question, Ike." I'm instantly tired, and ready to head back to my swamp. "Just call the interviews off. I'll set them up again myself."

"That's not acceptable," says Ike, his face red now. Kids across the street are out picking up limbs from a fenced-in yard, using the branches like swords on each other. "And don't think for a fucking second that you know more about this case or the justice system, okay. While you've been off playing Hemingway and Mother Teresa, some of us have been doing our jobs. Accomplishing things." He lets go of my arm, but I still yank it away.

"Fuck you, Ike," I say and get out of his SUV. Once I'm standing in the parking lot, I realize that if I don't go in with him, play by his rules, I'll likely never get an interview. After all, the people of Smallwood seem to like the idea of my brother becoming the next mayor, and I doubt that would be the case if he didn't already have their respect. As I take a deep breath, it also occurs to me that Ike has counted on my reaching this conclusion. He gets out, walks behind the vehicle, and draws up close to me.

In my ear he whispers, "Look, I want to help you with this. I'm glad you're home, but you can't run roughshod here. Just trust me on this. If you go asking questions about the Riley boy, they'll just shut down anyway. We've got to keep some perspective here, Gabe. This isn't a family . . ." He stops and leans back, his hot breath still dewy on my ear.

Now I'm the one to lean in close to him, and for a moment I wonder if someone watching out their office window would think we're lovers, or maybe the perverted descendants of a fatherly pervert. I almost want to mention our dad, even the memoir, get my brother to break a little, just as he's done with me. But instead I whisper into his ear, "Tell me, brother, you wouldn't happen to know something about that missing body, would you?"

I step back and fix my eyes on his. He's grinning sarcastically, and I can see his ire building. Then a warmer breeze washes over us and through the trees, jostling the unfrozen but wet leaves, making water flick onto our faces, and his anger dies down. He takes me gently by the arm and leads me toward the security door of the courthouse, as if he's a principal. "I love you," he says, and adds not all that quietly, "but remember this, I can have you arrested in at least ten different ways. You'd never leave Small-wood again. Ever." He throws his head back and laughs, and all I can think about is how this same person stocked his attic with all that I would need to stay here.

Chapter Fourteen

Later that afternoon, I ring my mother's doorbell and can't believe my eyes when a tall, white-bellied man in a towel ducks from the kitchen area into the laundry room. For a moment, I assume she's being assaulted, that I'll have to break down the door and will find her bloody and sobbing, her wrinkled body covered in this assailant's vile body fluids.

I yell now, "Mom? Mom, are you okay?" The door handle is tight, but I ratchet it back and forth. In one pathetic move, I slam my shoulder into the door just as Mom appears behind the glass, a cigarette in her mouth. She looks mad, even a little maniacal, her gray hair frizzy, cheeks red, her eyes moist and wide. A long, drab-colored robe is cinched around her as she opens the door.

"Gabe," she says, and not all that friendly. "My goodness what's the matter with you?" In person now, not over the phone when her voice comes across as sick and disinterested, she seems more lively, and that myth about her, the one that Gabe and I've constructed where she's given up, seems out of whack, un-synced. It begins to dawn on me what I've interrupted. I feel sick myself now, even as my mother hugs me lightly.

"Mom, I'll come back later, okay." I want to run away as fast as I can.

"Nonsense," she says, pulling me into the house. For one brief, awful second, I think I can hear my father, the sound of those HomeBeam Wares pans being loaded into the trunk, his voice telling us how today is the day when the sale of all sales will make his whole month. I try to shake the feeling, but the smell of our home has brought the auditory hallucination, and when I take a deep breath at the kitchen table, the scent of percolating coffee, and Crisco in a skillet, a trace of cigarette smoke, too, I actually believe I can hear my dad telling Ike how pricing something with ninety-nine cents at the end gets buyers excited, makes them think the price is a bargain. It's all perception, boys.

Mom reaches over and pats my hand. "When'd you get in, son?" I look at her and can't remember when my mother turned into a grandmother; her skin is paler, except for the sag under her eyes, where tiny folds of flesh the color of walnut seem to weigh down her entire face. Still, her eyes seem hopeful, maybe even passionate.

"Uh, yesterday," I say. "Listen, let me go, Mom, and I'll call tomorrow and we can have some coffee." I sound even to myself like I'm begging her to release me.

She sits up straighter and turns to look behind her as the man walks into the kitchen in a flannel shirt, his dark denim jeans stiff. He's perfectly bald and pink, a little white goatee at his chin. He's at least six-two, and he smiles at me and nods, then goes to the cupboard and quietly pulls down three cups. "I'm Dick Gramlich," he says, and Mom just watches him, and I think I even see a slight smile on her lips. "You must be Gabe." I can't believe Ike hasn't mentioned Dick, if he knows about him, that is.

"Yes. I'm Gabe." Mom looks at me blankly, but I know the subtle look, which is supposed to tell me to be polite, engage the person, act interested, but all I can think of is that his name is Dick, that he and my mother were likely just . . . I have to shake my head to clear it, not allow some awful image to take shape.

He comes toward us now holding all three cups, the tops steaming. He places them on the table without a sound. Dick puts sugar and milk into my mother's cup and slides it toward her. She tells him thank you, and if I'm not still hallucinating, she actually lets out a giggle. Good Lord, they're in the throes of a new love affair. They're energized to be around each other.

"Sugar and milk?" asks Dick, and I nod. His big hands fix my coffee, and when he pushes the cup toward me, he calmly smiles. He drinks his black. He sits back and looks around the table and says with a booming voice, "I hope you don't mind me saying this, but I thought your book about your father and your family was real good, and I'm not just saying that because I'm with your mother. I don't have any feelings one way or another about your dad, but I thought you wrote that book with a real desire to get it right, not sugarcoat things, but not blame anyone either. I don't read a lot of books like that, usually read Crichton and James Patterson, you know, thrillers, mysteries. But I read your book all in one night." He tips back his cup and drinks almost the entire thing. Then Dick lights up and offers Mom a cigarette. She takes it, dare I say, demurely, and Dick leans over and gives her a kiss on the cheek. I pray for strength.

"Thank you," I say, not sure exactly what to make of Dick. He's not what you'd expect, and I find myself strangely drawn to him as I sneak peeks in his direction and Mom tells me all about seeing Wendy in the grocery store with her boyfriend. I try to pay attention, but I'm mostly distracted, watching Dick smile at her, admire her, even as she rambles on about casual sightings of my daughter around town.

"Well, I guess you wouldn't call it a double date, that wouldn't be the proper way to describe it, but all four of us went out to eat at Stromlini's by the square. . . ." I finally come to, tune into what she's talking about, her voice barely fluctuating, a reporter providing the facts.

"What?" I ask. "What are you saying, Mom?"

"I was telling you about Dick and me going out to eat with Wendy and her boyfriend. We had a nice time. He's a good boy, and for what it's worth, he treats your daughter well, pulls out the chair for her and makes sure she's comfortable." Dick is smiling, nodding. The kitchen feels hot, and more than anything, I need to be gone from here. I'm happy for my mother, but somehow embarrassed, too, a selfish thought, but true. I don't want anyone saying how cute Dick and my mom are together, or for people I don't even know to see Dick and Mom out with Wendy and her boyfriend. I want to tell her all of this, but it would be cruel and unforgivable. Instead, I stand up and look at my watch.

"You know, I told Ike I'd be home for dinner." I move toward the door, and Dick and Mom follow, him standing with his big hands tucked into the front pockets of his jeans. He's a nice man, but he's sleeping with my seventy-year-old mother.

In my truck I honk and wave, but don't know why. The two of them stand now in the driveway and wave back, and I can't wait to see my daughter; I need to see her so things make sense, follow some logic. I drive straight to my ex-wife's house, thinking along the way about my day with Ike, how it all seemed too fixed and simple. We sat in a large conference room next to his office in the courthouse. The defense attorney, a woman about our age, was gracious and excited at the thought of a book on the Riley murders. She talked openly as Ike furtively snuck glances my way. He seemed a little on edge for a guy who claimed he could have me locked up. Still, the attorney talked about how she first came to meet the killer. "He isn't that impacted by his disability if you want to know the truth. I mean, we tried to play his IQ up with the jurors, but there are plenty of people in Smallwood walking around with brains that can't think beyond an 82 quotient." At this comment, I felt less satisfied with her, as if she'd somehow insulted Browder or Smallwood, or both. It's silly, but I started to believe she couldn't give me much more than what was reported in the papers. Over the next few hours we talked with the DA and had lunch with a sheriff's deputy named Will Williams, whom Ike playfully called Will-Will during our meal. Ike was careful to order a mixed drink, something that appeared to be just cola but was half whiskey. Deputy Williams was also gracious with his time, and Ike, more focused on his alcohol, let me ask a few questions.

As I drive to Kate and Cal's house, taking the turns slowly, my mind is running rampant, calculating and rehearsing what I will say. The curbs I pass are piled neatly with fallen limbs; Midwesterners like to tidy up, take on both minor and horrible disasters with a housecleaning mind-set, a place for everything and everything in its place. Once, after a tornado hit right outside of town and actually killed a man when one of his own dairy cows landed on him, his wife told the newspaper, "We're sad, but things have to be picked up, cleaned. We have to get it back to the way it was." I think of her picture in the Smallwood *Plain Dealer*, the black-and-white photo like a wanted poster, her face serious but defiant, as if the photographer would never catch her sadness.

It's just before 8 p.m., and the sun is starting to set as I pass the county golf course. The center of the horizon holds a tangerine wheel, spokes of blue-gray spreading across the sky. The green hummocks and darker green sugar maples give the course the look of a game board; something Wendy and I might have played on together ten years ago.

As I turn onto their street, I can feel the nervousness in my hands, something electric and slightly painful. I pull up behind a solid sedan, maybe a Lexus. It's almost dark now, and with the window down it's hard to believe just eighteen hours earlier ice covered everything. The night air is chilly, but it won't last long. In a month the spring will edge into summer, the weather growing warmer by early June, then awfully hot, unbearably muggy, the corn growing so quickly they say you can hear it, a kind of crackling maturation.

I wish Pascal were with me. When I get to the front door, something sort of builds me up, and for a moment I think it might have been Dick's acceptance of me, his nice comments about the book. I've doubted myself for so long, living in my swampy exile, that it's comforting to have a stranger tell me the book is good.

I punch the doorbell, and Kate is opening the door and giving me a fast hug before I can even say hello. Cal is now behind her, standing there in a pastel spring sweater, looking as if he's just left the golf course. Together they make a striking couple, lean and healthy, their eyes clear, rested. I rub my own face quickly, and the stubble feels grungy, and I believe my eyes are laced with red, and that maybe my skin is sallow and dry, my posture slumped, shoulders rounded, my hair dull and thin.

"Come on in," says Cal, his meaty hand dwarfing a tumbler of ice tea. He steps back as does Kate, and for a second I think that maybe I'm a surprise for Wendy, that the two of them are going to escort me into the living room where my daughter sits unaware, and Cal and Kate will say, "Voilà!" when they present me. A big joyful homecoming will ensue, and I'll have lip gloss all over my cheeks from where Wendy has pummeled me with a series of smooches. A writer's imagination is sometimes selfish.

When I sit down though on the huge wraparound sectional, covered in black microfiber, I can see I'm thinking stupidly. For ten minutes we talk about Ike and the possibility of him running for mayor. Cal stands up at what seems a planned moment and excuses himself. "I've got to dash into the office, Gabe. It was good seeing you. Maybe we can play a round before you run off back down South." He means no harm by the comment, but still, he cuts his crystal eyes toward his wife, my ex-wife, and shrugs his shoulders, then turns and leaves.

"So," I say. "I assume we've been left alone for a reason. Did I miss a support payment?" I can tell Kate is in no mood to joke, and I try to laugh a little to show I'm harmless, but she ignores it and cuts right to the chase.

"Gabe, Wendy doesn't want to see you. She's in a difficult place right now emotionally, and it would be best if you just stayed away. Can you do that?"

"Oh sure, Kate. No problem," I say sarcastically, standing up, pissed off. Their house is very similar to Ike and Susana's. The woods are rich, heavy copper ornamentals rising up from polished end tables, the smell of rose potpourri heavy in the air, and stainless steel appliances in the kitchen off the living room. "I mean, I can just forget about her until she's forty or so, then I can have her visit me in the nursing home."

"Don't be so defensive, Gabe. All I mean is, this visit has sort of come out of nowhere, and talking with her on the phone is different from seeing her in person right now."

I interrupt. "I haven't even gotten to talk with her on the phone in the last six months, and before that it was hell to get her to say much on the phone anyway."

"Exactly. She's busy with school, and they don't even talk on the phone to their friends. It's all texting now. Wendy sends me texts; her boyfriend texts. It's the way they communicate. The phone from our youth is dead."

I head toward the door, talking over my shoulder. "Perfect. I'll just text her something like, OMG let's be BFFs!"

Kate actually laughs out loud, brings her slim hand to her mouth, eyes smiling. "Right, and she'll send back, LMAO." I can't keep from smiling myself, but I don't know what her acronym means, and I must looked confused. "You know," says Kate, now more reserved, "it stands for 'laughing my ass off'?" I shake my head no, I didn't know. But just then, as I'm about to tell Kate I'll be back whether Wendy wants to see me or not, I catch movement outside in the driveway. It's my daughter, jogging toward the street, phone in hand, and a large zebra-print bag slung over her shoulder, obviously having snuck out the back door. She looks like an arsonist running from her burning secret.

"Hey," I say intensely to Kate. "There she is!" Kate sidles up next to me, and we watch as Wendy looks back toward the house and waits as a sensible car, some kind of hybrid, and absolutely safe-looking, pulls up to the curb. It's dark now, but the lights on the street cast the scene in a yellow glare. I'd hoped for a crisis, a boyfriend who was mean and tough, wore black leather and had a tongue pierced, his black eye makeup and ebony fingernails the cause for great concern by Kate. But instead, we watch as a stocky boy with luminous brown hair, cut modestly above the ears, gets out of the car and holds open the door for Wendy.

"He's a smart kid, Gabe. Scored almost a perfect SAT. His grandfather owns a seed corn company, and his dad is an agronomist for Monsanto. His mother is a nurse, too. Works for Dr. Clemens in Fort Wayne. Oncology." Wendy stands for a moment instead of getting into the boy's car; she stares toward us. He says something to her and then looks back toward the house, too. It seems he can make eye contact with me through the window.

"She hates me, then?" I say, and just stand and stare as Kate puts her hand on my elbow. I feel as if I'm being escorted out of my daughter's life.

"She read the book last summer, Gabe." The term, The Book, makes me think of something related to fundamentalist Christianity. "I talked with her about it, and tried to get her to call you to discuss it, too, but she read it in one night, then I caught her the next day in her pajamas burning it in the fireplace. You know someone spray-painted your dad's headstone with the word *pervert*. Ike had it removed, but Susana said he won't admit to having it sandblasted off, which seems weird." All I can do is watch Wendy bend and slip into the car. The boy rounds the front of the vehicle and gets in, too, and the red lights of the car burn brighter, then lessen, as the car pulls away from the curb and disappears down the street. I strain to see them, but all that's visible are warm lights pulsing from the interiors of homes.

"I want to see her, Kate," I say, turning toward my ex-wife. "Even if she hates my guts, I want to spend some time with her. You tell her that, please? Tell her I don't care if we just sit and she spits on me before dinner. I want to see my daughter."

"I'll try," she says, and walks me to the door. "You look really tired, Gabe."

"Yeah, well, the first day back in Smallwood is a chore."

Kate frowns, opens the door into the nippy spring night. "A chore, huh? Well, it's just a town, Gabe. Maybe if you stopped thinking of it as something bigger than what it is, you'd be able to manage a little better."

"I can't," I tell her, walking toward my ridiculous truck. "Besides, if my brother becomes mayor, you might just be looking at the next poet laureate of Hartford County." As I back up into the street, shift into drive, and push the pedal to accelerate away, Kate is still standing on the front porch waving, and for a moment, under the contained light of the entrance, she looks like Wendy, and even her good-bye seems like encouragement.

Ike is in a large, leather recliner, his shoes off, the pair of expensive loafers sitting primly at the edge of the chair. Pascal and Ruby are passed out by the fireplace, which is dancing with a low gas log flame. I walk over to the dogs and begin petting them. Pascal opens his eyes and lifts his head, a drowsy almost deathly look on his face, as if he's run his last race. His big head makes a subtle thud when he goes back to sleep; Ruby is dead to the world, too.

"They're tuckered out, Hemingway." Ike looks at me and smiles, rubs his socked feet together. He's got a documentary about Walt Whitman on the public television station. It's muted, and as I sit there returning his smile, I can hear Browder and Susana in the other room.

"What are they up to?" I ask, rising from my spot by the hearth.

Ike sips his drink and doesn't shift his glassy eyes to me this time, just stares at the television and says, "Pictures. They're looking at the ones they took today at the reservoir. Apparently your boy likes to photograph dead things. You haven't made that poor man morbid, have you, Mr. Burke?"

"Hope not," I say. "So tomorrow?"

Ike looks at me directly, then starts to get up from his reclined position. Compared to the night before, he's subdued, the liquor in his glass settling over his mood. When he finally is up, I watch as he stumbles slightly toward the bar, which is a heavy oak Amish table against the wall, with all manner of chrome tumblers and elongated shot glasses, a matching ice bucket and platters with smooth stone coasters. He pours himself a gimlet, stirs it with a long stick that reminds me of an old thermometer. "You are free to use the records room all you want tomorrow, for the rest of the week really. Whatever," Ike adds, waving the glass. "I gotta dig into a goddamn records request tomorrow in the archive room. Fucking due process and appeals. I'll be swamped until late. I'll make sure Jeanie helps you." Ike stops in the middle of the living room and offers me a drink. I decline, and he shrugs, crawls back into the chair. "I'm fucking beat." It's odd his letting me off the leash now after wanting so much control before.

We watch TV in silence for a while until Susana comes in with Browder in tow. He walks over and stands next to me and smiles. It's hard to believe we've only been here a little over twenty-four hours. Susana tells us all about their day of photographing the Salamonie, the driftwood and piles of stones, two arrowheads and the remnants of the old church that was flooded when the reservoir was made. It's called First Hartford Baptist, and back in school, kids used to say when the water was down, you could see spirits rising from it, drifting up from the muck toward the sky. Then when the floodgates were opened, all the phantoms would once again be submerged under brown water.

"Where are the kids?" I ask, after Browder shows me on a laptop his pictures of a squirrel skeleton and the hide of something that looks like an Irish setter.

"In bed already. Early practice again tomorrow," says Ike. "When they get this age, it's like they're already gone, or maybe practicing to be gone. Having teenagers is like living with ghosts. You rarely see them, but when they are here, it's all emotion." Susana looks at me and then back to Ike. He's not belligerent, but it's clear he's allowed the drink to somber his view. He doesn't even comment on the pictures, and I can tell it hurts Browder's feelings a little as he returns to stand next to Susana, who has in one short day won him over.

In the living room, we sit and yawn, talk about how quickly the ice came and went, and then Ike sort of blurts out, "By the way, where have you been?"

"Is there a curfew I should know about?"

He pretends to slap the arm of the chair. He seems more volatile now, on the verge of something. His teeth look bared, but I blink and stare more at him. He slurps from the drink again. I decide to defuse.

"I went by to see your mother. You didn't mention she had a beau."

Ike crunches ice with his teeth as Susana and Browder look at pictures on the laptop. I can hear Browder say how pretty her picture of a sunken canoe is. His gentleness gives the room a better feel, and I have to believe Ike has sensed it, too, as he smiles some.

"Are you talking about Dick?" And he almost allows ice pellets to explode from his mouth when I tell him about seeing the man in only a towel. When he can talk, he adds, "Your mother must like her afternoon delight, Gabe." At this Susana joins in, saying we're awful, that it's wonderful mom's found such a nice man, and I can't disagree.

"I thought you believed she'd just given up, Ike?" I say.

"Well," he says, finishing off the drink in one big tilt of the glass, light from the floor lamp sparkling off the tumbler, giving Ike the glow of some kind of saint, Saint Hartford of County Clerk. "All I know is she hangs around that house every waking hour, fucking Dick and smoking." He grunts when he rises from the chair.

"Ike," hisses Susana, turning on him wildly. "That's vulgar. Grow up." She glares at him as he bumps into the bar to pour another drink. I try to think of something to soften the moment.

"Maybe it's love," I say, and as soon as I say it, I realize I might as well have poked him hard in the ribs, his grave frame of mind just begging for assault.

"Yeah, right. It's all roses and champagne and candlelight over there. More like weeds and Pabst and ashtrays. The thought of the two of them fucking is revolting." Ike gulps down the glass of gin without ice, and Susana calls him an ass and tells Browder and me we better go to bed. As it turns out, it's not Mom who's given up.

Chapter Fifteen

In the morning, while Browder snores, the rich coffee brewing downstairs wafting up into the attic, I sit at the desk and open my laptop. It's strange to be writing again, or rather thinking about writing again. I find Ike's Wi-Fi signal and log on, check my e-mail. Michael has sent me a message, asking if I've made it to Hoosier Land okay, and did I see Gene Hackman coaching high school boys already in their midtwenties. He adds a line at the bottom of the e-mail: "I need a draft of the new prologue to the memoir soon. Shoot for around three thousand words and zip it over to me. I can read and provide feedback PRONTO!"

My fingers are loose on the keyboard, the tips clammy, almost hot, as I enter a kind of meditative zone. A memory comes back to me, the sound of leaves fluttering in the breeze, the smell of earth and cold, rust-colored fields and lawns of dark green at the periphery of my vision. I'm writing, and it feels good, medicinal, promising.

For the next half hour time slips into the closet, hiding, unable to move without me, unless I give it permission on the computer screen. Writing the prologue feels like hiding contraband, marijuana joints under a mattress or a vodka bottle tucked under a floorboard. Ike calls up to us, saying breakfast is ready, but he sounds hung over, hoarse.

Finally, when he starts to climb the attic steps, I rush to finish two lines, knowing Ike would consider what I'm doing blasphemy. The screen fades to a light sky blue, then vapid gray, and I close the laptop just in time. Behind me I can hear footsteps, and it's not until I really listen that I hear the sound of women's heels.

I turn slowly in the chair, and my breath comes out in a deflated exhale as Susana stands five feet away, dressed up, and looking every bit as beautiful as fifteen years ago. Her hands are in front of her, cupped at her waist. She has on an emerald-green dress and the heels I heard, gold loops at her ears.

"Hey. Good morning," I say, my voice hitched.

"He's not going in today, Gabe. He's sick. He tried, but he vomited in the kitchen sink." She clip-clops closer and smiles when she notices Browder still sleeping. Susana sits down on my bed and crosses her legs. "It's getting worse. I thought having you here might help, but last night is pretty much the way it always is now. He drinks as soon as he gets home, and I know he's been drinking during the day, too. He's always been a drinker, socially, sometimes on the weekends when we cook dinner, have people over, but never like this." She lets one shoe dangle from her foot. "You know what he did last week? He started drinking beer at noon during a cookout, then switched to wine, and then gin after it got later. I found him after our guests left. He was passed out up here. I thought he was dead. He had a picture of you and your dad and him when you went to Michigan to ski and sled. The funny thing is he had taken it out of the frame and rolled it up and was clutching it. I don't think he's going to get better, Gabe."

"Is there a reason he's drinking more? Maybe it's this thing about running for mayor." Even when I hear myself saying these things, I can hear the denial, the absurdity of my own obvious disconnection.

Susana smiles weakly as outside in the street a school bus pulls up with a moan and a grind. She seems grateful that I'm trying to figure out Ike's motivation, even though we both know the answer. Browder's snoring has reduced itself to a series of tiny clicks. He has his camera around his neck.

"No," says Susana, sounding like a confident but soft-spoken prosecutor. "I think it's what has caught up with him if you want to know the truth." Then she squints at me, and her face softens even more. Of all the things that have changed in Smallwood, maybe Susana's personality has been the biggest surprise, more so than the annex to the high school, or Mom's new love, even Wendy's hatred of me; all of that seems logical compared to my sister-in-law's presence, her essence. "You know, I know you know this, but I hated you when you wrote that book. Even Ike would defend you when I ranted and raved about how slimy you were to have told your family's, *our family's* secrets, and I really did hate you, Gabe." Susana's lip quivers, and she arranges herself more compactly on the edge of the bed, slumping into herself, putting her shoe back on. "I'm sorry about that now though. I can see some good in it now. I still get upset sometimes, and it's difficult to talk with the kids about it, but in the end, you got it out. He can't. Ike's locked into a box, like a magician, and he can't find the combination or how to get free of the chains, and he's losing air all the time." Susana lets out a sob, and I get up and walk across the room and sit down with her on the bed and pull her close. It's funny how she really does seem like a sister to me. For some reason, I rock her, and I realize it's set to the tempo of how I would rock Wendy when she was colicky. When the bed starts to squeak, I stop and ease her back as she looks for something to blow her nose on. I offer her a sock, and while she makes a grossed-out expression, she takes it and blows anyway.

"What can I do to help?"

"I don't know. I don't know what to do. But for today, could you take Browder with you to the courthouse?"

"How can I go there without Ike?"

She tosses the sock onto a pile of my dirty clothes and stands up. "He's already set it up for you. When he called in sick, he made sure to tell his secretary to help you today." Susana's heels are clicking over the attic floor again, now starting to go back down the steps. She adds, "Browder is a lot of fun. Make sure he gets to help you today. He sure likes you, Gabe."

The file room in the Hartford County Courthouse is so quiet it feels like a church, and the lighting lends itself to the effect as well, low and golden. There are rows and rows of crime-scene files, all labeled by the victim's last name and corresponding dates. While Browder goes off to use the rest room, I pull a random file and open it. The label reads: "R. Paulding/December 1998." There's a picture of a middle-aged man, bloated, lying nude on the banks of the Wabash River. His skin in spots is maroon, and he has a large, puffy slice across his neck, some kind of gelatinous substance coagulated over the busted seam, looking like fat fish eggs. I shove the file back on the shelf when Browder drags himself toward me. I tell him we better get to work, and we load up several boxes onto a handcart, which he struggles to pull behind him. But I don't have the heart to take away a task he seems proud to be doing, even if it's taking ten times longer.

Finally, we make it to the area Ike has designated as our work space. As we sit at a round table in the large break room, Browder is clearly bored. There are no fewer than fifteen boxes of court documents, and I'm surprised to find more than just photos of the crime scene. In envelopes with gold clasps, there are clear bags with shotgun shells, and items from the home: a large Goody comb; two bills from the Rileys' mortgage company, blood splattered like paint; a takeout Chinese menu from Emerald Palace also flecked with tiny dark spots; and a bag that looks empty, until I hold it up to the light. I search, looking every bit as if I'm trying to detect a hanging chad, and finally spot a fingernail. It's grayish, and thick, almost toelike, but it's clearly not wide enough. Browder sits in a chair next to a vending machine and tries to make the best of things.

"Hey," I say to him. "Why don't you use your camera to take photos of this stuff?"

He suddenly looks as if he might pop with excitement. "Yeah, and then you can read and let me be the photo man!"

I set him up a work space and tell him I need several shots of all the bagged items.

"Don't be afraid to take shots from every angle, Brow."

"Ike calls me that," he says.

"I know."

"Why isn't he with us today?"

"He's sick at home."

"He's sick from drinking those beers."

I can't help but smile, but then I ask Browder to also lie, the trademark of a family in denial. "Just don't say that around here, okay?" But he's too busy, precisely photographing a plastic bag with a squashed beer can in it.

The trial transcripts are methodical but boring. I need information about the killer's background. Michael the agent has made sure to remind me that true crime readers like their killers to be understood. "They don't want to like them, Gabe, that's not what I'm saying. They just want to know why they did it, that's all. Could be anything: drugs, cult, mental illness, abuse, fit of jealousy. In this case, I guess you'll have to go with the retardation." When I told him that was stupid, he just got quiet, then said, "Well, why did he do it?"

I burrow deeper into the court records and find the testimony of two forensic psychologists. One is named Dr. Brady, who at the time was working on a locked-down ward at Central State Hospital outside of Indianapolis. The defense lawyer, the same woman I met with yesterday, is referenced throughout the next ten or so pages. I flip through them, seeing her name, Heather Godshalk, jumping from the papers.

Godshalk: And Dr. Brady, after you examined the defendant, did you come to any conclusions about his state of mind?

Brady: Yes, he's borderline developmentally delayed. He would fall into the dull category, which really only tells us he can't learn well and that the written word isn't his cup of tea, so to speak.

Godshalk: Did you find anything else out about Mr. Finch's abilities, his personality?

Brady: Yes. Mr. Rodney Finch had what we'd call a trauma-laced childhood. He was often moved from one home to another, and his birth mother would frequently send him to live with relatives in other states. To the best of our abilities, we've determined he lived in six states and nine different homes from ages 3 to 10. And he had a long-standing sexual relationship with a much older caretaker, female, which started as early as age 11.

Godshalk: And what did this do to him, in terms of his development?

Brady: Whenever a child is living in transient situations like this, they tend not to develop normally, either socially or in their personality. His frequent moving, coupled with the fact that two of his mother's boyfriends molested him prior to puberty, produced an antisocial personality, and a severe and persistent fear of rejection. He exhibited this when Mrs. Riley turned down his advances in the weeks leading up to the murders. While she had been friendly to him at the grocery store and often tipped him, her rejection of his desire to make her his girlfriend unleashed an age-old fear of his that those around him for whom he had affection would ultimately deny him. He meets 7 out of the 10 indicators of a sociopathic personality.

In the transcripts, the DA objected to the doctor's statement, calling it speculative and prejudicial.

As I rustle through the documents, feeling overwhelmed, trying to find a strand where the story starts, the flash of Browder's camera feels like progress, even if it isn't mine. A kind of anxious focus climbs higher in me as I separate sheets that I want to copy. In a rush to create a pile of transcripts to read more thoroughly, I bump a foot-high stack of notes, and they fall with a whump to the floor. I feel sick.

"Stay here, okay?" I tell Browder as I duck out of the office and into the hallway. I make my way to the rest room and splash water on my face. Today I'm not dressed in Ike's clothes, and I ponder if I look as stupid to Ike's staff as I do to myself, in faded blue jeans and a pullover cable sweater from college, a little too tight. As I examine myself in the mirror, I realize how unbalanced this place feels without my brother. Back in the hallway, I notice for the first time the photos of Ike. There's one where he's being sworn in, another at the ribbon cutting of a new justice center outside of town. There are numerous snapshots of Ike posing with men and women from Indiana's Thirty-Second House District. There are photos of my brother at all the important Hartford County trials: the man who fire-bombed an ACLU office, killing an elderly woman on assignment from a senior citizens center; a woman with a cleft palate who flushed her premature but alive baby down the toilet, only to have it found by a Smallwood city sewer worker; and the man named Rodney Finch who killed the Rileys.

"Where," I say to myself, "could the Riley boy be?" I'm examining each photo of Ike as if I might find the body at the periphery, like those games you can play on the Internet, searching and comparing similar photos to discern how they are different. Maybe the body is hidden behind the flags in the photos, or stuffed under the judge's bench. I'm about to go back inside the break-room area when Heather Godshalk comes out of the rest room, her heels sounding like more authoritative versions of Susana's. She smiles at me and stops, even though I try to pretend I've not been looking at the pictures of my brother.

"He'll make a great mayor. I sure hope he runs."

"Uh-huh," I say, leaning back on my heels.

"You know," she says, "I double-dated with you back in high school. I was three years younger than you though. I dated your old girlfriend's cousin. Casey Wilcox?" Heather smiles at me and shrugs, and looks back at the photos, too, her face soft, the low light in the hallway giving her the look of a young nun. I remember Casey, of course. He bought us weed, and since Becca and I never double-dated but once, the image of a skinny, way too young Heather Godshalk comes back to me.

"You were way too young to be dating Casey. What was he, twenty-two? And you were fifteen?"

"Yeah," she says kind of proudly, which throws me, makes me think she's likely a very hard-nosed and competitive litigator. "Stupid, I suppose, but what can I say?" She straightens up and tosses her hair, clears her throat. "Did you stay in touch with her, Becca that is?"

"Not really. I mean, I've been living in Georgia for a while."

"Well, she works just across the street, you know. Casey's in business for himself, a contractor. Kind of took a hard hit with the housing mess, but they've done all right. Becca is the office manager. You should go see her sometime. It's a small town though," she adds as she clomps down the hall. "Better surprise her quick, or word will get to her by nightfall that you're here." Heather disappears into one of the dark walnut courtrooms, and the doors slowly ease shut behind her.

When I return to the break room, Browder has two secretaries helping him stage the plastic bags with evidence inside them. One woman is arranging a blue cloth under the item and telling Browder to back up a step. "Just one more now, hon." The bright flash assaults my face, burnishes my pupils, and I think of school pictures and the time a boy behind me in line said, "Your dad is a perv."

Now, I'm ready to move things forward, make my time in Smallwood pay off. One of the women actually tells me, "Your photographer is taking care of you, I'll tell you what."

Back in the files, I go on a search for where Rodney is housed. The paper in the file smells like iodine and pencil eraser, the edges tinted gray.

At lunchtime, I don't have any idea where to go except the wing joint Ike took us to yesterday. I think of taking Browder to meet my mother, but I'm afraid of what we might see, maybe Dick in a Speedo or ensconced in a velour robe, hair greased back, their love on display. I actually have to shake my head to lose the images.

The wing café pulsates with people on their lunch break: courthouse staff, sheriff's deputies, county road workers in orange vests, and two teachers I recognize from the high school. I know one of the teachers, a man with a large stomach and tree-trunk thighs, taught shop, and for some time was the JV wrestling coach, until he went Bobby Knight on a kid who wouldn't wrestle, just lay there and got pinned. The rotund teacher body-slammed the boy himself, and I can't comprehend how it is that he has kept his job.

Browder and I sit in the same booth as before, and he orders the wings again, along with a to-go cup of iced Coke. More people file in; other faces that hold some feature that I think I recognize: a bent nose, or a set of squinty green eyes; the vacant, lonely look of a woman who has stayed single, someone I maybe danced with one time at a party near the fairgrounds. Sitting here is like experiencing a watered-down version of memory lane; they all look aged and loosely familiar, melted faces out of focus, caricatures of Smallwood, fictional cutouts ordering faux food.

When the wings arrive, I can't believe my eyes as Ike walks up to our table and smiles broadly, his face scrubbed clean, hair still wet, smelling of spicy cologne and fresh soap. "Well, well, well," he says, "did my boys clock in without me today?" Ike sits down at the table, and I can tell Browder has cooled on him. Ike tries to engage him, but it doesn't work.

"Are you okay?" I ask, and Ike slaps my back and takes on the persona of the citizen servant alive and well in his admiring public's view. He's campaigning, for office, for himself, for the chance that he might not fully crack.

"I'm fit as a fiddle and better than I deserve to be." Ike looks around as the bustling crowd starts to frighten me. They wave and smile and holler over at my brother; they debate and order food and throw back soft and hard drinks. And while I'm watching Ike do his best to sober up, a woman comes through the door. I recognize her companion first, his broom-bristle hair gelled and mirrored sunglasses hanging around his neck. There's gray at Casey's temples, but he looks boyish still. Becca is at her cousin's side, and she appears nearly the same, too; some small wrinkles at her eyes, hair long and her body trim and managed. I wave, and she does the same back, and for the life of either of us, we can't seem to do anything else.

Chapter Sixteen

I slip out during the night and sneak away in my truck, first putting it into neutral, then pushing the junker down the street so I don't wake anyone. If Ike looked out the window and saw me, I know he'd think I was running away again, ditching Browder and heading off into the cool, dark spring night, Indiana twinkling in flat quadrants all around me, as I speed effortlessly down a weathered tarmac road, the ditches alive with rampant fescue and, behind sagging wire fences, the dark figures of Holsteins grazing under black skies. It's tempting, but I just need to get out, drive around my old town, maybe make my way to her house, find out if she's still spontaneous, still willing to break things; let destruction move life around, clear some of the clutter.

After fifteen minutes though, I have to admit I'm lost in my hometown. The darkness and my faulty recollection have left me parked alongside the road, the truck idling. The Google map showed Becca's address just outside the city limits, on a road called Pike, which stretches all the way into the river-bottom area where black loam lies like cold lava, giving rise to corn and soybeans that defy understanding; if you didn't know better, crops from here would look as if they'd been bioengineered, but it's just the nutrient-rich Wabash River basin that has flooded and reflooded for centuries, leaving behind what farmers call black gold, Indiana oil. But I can't find the road; I'm stuck on some kind of perpetually looping side street, and every time I think I've gotten off it, I'm circling right back around, ending up at the same four-way stop.

Finally, I manage to maneuver back onto the main drag, Highway 15, where I pull into a gas station and just sit and think. My head is filled with a map from twenty years ago, Smallwood saved in my memory, its old schematic, the intersections that are no longer there, rerouted and redirected toward a bypass. As I sit in the truck, I find it hard to believe that Smallwood would need a bypass. For what? To avoid the quaint streets, the nicely coiffed town square, the washed-up writer sitting stupidly in his truck, the Mylanta-mobile?

Once I get my bearings, the surroundings seem to coalesce, form into a semblance of the landscape of my long-term memory; it's not a perfect match, but I manage to drive and turn and stop and peer out the window, until I'm actually on Pike Street. It's late, and most of the duplexes and modest houses don't have porch lights on. As I try to make out the numbers, it occurs to me that this is a ridiculous idea. It's been a lifetime since Becca and I rollicked in and out of each other's beds. Still, I decide the small house on my right, the one with its porch light off, but some type of light burning in a small room at the side, must be the one. I can imagine her up at this hour, reading a mystery, flipping through a garden magazine.

I step out of the truck and stretch, a kind of involuntary postponement of what I've come for. I'd thought about bringing Pascal, but he was curled up next to Ruby, and it was actually that image that provided the impetus to drive here. My dog was enjoying the closeness of a warm body, and even while I thought about it, I knew my actions were cliché. I couldn't help myself though. Tracking down your old flame is akin to visiting your hometown cemetery; you want to be sad, you need your memory to have dead ends.

The night is clear, stars overhead, steady and beyond comprehension. I look up at the sky as I walk down the limestone path. I'm excited to see Becca, but even more curious about why we only had a cursory eye meeting at the wing café. Had she soured on me? Or likened my presence in Smallwood to a ghost?

There's only one car in the port, and I don't see anything masculine on the door, the entryway, like an IU banner or some kind of classic-rock radio station sticker. I wish now that I'd slammed a beer or quickly sipped some liquor, but I ring the doorbell anyway and wait. I tuck my hands in my pockets and look around, acting as if I might be on video, as if I were being watched. A car from a street over peels its tires, and a sudden yell follows it, then the roaring engine is blasting, growing more faint, until once again it's quiet, and the little porch settles around me, almost absorbs me. The smell of wet wood and old smoke wafts up, and I notice in the corner an outside fire pit, turned on its side, rusted, and a single scorched log lying next to the wire-mesh top. The sound of a trapped fly buzzes from somewhere above my head.

I told myself I'd ring once and let the fates figure out the rest. Still, I haven't turned away. I just stand there and wait. Waiting. Behind the door, I can hear some cautious rustling, then the sound of someone standing still, breathing, actually more like the paused essence of a human being than silence itself, little creaks and pops, the shallow breath exhaled.

Slowly, the gold handle turns down, then stops, and through the crack of the door, Becca's familiar throaty voice: "Are you selling HomeBeam pans, mister? I can only afford a spatula, maybe a pack of scouring pads." I'm relieved and let a big, hearty laugh blow from my lungs, sounding to my own ears like my father. It gives me the chills as Becca flips on the porch light and reaches out and pulls me inside.

She hugs me, and I can smell the heat of sleep on her, the static in her hair clinging to me. "I saw your daughter earlier this week," I say, and she pushes me back and smiles.

"That's weird, because last month I saw yours on a tour of the courthouse. Wendy didn't know who I was, of course, but she has your mouth, which should worry you." I'm a little embarrassed, but pull her back to me and take another hug. We sit down, and I can't help but feel more optimistic.

"You're in town to do a book about the Rileys, huh?" says Becca as she snuggles into me on the couch. If I close my eyes, I can see us in the basement of her parents' house, the first time we kissed, warmed then, too, under a quilt, but I can't think of it long or my mind plays that cinema of Dad filching her private things.

"I guess. But it's not going that well. Ike is . . . Well, he means well, but I can't seem to get a real start. Everything is stilted, mired in. . . ."

"Smallwood?" she asks, and kind of chuckles.

"Right," I say. "Hey, why didn't you come over to my table today? You looked at me like you could care less."

Becca starts laughing uncontrollably, and the couch actually bounces. She puts her hand to her mouth and sucks in twice as she sits up some, turns to me, and tries to get control, now fanning her hand in front of her face as if something were too hot to swallow.

"What?" I say, getting that feeling of isolation, the other person privy to something you should know; it's all so obvious, if you weren't such a numbskull.

Becca gasps, eyes watering, then she points to her eyes. "I can't see very far away if I don't have my glasses on. I forgot them today," she says, her amusement cooling, catching her breath, as she settles back into me.

"Well, who did you think I was?"

"I dunno. Everyone sort of looks the same without my glasses. I just thought you were a builder that we'd worked with." I smile and suddenly feel uncomfortable. Only a writer would think he should be welcomed back in his hometown, as if he'd been on some long and important sabbatical.

"It's great to see you, Becca."

"It's always good to see you, Gabe. Even if you look scared as hell."

"What? What do you mean?" I ask as I rearrange myself so I can look into her eyes.

"Well, who wouldn't be? There's your daughter, Ike, your mom, and her new man." I laugh with her as she continues, "Not to mention the murders, or The Book," which Becca pronounces in a deeper voice for the effect.

"I guess."

"It could be worse, you know."

"How's that?" I ask.

"The guy I'm seeing could've been here." She doesn't say it as a nasty, taunting remark, more like she's trying to slip back into how we teased each other, how sarcasm and our cynical worldviews meshed so well, drove us to care less, to carelessness.

"Yes," I say, feeling the energy drain from me. "That would certainly make things worse, since I suppose your beau is kin to Mother's new man. Maybe a nephew? They grow them big in Smallwood, don't they?" Becca lights up some, takes the baton, and runs with it, goads me.

"Right. He's actually a killer himself. The other guy that got away. They've been looking for Rodney Finch's accomplice for years. My new boyfriend is that guy. Butch Butcher." I tense up and feel abruptly betrayed by Becca's sarcasm. I twist to move away from her, pouty.

"Hey, I was just kidding, you know," she says, now slipping off the couch, kneeling before me. I want to kiss her hard. "I thought we were playing around like we used to. I'm sorry."

I feel stupid. "No, it's me. I'm starting to think I need to just turn around and head back down South."

Becca pats my leg, tosses her hair. There's not much light in the living room, but her lips glisten from something, maybe bedtime Vaseline. "It'll be okay." She climbs back onto the couch, and I lean in for a kiss, but she averts her head. "I wasn't joking about seeing somebody though. He's an excavator for our builders. It might be something serious."

"Oh," I say, wounded.

"Gabe," says Becca, "you didn't really think you could just come over and I'd be available and willing to start up something from twenty years ago, did you?"

I shrug. "Well, what was this?" I ask, pointing to us on the couch. "You let me in."

"This is me missing an old friend. This is two people from Smallwood hoping the best for each other." She smiles and stands up. "Hey," she says. "Are you hungry? I wasn't when I got home from work, but I'm starving now. Want an omelet?"

"I'm sorry," I say. "You're right. I guess I'm just, well, lonely."

"I can help with that. What are friends for if not to help with loneliness?" I nod, realizing I'm too late here. She's better off for it, and I'm not.

As Becca chops onion and I whisk four eggs, we talk about our girls, their boyfriends. And it occurs to me to ask, "Hey, do they know each other? Our girls?"

Becca dices tomato, moving the knife quickly under the soft light. "Not really. I mean, sort of. They run in different crowds. They were closer I guess in middle school. They had a dance class on Saturdays and they'd sometimes talk. It was always fun to see them together. Made me smile every time." Becca throws the onion into a pan with olive oil, and the smell instantly makes me feel safer, as if this were all that would ever be needed. We chat and laugh, sip beers as Becca flips the omelets, makes toast. I get out the plates from her tidy cabinets.

"Where is she now, your daughter? In bed?" I say, whispering. Becca laughs.

"Nope," she says, her mouth tightening, becoming more focused, a serious parent. "Oh, we went round and round about it, but she stays at his parents' house. They're not awful people, but I wish they'd been stricter. It's not what I wanted for her, but she's almost eighteen. What can you do?" I think of Wendy and feel a panic as I arrange the plates on neatly pressed place mats.

"I think Wendy is hiding from me," I say, and I can't help but laugh a little as we sit down at the table. Becca smirks and drops again back into our history, her teasing a relief, something that feels benevolent after I've embarrassed myself so much.

"Well, that can be problematic. Particularly if there's a father-daughter dance. It takes two to tango. Maybe she's nearsighted, too. She could think you're the UPS man."

We eat and talk, and I admire Becca's appetite, both for her omelet and the life she leads. While she talks about her job and the new hobby she has with her man—learning to ballroom dance—Becca's face glows, and I wish I could bottle her upbeat attitude, her ability to accept and enjoy. In the low light of the kitchen, we sip tea she's made in the microwave, honey and lemon, the tart sweet taste in my mouth making me want to try and kiss her again, but it's selfish.

"How's Ike doing?" she asks. And I can't help but notice how she asks the question a bit sheepishly, just like she used to with my dad, her voice lowering a little, eyes squinted, as if merely asking the question would somehow harm me.

"Well, he's gonna be a drunk mayor if he gets elected."

"That's awful," she says, smiling, then patting my hand.

"I really don't know what to do. Susana seems lost, too. It's like he's taken up alcoholism as a pastime." I tell Becca about how much work Ike put into the attic, the way he's been so welcoming to Browder. I think she might be a good person to start with, a local interview about the Rileys, someone I can trust to let me fumble.

"What have you heard about the murders?"

She pulls her robe tighter and blows on her tea. "The usual stuff, I guess. You know how people talk. Everyone says he'll get the lethal injection, but others say it's unlikely because of his disability. I mean there's no question he murdered them, but without the boy's body being found, there'll always be doubt and rumor. Did you meet with his attorney?"

"Yes, Heather Godshalk. She's the one that told me where you worked."

"Right. I used to babysit her. Kind of weird to think the kid that liked to eat boogers is now a lawyer."

"Gross," I say, smiling. "So what does the booger-eater have to say about the missing body?"

"I think everyone involved would like to forget about his body. The defense tried to bring it up during the trial to make the case of reasonable doubt, but I think they just ended up focusing more on his IQ. The DA didn't want to lose the case because they didn't have the fourth body, so they just ignored it."

"Where's it stand now? Is anyone still looking into it?"

"Finding the body, you mean?" asks Becca. "I don't know, but last year about this time Heather and I had lunch at . . ."

"The wing café," I say, finishing Becca's sentence.

"Right, Smallwood's gourmet mecca."

"The place to be if you want to see Smallwood's next mayor two sheets to the wind."

"Anyway," says Becca coyly, but focused on the discussion. "Heather said they found a new substance on something from the crime scene. It was like limestone dust, but different. They couldn't really determine what it was because it was old." The information makes my heart race.

"Did they do anything with it?"

"I don't know," says Becca, now slurping from her teacup. "But you know the Riley boy was gay, right?"

"No," I say, a bit perplexed. "What do you mean though?"

"Nothing really. It's just that some of the rumors that float around are about him being targeted because of the Ryan White thing. You remember that group of people in Kokomo back then that protested Ryan and wanted him quarantined and thought he was going to infect the whole state? I think it was called Americans with Values or something. Some people say Rodney Finch went to the house with a buddy who had been part of that group, and that Rodney killed them all but that the buddy kidnapped the Riley boy and tortured him somewhere around Kokomo and then fed his body to pigs or something. The group that hated Ryan was like a cult. But you know how people are here. They love rumors; hell, I like listening to them," says Becca, "but still, I think most of it's just talk. You can ask Heather though about the dust and the tests they did on it."

It's nearly 3 a.m. when Becca walks me to the door. She snuggles up to me, and we stand and hug, and the room buzzes around us with heat and the electricity of time together. She invites me back to meet the man she thinks she'll marry if he asks. If I come back for dinner sometime next week, we'll have salmon and good wine and I can see the video of them ballroom dancing last year in Indianapolis.

Time seems to bend and fold, swirl around, collapse. I think of the stars outside, of Wendy's birth, Dad's death, Ike's anger, the way Smallwood will really never change, the way it has already gone against me and morphed into an image of its dislocated past.

"I don't think I could stand doing that," I tell Becca as I step back from her. "The truth is, I'm happy for you, but I won't lie. I had visions of us living happily ever after, or at least making wild love."

She laughs and kisses my cheek. "A year ago and I would've definitely taken you up on that, Mr. Burke. But today, well, Smallwood actually feels really good for the first time in a decade."

On the walk to my truck, it feels as if the temperature has actually risen. I drive along the empty streets, wide and well lit as I enter the city limits. The spaces where cars are usually parallel parked seem naked now, obscene and vacant, the lines canary yellow, the meters preposterous, long necks giving way to bulbous heads, replete with eyes and mouth. I slow down and feel so silly stopping and waiting all alone at a red light that I actually look around to see if anyone else finds this funny. It's called Hill Street because it's on the town's biggest hill. The high schools outside of Smallwood—the county ones we used to play in basketball—are called Northfield High, because it's north of a big field, and Southwood High, for a similar reason. We Midwesterners are stereotyped for the same kind of thinking behind those schools' names.

I drive around awhile, not feeling like going back to Ike's. It's three thirty in the morning now, and as I loop back around the park, I see that the ice storm has killed the jonquils, spotlighted by a security pole. Their yellow heads, browning at the edges, lie flat on their green leaves, looking as if the ice had a big foot that mashed their beauty to the ground. For some reason, I sit and stare at the flowers, for how long I don't really know, before shifting gears and heading back to Hill Street.

I'm a mystery to myself tonight, and I can't say why I don't want Ike or Susana or even Browder to know I've been out. I leave the truck on the street, park a few houses down and just walk. On the rise I can see the attic window, light burning inside. I think Browder is awake, maybe worried, or scared to be by himself, but it doesn't seem likely. He sleeps like a dead man; light or sound doesn't wake him. I pick up the pace and realize I don't have a key. I'm busted. There's nothing I can do but ring the doorbell. The old Susana would've had me arrested, but these days she might even relish having a disturbance other than Ike. I try to think of some excuse, but nothing comes, so I decide if asked I'll tell them I couldn't sleep, went for a walk. A weak cone of lemon light falls on the yard from the attic window, and when I ring the bell, Pascal and Ruby bark like mad, and the light in the attic goes out, leaving that spot in the yard pulsing with light that has vanished. I think I can hear some elongated response inside the house, a rumbling, maybe a squeak of the attic stairs, and the dull thud of feet to the carpeted stairs that lead toward the front door.

"Shhh, shhh," I can hear Ike saying. "Go lie down, now. Lie down." The dogs hush, and their nails on wood floors fade away from me. Ike opens the door, and I realize then he's been upstairs; how else would he know I'm not there, that he's not opening the front door to a Rodney Finch wannabe or someone he's pissed off as county clerk? The question is: what was he doing up there?

"What the fuck are you doing?" he asks, his pinstriped silk pajamas swallowing him up. His eyes are bleary, and he's tried to cover his night's booze with Listerine. I eye him for a moment and think of asking my brother the same question, but it's late, and I'd rather have a look around for myself upstairs before accusing him of something. His hair has static, and I can't even believe I'm saying what I am until the last sentence trills from my hysterical mouth.

"I just really need to see her, Ike. Can't you do something?" I say as he pulls me inside. Why the fact of not being able to see Wendy has come out like this, here at this particular moment in time, I have no idea.

"What, you mean you want me to subpoena her or something?" Ike can't walk a straight line as he tries in vain to escort me to the living room, his warm body bumping into me, his grip a little too tight on my arm. He plops me down in his own lounger and sits on the edge of the fireplace hearth.

"No, I just . . ." I say, then starting over, "can't you try to call her or something tomorrow, try and talk some sense into her? I just want to take her out to eat or go for a drive."

"Jesus," says Ike, now seeming more sober than before. "My kids don't even let me do that, and I'm around all the time."

"You'll call her, then? Please, for me?"

"Sure," he says, face a little amused, softer. But a sudden change sweeps over him, seems to plunge him back into a funk, and I think he might be experiencing withdrawal or possibly an early morning hangover. Or both.

"How much have you written so far?" he asks as he moves away toward the bar. It seems he spends all of his days either in this living room or the file room at the courthouse, his two rooms, existing in only two realms.

"Nothing, that's not the way it works, Ike. I'll do interviews and read all the files; there are even some newspaper pieces I've not read. I probably won't write a word of it until I'm back in Georgia."

Ike is about to say something, something he appears to be pissed off about, his face scrunched into a wicked little red beet, but in the entrance of the living room, standing there with blank blue eyes, arms down at her side like a marionette, staring straight ahead, is his daughter, my niece. More than the fact that she's clearly in a solid sleepwalk, I'm nearly bowled over by how much she looks like Wendy. They have the same red bow lips, and long necks, and judging by the quick glimpses I've caught of my daughter running away from me, they appear to be the same height and weight.

"Katherine," says Ike, his voice calm and measured. "Turn around and go back upstairs, sweetie. You're sleepwalking." Ike moves toward his daughter slowly, almost as if she's wearing a dynamite vest. "Here, let me help you."

Katherine's eyes seem to look right through me. She points and says in a monotone voice, "He's my uncle. He's been gone." Ike nods and turns her slowly toward the end of the staircase, and they seem to fade away like some poignant moment in a movie. I sit in the living room alone for quite a while, until it's clear Ike is not coming back down. I stand and head up the stairs myself.

On the desk, my laptop is open, but not on. I know for a fact it was in the travel bag when I left. I look around the room and notice my backpack seems to have been searched. Browder is asleep in his twin sleigh bed, head under the covers, and it's not until I crawl into my bed and the room is nearly dark that I notice light from outside playing over the surface of a crystal tumbler on the desk, my brother's melted ice and booze forgotten in a rush to leave.

Chapter Seventeen

Two days pass, and Browder leaves me again for Susana. At night, in my brother's home, we review the photos Susana and Browder have taken. There's the old Kranston Mill Brewery, the Shanty Falls, and the faces of old people at Thompson's Merry Manor Home. These new photos though have taken a turn, and Browder is seen in some of them, posing in front of a brick wall where two rusted beer signs look as if they might fall on his head; then standing at the edge of the cascading creek, hand dipped into the silver cold water; and finally Browder with Pascal and Ruby in the old folks' home, a group of elderly people smiling, reaching from wheelchairs to pet our dogs. I'm ashamed I once thought Susana was shallow; she's clearly grown more mature, volunteering, while I've been the one who's let fear stifle growth.

Last night, Katherine and Evan, Ike's kids, joined us for dinner, both of them free for only one evening. They are lean and beautiful, and I can see my father in Evan's eyes, the flicker of intensity when someone says something he doesn't agree with. He doesn't talk much, but when he does, it almost breaks my heart; his voice, or rather the cadence of it, sounds so much like his grandfather.

Now, back in the file room at the courthouse, I feel trapped, cut off from my daughter, from writing, from our town. As I photocopy yet another stack of transcripts, I peek out the window and see Ike heading for the wing café. I can't stand being here anymore and decide right then to make a break for it, hit the road again and hopefully inject some real-life energy into the story. I put the papers down and walk to Heather Godshalk's office in the adjacent building.

In the waiting area, I have to sit for fifteen minutes while her secretary briefs her on one Gabe Burke sitting on the mauve love seat near the ficus tree that may or may not be real. The weather outside has completely left behind the ice storm of nearly a week ago, and I can see the clear blue sky behind the shimmering shamrock leaves. I stand up and walk to the window and peer down at Smallwood. Sunlight is glinting off cars and the flat window fronts. The circus used to winter here back in the early 1900s, and someone has employed the theme in the downtown renovation. I spot elephant statues on each block, and a colorful mural of men on stilts, two smiling lions, and a legion of intelligent-looking clowns performing for a crowd of jubilant faces, cheeks red, hands in mid-clap. On top of the old Witchell Loan Building there's a replica of a big top, and even a moving miniature Ferris wheel. Ike could have all of this, become the next Mayor of Smallwood Past. When we're dead and gone, what will they use as a metaphor to revamp the town in a hundred years? The renovation just feels like a dying animal's last kick, although it's likely that it's just me feeling this way. Everyone else is too busy with life to sit around thinking about what a clown mural means.

"Mr. Burke," the voice calls. "Mr. Burke?" I turn from the sunny window and stare at the receptionist. She smiles. "Ms. Godshalk can see you for a few minutes." I feel like my niece, Katherine, as I sleepwalk my way into the lawyer's office, deep walnut decor, forest-green paint, the crown molding the color of avocado pulp.

"Hi," says Heather. "Sit down." I feel too low in front of her desk and try to push myself higher, but it's as if I'm in quicksand that's pulling me deeper into the leather lounger. "I thought you might come see me." I must look perplexed, as she folds her hands together, smiles politely, and explains. "I saw Becca this morning. They're building our new house out near Richvalley," she adds.

"Oh," I say, now feeling even sillier than the chair has made me look. If they're close, did Becca tell her I made a move? But the thought quickly recedes; Becca is a loyal friend. I speak up. "Okay, so there was some dust, or something that was recovered? Can you tell me about it?"

"I will, but listen, I don't want any complications with the court. You know the rumors about the Riley case, and as far as I'm concerned, it's been tried and put to rest."

"That's not much of an advocacy point of view though, is it? I mean Rodney Finch could hear that comment and interpret it as not exactly in his best interest."

"Cute," says Heather, an intensity revealing itself in the way she swivels in her chair, her face lovely in the soft light of her office. "Though you might want to leave the legal wrangling to experts. After all, you don't see me trying to edit your memoir after it was published, now do you?"

"You've got me there," I say. "All I meant was that I would think you'd want to look into any possibility that he had help in the crimes. Becca mentioned there's information that the Riley boy was gay, that the group that hated Ryan White may have had something to do with his murder."

"All gossip, to my knowledge anyway," says Heather, dismissing the notion with a wave of her slim hand. She wants to make sure I stay in my place, and she pulls a Midwestern tactic, edges me out of bounds with innuendo. "You, I would expect, are sensitive to how rumor and implication run rampant in Smallwood. We have to be careful not to compare too many things to other things, or people for that matter."

"What did the tests show on the dust?" I say, acting as if she's not just insulted me and been cruel at the same time.

"Not much," says Heather, shrugging her shoulders. "It was old. That they could say for certain, but the origin was unclear. Just because something turns up new doesn't mean the gates of heaven open wide and the case is solved. I'm afraid real-life crime has little in common with television."

"Where was it found?"

"In samples of Mrs. Riley's hair," says Heather, looking at her desk phone as it trills twice, then rolls back to her assistant, like an echo in a valley.

"So it had to have gotten there somehow, right? Was any of it found on Rodney?"

"No, it wasn't. We had his clothes from the night of the murder reanalyzed, and the samples from his nails didn't show traces of the substance, but that doesn't mean I can get him a new trial, Gabe. He did confess to the murders; anything we petition the court with has to have a connection to getting him off death row. I can't do that with new dust evidence."

"But there are two issues, correct? One is his death sentence, but the other, the one I'm talking about, is that there is potentially another killer involved, one that maybe could be found if this dust were fully analyzed."

Heather smiles, then actually lets out a forceful laugh. "You sure know how to complicate matters. If I were you, I'd write the book with the scenario we have. If you think you're going to solve the case of the missing Riley boy's body though, be my guest, but take some advice and accept what we all have to accept."

"What's that?"

"That as much as we'd like to have the answers to every unsolved case, sometimes there just aren't any. Maybe in the next life everything will be laid out before us, but here, here in Smallwood, we do our best and move on."

I nod and actually find some comfort in her words. "What's his fascination with dinosaurs?"

"Oh, I don't know," says Heather, becoming pressed for time. "A hobby, I guess. He talks about them when he doesn't want to answer other questions. Could be a defense mechanism. He has posters of different ones in his cell. When he's allowed books, they're usually about dinosaurs." Heather shrugs and rearranges her pearl bracelet below the white and blue cuffs of her shirt and jacket.

"Can I talk with him, today if possible?"

"Who," says Heather, "Rodney?" as if I've asked to sit down for a rap session with the Pope.

"Right. I'll need to interview him for the book."

"It doesn't work that way, Gabe. You have to make a formal request, and have it signed—"

"But you could speed it up, right? You could help me meet with Rodney. I just want to talk with him." Heather nods. She stands and lets me know my time is up.

"I'll help you, yes. But . . ." Her face seems flushed, and her mood a little downcast, but only for a second, then she's unflappable again, her expression set purposefully, determined.

"What?" I ask.

"I really admire your brother. He's been a good public servant, but it's more than that. He's survived what happened to your family. I hope you don't mind me saying so. And since I've said that, allow me this: He also handled your book with what I would call grace."

I think of defending myself, telling her how my brother didn't exhibit much grace when he'd call and badger me about the book, but I realize even now that Ike had the right to react any way he wished. "And?" I ask, walking with her toward the door.

"And he's at a critical moment in his career. If the committee gets behind him, he'll be running on the Democratic ticket for mayor. The last thing he needs is his brother playing detective." The comment hurts, but she's right.

"Thank you, Ms. Godshalk. I'd like to visit Rodney if I can." She nods and holds the door open for me. "And for the record, I'm not trying to be Columbo or anything. I just like the truth."

Heather licks her lips and says politely, with just a tiny bit of her justice wrapped around the words, "Then you'll need to be prepared to not like it, too." And something about the way she looks at me makes me think she's sincere.

My energy from just an hour ago has waned. I'd thought arranging to visit Rodney Finch would be as simple as asking, which was naïve. Now, I'm once again tied to the copier and can't keep from walking to the window and peeking out while the Xerox pounds away, the collating and stapling actually vibrating the room. As I stand and spy on my brother, hoping to catch a glimpse of him leaving the café, walking this way, head down, stride wobbly, the copier makes easy, yet intense work of the files. When I turn around after daydreaming, the floor is littered with loose pages, and there are no fewer than four lights blinking on the copier. I've managed to jam the process, clog the machine with my need to duplicate and record.

I stoop and gather the papers. I must look like an angry chimp when a woman enters the room and asks if I'm Gabe Burke. I'm looking up at her, squatted as I am on the floor, and I divert my eyes from her legs. "Here," she says, handing me another sheet of paper, and for a moment I think she's found one of my strays, that maybe the papers have blown into other offices. "This is from Ms. Godshalk's office. If you will sign it, I'll return it to her staff to process. He'll have to agree, but he usually does with other reporters. He likes attention."

I stand up, back knotted, clutching the wad of crinkled papers to my chest like a mad professor. I tilt my head and read the top of the memo as the assistant waits patiently, examining her nails. It's a form letter, requesting permission to visit inmate Rodney Finch on death row at the prison in Michigan City, Indiana. The information is jolting: one, because I thought death row was in Indianapolis, and two, because I didn't believe Heather Godshalk was really going to help me. I scratch my signature on the line and hand it back to the assistant. "We'll call you when it's approved," she says. "You never know though. Sometimes the warden up there gets finicky." And with that she trots back through the door and down the hall, her heels clicking the floor, a sound I've come to associate in Smallwood with dread.

As I try to straighten the papers, my cell phone rings.

"Hey," says Ike, and I can hear the noise in the background, the patrons, his voters at the café, eating fried food and sneaking drinks before clocking back in at the tile mill, the used-car lots, the real-estate offices, and government complexes.

"What is it, Ike?"

"Good news. Susana got in touch with Kate, and she's bringing Wendy over tonight for dinner." My throat tightens, but I don't believe it.

"Are you sure she agreed to come?"

"Jesus, Gabe. I mean I can get her picked up by a sheriff if you want. She'll probably bring her boyfriend."

"Okay," I say. Then all there is on the line is the sound of people milling about, chatting and coughing, cell phones ringing.

"But I'm afraid there's some other bad news to go with this," says Ike, and I can tell his words are starting to lengthen, that if he has another two drinks, he'll be officially drunk.

"What?"

"Dick and your mother are coming over, too. Susana set it all up. A real fucking family reunion." Ike cackles, and then tells some supporters thank you, that he's not made a decision about running, and then he's back on the phone. "Sorry about that."

"You should be. I don't really want to see Wendy for the first time in front of everyone."

"Oh, why don't you cry me a river, brother. Take it or leave it. This might be the only way you'll get to see her. Suck it up. You're not the one who has to be pleased in this situation."

"Ike," I say, "what were you doing up in the attic the other night?"

The phone rustles, and I assume he's moving it to his other ear. "Well, I suppose I can go anywhere I please in my own goddamn house, Gabe, but from now on I'll let you know my every movement."

"Why did you want to help me in the first place with the Riley book? I mean, you hated me."

"Well, I suppose," he slurs, ice tinkling, "I'm a real Burke Man, Gabriel. I want to watch you. You know, really watch. Keep my eyes on you. It runs in the family." He laughs to himself.

"Fuck you," I say.

"If only it were that easy, memoirist."

Then I imagine him clicking shut his phone as the empty connection hums in my ear.

Chapter Eighteen

Up in the attic I help Browder knot his necktie. Susana brought up one of Ike's old suits; why, I'm not sure. Getting dressed up for the dinner doesn't make much sense, but I've pressed a shirt, too, and tucked it in, put on some boat shoes. I've shaved and splashed on some cologne; it seems Browder and I will be at the dinner table with pieces of Ike on us, and the idea makes me think of the crime reports, the technician who stated, "Pieces of Mrs. Riley's brain matter were found on a grandfather clock, on the family photographs in the hallway, and in a potted plant." If I'm not careful, I'm going to have a panic attack.

"You look great," I tell Browder, who smiles, his camera around his neck.

"Can I play them a song tonight?" he asks, and I look at him, a little confused, already having forgotten the instrument he bought at Cracker Barrel. He pulls his harmonica from his zippered camera bag, and I realize he's likely been playing it on the car rides with Susana. I miss being with him, him and Pascal, the three of us just watching birds and spotting things both dead and alive in the swamp. Georgia seems so foreign now, it might be the country of the same name, the one next to Russia. When the armed conflict occurred there, Browder greeted me at the door of the group home, telling me Russia had invaded the state of Georgia, but then again, he wasn't the only person in the country to think that. I had to get a map to show him we were safe.

"How about we just eat good tonight and try to help each other out," I tell him. "You remember Wendy. She's coming tonight with her mother, maybe her stepfather, too. I'm real nervous. I've missed her so much, but I'm scared she doesn't want to really see me at all."

"She's your family though. Families love each other." Browder smiles again, his large eyes gleaming with light.

"I sure hope so," I tell him, and my hands are actually shaking. Browder gives me a hug and pats my back. He goes first down the attic stairs—now a pro at it—and I follow. At the top of the staircase that leads to the first floor, I straighten his tie again out of nervousness. The food smells wonderful, and I make a mental note to thank Susana for all she's done.

It's just about six thirty, and the dinner date is set for seven. Susana is in the kitchen, putting the final touches on what looks like a delicious meal: a spinach salad with tangerine slices, candied pecans, Roma tomatoes, red onion, and crunchy croutons; French bread; salmon steaks and tuna teriyaki served with peach chutney; and for dessert a lemon-lime cheesecake. "It's from a woman near the reservoir, an ex-Amish lady. She left the order and now caters wonderful meals," says Susana. Browder asks if he can have some cheesecake now, and before I can intervene, Susana has told him sure he can, already placing a big slice on a plate.

I leave the two of them in the kitchen and walk into the living room where Ike is watching CNN, both Pascal and Ruby asleep near the fireplace.

"Hey," I say. Ike shifts in his leather chair; tonight he's wearing a spring sweater, yellow as a canary, and perfect cream-colored slacks. He's smoking his cigar and drinking from a tumbler. His cologne is strong, the Royal Copenhagen he's worn since college, the scent woodsy, like toasted moss.

"You ready for this, brother?" he asks, not really making eye contact. What started out as a congenial visit with him has taken a sour turn. Now, we are cautious with each other, sensing something that's age old, as ancient as it gets, brothers who don't trust one another. I can't stop thinking about him going through my belongings, and I'm certain he's put out with me for pushing things. Still, I'm so grateful he's helped me get to see Wendy.

"Thank you, Ike." He waves me off, the ice in his glass clinking.

"I saw some more crime-scene photos," I say. "I don't know how you can look at that stuff every day." I try to make it sound like a compliment, but there's an edge to him.

"It's my job to look, Gabe," and he still doesn't make eye contact, but rather peers inside his glass, where the liquid is now tea-colored, and nearly gone.

"Huh, that's funny. It's my job to look, too, then write."

"Uh-huh," Ike says sarcastically, as if I've just described my work as something akin to curing disease. Ike rises from the chair, but gets hung up, his pant leg snagged on the recliner. He yanks his leg hard, and a small, audible rip seems to tear more than the fabric of his slacks. I'm shocked he's being so careless with his appearance, shocked and scared by it, too. "Fucking chair," Ike mumbles as he makes another drink at the bar. I can feel my hands still shaking, and the clock ticking on the wall seems like it might be attached to a bomb.

I watch his back, then add, "Hey, maybe I should have one of those."

"Be my guest," he says.

We sit and chat now over our drinks, and for a few minutes it's civil, then he takes a big gulp and looks at me with what I'd call dire amusement.

"You talk with Heather Godshalk today?" Ike sucks a piece of ice, then spits it back into the glass like he might be puking it up.

"No harm in talking with someone, is there? Free country, right, like we used to say as kids."

"Free country maybe, but not a free Smallwood. You stay out of her office and the DA's, you understand?" I'm stuck now between needing to keep him cool and on my side for the Wendy visit and wanting nothing more than to punch him in the face, or at least argue with him.

"Whatever you say, Mayor." The comment brings a smile to his face, but I can see how tired he is, how much he looks as though he is on the verge of something. Just as I'm about to reach over and pat his hand, Katherine and Evan come into the living room, dressed nicely, too, wearing slim jeans and colorful spring sweaters. Evan and Katherine sit down on the hearth, and the dogs wake, yawn, and sort of crawl toward the kids for petting. Ike grins as the two of us watch his nearly grown children rub the ears of two of our favorite creatures.

When the doorbell rings, Ruby barks once, followed by Pascal. Ike and I shush them, and the house takes on the active, jittery atmosphere of a fractured family attempting (however briefly) to heal its wounds. I feel my stomach turn, but stand up. Katherine and Evan leave ahead of us. Ike and I stand in the center of the living room, and he looks at me and says, "You might want to down that," pointing to my nearly full glass of bourbon. "It's showtime," he adds as he slugs back his own drink with real passion.

I creep into the kitchen. In a bustle of jacket shucking and agitated chatter, I scan the faces as stiff hugs are given, received. There's Dick and Mom, but I don't see Kate or Wendy. Evan and Katherine are standing before the adults, allowing themselves to be surveyed, inspected. Susana and Ike are side by side, but he seems to be leaning on her. Browder is introduced to my mother as "Gabe's friend from Georgia," and I wonder if Dick thinks the phrase means we're in a relationship. I watch as Ike extends his hand to Mom's large boyfriend. In the light of the spacious kitchen, the shiny onyx countertop reflecting the stainless steel appliances, this family is rearranging itself, divergent beings brought together by blood and history, shame and uncontrollable love. Smallwood, Indiana, Our Shattered Hometown USA.

Watching their faces, tense, smiling, sometimes letting real joy enter, I again feel saddened by all that I've missed, the ugly parts of living like this, fully realizing my cowardice to stand and take it. I have to fight the sensation of having slept too long, fuzzy and feeling as if this scene has been played out a thousand times before. When you're a spectator, our father used to say, don't expect anyone to ask you to join the game.

As Dick removes his coat, an expanse of denim trimmed in leather, he does a double take and looks behind him, smiles broadly and steps out of the way for two figures to enter the kitchen. First, Kate comes into focus, going directly to our mother and hugging her, kissing her cheek. I strain to make out the other person, until, stepping into the fuller light of the kitchen, Wendy tosses her hair and smiles at her cousins. She's not looking around for me; she's engaged in telling Katherine how much she loves her jeans. I had thought my daughter would've shown up somber and detached, but she's comfortable here, and when her cousin Evan says something to her in an apparent tease, she sticks out her tongue at him and laughs. All three of them are holding different phone devices, every moment or so checking them, quickly firing off a text. More coats are removed, and I can't say that I've ever felt more out of place, more afraid to move or speak.

Finally, Kate makes her way to me and hugs me. She whispers in my ear, "Don't go all out here. Let her come to you." It sounds like we're trying to trap a dog that's gotten loose, or some kind of delicate but finicky bird, out of its cage, skittish and on the verge of simply up and flying off. Kate moves away from me, and then steps forward, tells me to introduce her to Browder.

"Where's Cal?" I ask as we walk toward Browder.

"He's doing the sensitive thing and stepping aside tonight," Kate whispers. Browder immediately tells her she's pretty and snaps a photo of her. When he asks to show it to her, I have to remove the strap from his neck and hold the camera where Kate can see it. Browder pushes some buttons, but different pictures appear, ones of Ike. They're of Ike in various stages of drunkenness; ones of Ike snooping in the attic, so drunk he must have not noticed Browder hiding somewhere taking photos. Kate kind of widens her eyes and contains a slight grin, then gets serious again, deferring to me as Browder smiles and keeps advancing the pictures.

I make sure Ike and Susana aren't nearby and then quietly ask Browder, "When did you take these?" He shrugs, doesn't offer much insight. The ones of Ike snooping are sort of funny, but they're scary, too, and I have to try hard to recall if I've seen my contract folder, the one that spells out how *Leaving Smallwood* will be reissued. It dawns on me that Ike may have already read the draft prologue I've written. "Why don't you put the camera back in its case for now, Browder, okay?" He agrees, even if he does give me a perplexed, almost irritated look.

Ike escorts us all into the living room, and I'm glad Kate stands near me as the family becomes stuck in that old quiet dysfunction. Mom and Dick agree to have a glass of wine, and the kids all sit on the sofa, texting, sometimes laughing nervously.

"Shouldn't I at least say hello to her?" I ask Kate, who shakes her head no. I whisper even more quietly, "So I should just pretend I'm not related to her, that I'm not her dad?" Kate raises her eyebrows, and I know the gesture is meant to indicate I have no moral ground here. After a few awkward moments, Kate returns to the kitchen to help Susana and Browder, leaving me to chat with Ike and Mom and Dick.

Mom is actually wearing makeup, and if it weren't for her fuzzy gray hair, she would look younger than her seventy years. I sit on the hearth and listen to Ike and Dick talking about the politics of Smallwood, how Dick's great-grandfather founded the first Democratic Farmer Labor Party. Ike is authentically interested, but he's now drinking the bourbon straight, almost as if it's iced tea. Mom seems to notice, glancing at the drink in his hand the same way I'm glancing at my daughter, careful not to get caught. I'm terrified to say anything at all as Wendy and her cousins roll their eyes and talk quietly, the sounds like pigeons cooing while their phones vibrate and screens flash reds and blues.

In the kitchen, Kate and Susana have music playing now, something that sounds like elevator jazz, tinkling piano and trilling woodwinds. For a while, things seem to mute and soften, the sounds in the kitchen, voices and music, dishes clinking, the drone of Ike's voice agreeing with Dick, as the house tries to accommodate our fears. Before long though, Kate and Susana enter and announce that dinner is served. For the first time Wendy looks in my direction, and my heart skips a beat, only to grow leaden when she uses my location to steer clear of me as we make our way into the large dining room.

The table is long and dark walnut, the place settings pale green, arranged perfectly over a thick russet tablecloth, the silverware like odd mirrors, shimmering glasses full of ice water, coffee cups turned upside down, and a towering row of tapered candles unlit in the center of the tabletop. The food is already served on the plates, the salmon and asparagus gleaming, salad bowls with spinach leaves bathed in shiny oil. The smells are delightful, and I can feel my mouth water. Dick asks, "If you good people don't mind, I'd like to say a prayer before we eat." He defers to Ike, whose eyes are glassy, and there's a look of sadness now, too, as if this supper were his last, the Good Shepherd of Smallwood with his disciples, breaking bread before the betrayal.

Ike at first shrugs, then pauses and musters up, "Please," and even bows his head.

Dick blesses everyone in the room, asking that Evan, Katherine, and Wendy be gifted with an uncommon ability to resist the temptations of the world, which apparently doesn't include boning our mother out of wedlock. His words are hypnotic though, and when he adds at the end, "And thank you for bringing Gabe home to visit," Ike clears his throat then coughs. Wendy acts as if my name means nothing. My hand shakes when I reach for a sip of water. The meal starts, and I try to focus on the small talk, the compliments about the food.

About halfway through the meal, the stilted talk having slipped into a more relaxed exchange of information, I notice that Wendy is suddenly free for a second, not engaged with her iPhone or cousins. I can't help myself and say, trying to sound nonchalant, "Wendy, where's your boyfriend tonight? I thought he was coming over, too."

She cuts her big eyes toward her mother, and Kate quits chewing and puts down her fork, dabs her lips and answers for our daughter. "Todd had a weight-training session at the high school, and he's got a big trig test tomorrow to study for."

"I see, and, Wendy, what do Todd's parents do for a living?" Wendy lets her napkin fall to her plate, covering up her untouched salmon, the asparagus that she's only pushed around. I want to hug her, tell her I'm sorry for not being a better father. My throat tightens, and those old images of our father come rushing back into my head, our trips on the road, him behind the glass at the jail, his hair much thinner, almost completely white.

Wendy sits back in her chair and lowers her head, makes the sound of someone truly disgusted.

"You remember, Gabe, I told you his mom is a nurse and his dad works at Monsanto," says Kate, and even she seems to be trying to keep from screwing up.

"Why don't you let Wendy tell me about the special person in her life?" I say, and Ike seems to pep up some, even if he's already drunk two glasses of wine on top of all the booze. The phrase "special person" is what has made him smile, knowing that I might as well have said "your lover" to my daughter, and I can't believe in front of these people that I've put my child in such an uncomfortable situation. Browder snaps a picture of Wendy, and I tell him to stop it, to put the camera away. "Come on, Browder, can't you leave that damn thing in the pouch for one night?" My voice is too forceful, sounding like nothing less than a reprimand.

Wendy sits up in her chair and looks directly at me, her eyes fiery, and her beautiful face alive with complete contempt for me. I have it coming, and it feels right to get it this way, to be worthy of such hatred at this particular dinner. Only families know how to hate with such utterly perfect precision. "Why don't you mind your own fucking business," says Wendy as Mom picks at her plate, begins to look around at the walls, searching for something that will make her appear occupied.

"Watch your mouth," says Kate, but Wendy doesn't allow her glare to leave me.

She stands up and points at me; I can't help but think of her as a toddler, pointing at animals in a book and trying to say their names. "Why did you come back here anyway? Did you want to make us all embarrassed again?" Kate stands and goes to her daughter, who is now sobbing, unable to deliver all the revulsion she has for me. I get up, too, and move around the table as the others start to edge away from their plates. Browder hangs his head as Susana tries to get him to eat another piece of salmon. I feel worthless. Before I can get to Kate and Wendy, my daughter pushes her mother back and runs to the front door and slams it behind her.

"Nice work," says Ike, pouring white wine into a tall water glass, gulping it down.

"Shut up, Ike," says Susana. Dick is helping Mom up and leading her to the door. His face is apologetic, and I can't be sure, but he seems to be teary eyed. At the door, helping Mom on with her coat, he bellows, "It's been a long night. Maybe we should all get some sleep." Ike rolls his eyes. I kneel down next to Browder and tell him I'm sorry, to which he responds by snapping a photo of me, the camera shoved up close to my nose, the flash blinding me, his expression almost angry.

"Well, if you ask me, this has been just about as good as it gets with the ol'

Burke family," pronounces Ike, his speech garbled with inebriation. Evan and Katherine look ashamed, scared, and hangdog as Susana tells them to go on up to bed, that she'll bring their plates up later. When they leave, their empty chairs, along with Wendy's, seem to symbolize the impossibility of reconciliation for the Burkes, for any family, and since my mood is now so defeated, for the entire family of man.

I head for the door, going after my daughter, but Kate says, "You've gotta be kidding, Gabe." She pushes past me and leaves the house, too. From the open door, I watch her get into their car, Wendy sitting curled up in the passenger's seat, jacket nearly over her head. Kate backs the car out of the driveway, and I'm left with Ike at my shoulder. When I turn to face him, he's fully drunk, almost belligerent.

I try to move past him to reach Browder. I'm thinking of how to get out of this house, out of Smallwood, free from the things I've written and the ones I'm contracted to write. I step up close to Ike's face, and he smirks. "You're a drunk, Ike," I say. "You have a serious drinking problem, and you've embarrassed your kids tonight. You need some help. I love you, but you need help."

"And you didn't embarrass Wendy tonight?" he says, swaying, an expression of contempt on his face.

"Of course I did. I was an ass. But that doesn't change your situation. I don't know if you want to be mayor or not, but whatever you plan on doing, you need to get sober." Ike burps, then seems about to throw up, but he swallows everything forcefully and for the moment gets control of his body.

"Fuck you, Hemingway. You think you can waltz back into town and we're all gonna forget how you used us? Is that it?" I start to walk away, but he grabs me, and even when I try to toss him off, his grip is like a vise. "Don't think I don't know about your fancy contracts, Gabe. You reissue that book, and I'll sew your face to your ass just like I should've done the first time." I can hear Susana crying in the dining room, and my heart swells when I catch a glimpse of Browder holding her, looking around at the walls, uncomfortable but present, right there for someone he's only known a couple of weeks. A much better man than I am.

Finally, I'm able to break free, but the force required to twist away from my brother nearly throws him to the floor. He drops his drink and cusses me out, the slur and violence of his words demonic. I hear him gag, spit. As I head into the dining room, I call back to him, "Get help, Ike. We're leaving in the morning. You need help."

Browder and I walk Susana upstairs and leave her at the door of her room. I want to go talk with Evan and Katherine, but what good would it do? People spray-paint their grandfather's grave with the word *pervert*, and I can't believe it would have happened without the book. Words, they say, can hurt or heal. But that's just a nice, compact way of saying what we already know. The question is, if the same words can hurt some and heal others, how do you proceed?

Once Browder and I are in the attic, I begin gathering our clothes, putting notebooks and stacks of the copied court files into an empty box. I can't look at him, because I'm ashamed, but I apologize. "I'm sorry. I couldn't have come here without you, Browder. You're my friend. I like that you take pictures. I was hurt that my own daughter didn't want to see me, and I took it out on you. That was wrong. I'm so sorry."

"You can be a jerk-ass sometimes," says Browder, and it makes me smile.

"I know," I tell him. "I'm sorry."

"Are we gonna leave?"

"Yes. Do you still want to come with me?"

He nods. "But if you are mean, I don't want to."

"I won't be. I promise." When I hug him this time, I wonder if he's thinking why he's had to hold two of us Burkes as we've sobbed, first Susana and then me. But he seems to answer my thoughts.

"Your family is kinda scary," he says, and my crying turns to laughing before we settle down to sleep one more night in this house in Smallwood, Indiana, the place where so much has been hidden away, where so much has been denied.

Sometime around 4 a.m., the steps to the attic squeak, and bright light wakes me. I sit up in bed and squint, thinking maybe Browder had to pee in the night and didn't wake me as he went down, but it's clearly Ike, still dressed in his dinner clothes, his yellow sweater soiled with brownish splotches.

"What are you doing?" I ask him as he walks toward me, arms slack at his sides, looking every bit the deranged killer. He stands at my bedside and doesn't talk, and for a moment I think Katherine has gotten her sleepwalking from him. "Ike, what is it?"

"Come on," he says, voice hoarse, the rasp in it possibly because he's been arguing with Susana.

"No," I tell him. "Go back to bed."

"Just come with me," he says, and something in his tone scares me, makes me think he might be concealing a weapon.

Without another word, I climb out of bed and follow him down the attic stairs. I notice once we're down that his bedroom door is open, and that the kids' doors are, too. I peek inside all three rooms in quick succession, then turn back to Ike. "Where are they?"

He's holding a Bud longneck now and says mildly, "She took them to her parents' house." Ike starts down the stairs to the lower level, and I trail after him. We walk through the kitchen and into a smaller room they use for a reading area. He opens a door that leads to the garage.

"What are you doing?" I ask him.

In the garage, he gets a ladder and puts it up, climbs it, and pulls down a large metal box with both a padlock and a combination lock. He slowly backs down the ladder with it, as if he's retrieving something holy, some sort of relic. I get out of his way as he silently pulls two plastic chairs into the space where Susana's vehicle should be. "Are you okay?" I ask him, but he motions for me to sit down, so I do. He sits, too, and first rolls the dial of the combination lock between his thumb and forefinger, unlatches it. Then he pulls a key from his pants pocket and uses it on the padlock.

Finally, he looks at me, his face tired and eyes red. "You remember his closet?" he asks me, a resigned sickness in his voice, and he repeats, "Do you remember the perv's precious closet?" I nod. He turns his eyes back to the box, and we both stare down at it as Ike removes a smaller box from the metal one. He opens it with another key and then begins handing me photos as if we're perusing the family scrapbook. The first ones are of women I don't know, their breasts and pubic areas, legs and buttocks.

When Ike hands me several more, I say, "Okay, I get it. I don't want to see this stuff, Ike. And why the hell do you keep it anyway? I thought they took all of it when he was prosecuted?" Ike looks at me, and I understand his expression, one that is meant to tell me that he's the county clerk, that really, all files are his.

I hand the photos back to him, but he lets them fall to the cement floor, which is cold on my bare feet. One of the photos lands in a little oil slick, sticks there, faceup, a dark-haired woman in only a pair of high-waisted underwear. I start to stand up, but Ike shoves a stack at me, actually pushes them into my hands. "Look at them," he says, teeth clenched, as he slaps at the air. The top photo seems familiar, even though it's only of a woman standing with her back to Dad's camera. All I can see is her torso from her shoulder blades down to her thighs, the picture obviously snapped through a window, or from some hidden spot, the border blurred with wood trim or maybe the crack of a door. I spot the beanbag chair and quilt first, then Becca's dresser in the background. The next photo is of a nude Becca brushing her hair, and the next of her bending over to put on socks. I throw them back at Ike and stand up so quickly it feels like I might pass out.

"You write about the truth, but you can't take it," says Ike. "You made it all so poetic and humanly flawed, but this is who he was, Gabe. He was a pervert, and if you let that book get published again, all you do is hurt our kids. That's all you'll do. He wasn't a complicated man with a personality disorder, or a good man with demons. He was a pervert who liked to jerk off to pictures of your first love, brother." I can't stop myself when I yank him up from the chair, pulling his expensive spring sweater so hard it seems to instantly shroud his whole head. I have to let up to see his face, eyes full of tears, but angry, too.

"What's this supposed to prove, Ike, that he was fucked up? I know that. I didn't try to make him some kind of misunderstood father with problems. I told the truth. I told it all the way I remember it. And that's all I did." Ike yanks away from me and reaches down into his secret box and rummages around for something, an envelope he has to rip open. He holds up a photo that's clearly Susana naked in their old house, then another of Kate in our apartment.

"He took pictures of them, too," he says, now sitting back down in the chair. "The sick son of a bitch." The garage smells of gasoline and dried grass clippings, and the floor under our feet seems as if it might open up and swallow us for good. I feel ill, and I sit down slowly. My chair feels like punishment, a current running through it, hot to the touch, burning me from the inside out. My throat is tight, and I know my lip is quivering. It's hard to understand how Dad's lecherous eyes could cost us all so much. I think maybe Ike has gasped, then let out a quick, one-note sob. He touches my arm. He's defeated and drunk and sick. "He would've taken photos of his granddaughters, too, Gabe," he says, and he doesn't sound sad anymore or mad, or even disgusted. He just tells me, "If he hadn't killed himself, I would've done it for him." His clarity, the simple statement of fact, frightens me more than all of what has come before. I stand up and manage to reach out and pat his shoulder. He grapples to clutch me and returns the affection to my hand, his head down. We hold hands, his skin cold, as if he might be cold forever. I have to pry his hand off mine. Ike doesn't move when I head for the door that leads back inside the house, where I'll wake Browder and leave before dawn. He does say though, as I pause, hand on the doorknob, my back to him, his voice almost like a robot's, "Make sure you take the packet I left you on the kitchen counter. Maybe you can use it." I nod but can't look back as he retches, sounding like something leaving the world for good.

Part Three

"The true mystery of the

world is the visible, not the invisible."

—Oscar Wilde

— *The Picture of Dorian Gray*

Chapter Nineteen

The drive out of the dark town reminds me so clearly of when I ran away before.

Pascal and Browder look out the truck's windshield with blank expressions. There's a dense fog, the lights of other cars coming at us like alien orbs, growing nearer and nearer, then rushing past, illuminated cannons of energy, as if the cars themselves were empty, powered by forces unknown. It's so early the sun has just barely started to rise. I think of Ike back in his empty house, his dog and wife and kids gone. I can see the empty attic in my head, that awful box within a box where he's kept our father's sins under lock and key, an explosive strapped to his chest.

When we pull into the cemetery, the truck lights make the entire lower section of Smallwood Memorial Lawns look as if it's about to float away; the foggy haze gives the impression that we are coming into a whole different plane, heavenly, yet too heavy for heaven, the iron and granite, the fat hills and thick paved paths the only things holding the place to earth. I shut off the engine and rub Pascal's ears.

"Browder, I'm sorry about all of this. I didn't mean for you to get caught up in my family problems. If you want to go back to Georgia, I can call Cindy." I have my hand on the door handle as Pascal barks once and then lies down in the seat.

"I want to stay with you. I wish your daughter could like you." He never fails to give me an entirely fresh take on relationships.

"I do, too, Browder," I say, and I open the door, which brings Pascal to his feet. He bounds out. "Are you sure you want to stay with me? We'll be going up north farther, almost to Michigan."

"To see that man that killed those people?"

"Yes, I hope so anyway. We still have to get some paperwork approved." I stand outside the open truck door. "Do you want to stay in the truck?"

"Can I take a picture of your daddy's grave?"

I nod. "I think that's a great idea, Browder."

We stumble through the thick murk, and at least three times I have to stop and look around, get my bearings. It's warm, and if the weather report is right, sunshine by noon should burn the fog off. The gravel under our feet is so pleasant-sounding, I purposely drag my shoes in it. Pascal runs from headstone to headstone and never once pees on them, just sniffs, then trots toward a fence line that separates the corner of the cemetery from a tall stand of sycamores. Their white bark, wet from the mist, shimmers in the growing light. Smallwood smells of wet pavement and burning leaves; of wool blankets clutched during a cold football game; of chlorine at the Bryston Community Pool; of softener sheets being vented from a hundred clothes dryers; of burbling spaghetti sauce; and the metallic, stale aroma of your own hands brought to your face as you stand before this grave.

"This is your daddy's place?"

"Yeah, it is. He wasn't a bad man, Browder. I guess I've never really talked to you about this, but he had problems. Things he did that embarrassed us. He was sick, or something like that. Ike thinks he was an awful man, and sometimes I agree, but my father also could be loving. He made us pancakes all the time when we were kids. He loved dogs and never went to work without a necktie, even when he was just doing telemarketing. I thought I'd forgiven him, but I don't know now." A red light blinks on and off in the sky, a plane moving slowly.

"My daddy and my mother threw me away."

"That's not true, Browder. They had to give you up. They loved you; they just couldn't figure out how to take care of you."

Browder shrugs and motions for me to step in front of the headstone. I do as I'm told, and I stand there as if my dad were actually alive, standing above the grave, and we're at some family function, maybe Evan's and Katherine's track meet, Wendy's prom at Smallwood High. I wish. I really, really do.

"Smile," says Browder, and I think I might have to step out of the frame.

"I can't. Can you just take a picture real quick?"

Browder is kneeling, using one knee like a professional photographer. A flash goes off in the pall of the dawn light, the quick burst of silver giving the impression of a haunted house. I hold my hand up as Browder says, "Say cheese!" Pascal barks and sits down beside me, and I finally relent, and there in front of my voyeuristic father's grave, I say dully, "Cheese," and Browder couldn't be happier, and for that I'm grateful.

I step back from the grave and look at the granite headstone. There's an obvious area near the center where it's been sandblasted, the word *pervert* removed, along with two or three layers of grit. A boat-shaped divot remains, and I can't help but let my fingers slip over the indentation, the wet mist fine on the stone. It's as if someone has removed a piece of it for a keepsake. Browder watches me, and I'll be darned if he doesn't crank off two photos, the flashes this time giving me blind spots.

All around us Smallwood is coming to life. Out on the highway semi trucks downshift and bounce; I can see them a hundred yards away, through the wrought-iron gate, and it makes me feel as if we're prisoners in this cemetery. To the east, the sun is a half globe of orange sitting patiently on the teal horizon, waiting for this town to notice it. Someone up near a white clapboard garage is opening the bay door, exposing all manner of yard equipment: a mower, wheelbarrow, leaf blowers, and rakes. The man looks up at us, waves kindly, then returns to preparing for his day, shuffling items in the garage. I revolve a click or two and see the yellow arches of McDonald's towering above a line of redbuds, the long procession of cars, taillights ruby red, also waiting. I swear I can smell coffee, the grease of bacon.

"I guess we better get going." But I can't take my hand from that damn divot. Dad will lie here for eternity without Mom, and Ike and I won't be buried next to him either. Even in death his well-deserved stigma will keep him ostracized. Maybe a new generation of kids in Smallwood will spray-paint awful epithets on his headstone, but the truth is actually sadder than that. He'll likely lie here forever, and no one will visit, and no one will want to be next to him, and no one will even remember our shame a hundred years from now.

"Sun's coming up," says Browder, snapping it from four or five different angles. He eases the camera back down to his chest, and it dangles there. "It's pretty, huh?" We stare at the sunrise, clean and orange, a little warm breeze kicking up. The air smells of spring, pollen and grass clippings, the damp earth.

"It sure is," I say, and it's Browder who finally turns and walks toward the pickup as I stand staring, lost in that strange portal of the past, an image of Dad clapping his hands, squatting down, opening his arms as Ike and I run to him. I stand there missing him and wishing I'd put this image of our father down on paper. That's the trouble with writing; it can't all be remembered; it can't all be recorded.

Out on the highway, the flat fields of corn stretch out in huge expanses of gentle green, the plants just ankle high, vulnerable and shuddering in the brisk spring wind. There are red barns with white trim in such dramatic contrast that the structures themselves seem to be etched into the backdrop of sky blue, pulsating with color. We have the windows down, and the combination of spring air and the wind whipping through the openings give us chills. Pascal's curled up, and Browder wears his jacket hitched up to his chin. I fiddle with the radio until I find a station that doesn't pop, and John Mellencamp croons about paper and fire, asking how should a man spend his days, should he let them smolder or let them burn up.

The envelope Ike left for me on his gleaming kitchen counter is tucked into the crack in the dash, and I reach to move it so the wind won't blow it out. There are only two pages, the initial dust analysis and the name of the forensic examiner in Indianapolis. As far as today is concerned, I have no real plan. If Heather Godshalk can work her magic on the wheels of justice and actually get me approved to visit with Rodney Finch, it won't be today for sure. So we travel along the highway at a leisurely pace, listening to music, feeling the cold, clean springtime air blast our faces. The sun is up, and as we pass another homestead of red barn and green field, a boy and a girl stand in an open pasture, waves of rye around their feet, holding on to the end of one kite string, staring up at the sky where a green-and-orange diamond dives, then pitches upward again, its long single black tail like a scar against the blue. Browder tries to snap a photo, but I'm sure it'll turn out to be a big and colorful blur.

We pass through towns like Mentone and Etna Green, Bourbon and Plymouth. Outside of La Paz, Indiana, we stop to eat breakfast at a café called Wymon's. A placard on the tabletop boasts: "La Paz has 90% more tornado activity than the overall U.S. average." The waitress smiles and nods when she spots Pascal in the back of the truck, parked right up next to the plate glass window. I tuck two pieces of bacon in a napkin and put them in my jacket. The café and the smell of coffee and hot grease remind me of the trips with my dad, and with all that's transpired in the last twenty-four hours, I'm having trouble remembering how old I am, what I'm doing here again, on the road in Indiana, all the people I've known jumbled into the present, the image of Dad's grave seared behind my eyelids.

"Where'd they all go?" asks Browder, pushing a half-moon of sausage over his plate, flicking it with the fork tines.

"That's a tough question," I say, feeling philosophical. "Some people believe in heaven. I do. Others think that once you're dead, there's nothing. Religion, of course, has a lot to do with it, but in the end you have to believe in something." Browder stares at me as if I've just spoken Czech.

"Where did Susana and Ruby and their kids go?"

"Oh. Well, they went to Susana's parents' house. Don't worry, they'll be fine." I wonder how many times in Browder's life people were there and then just gone. My cell phone rings, and I see that the prefix is not Georgian, but Hoosier.

"Hello?" I say as I watch Browder finally spear the sausage and gobble it up. Phone pressed against my ear, I struggle to write down all that Heather Godshalk is saying. There's the name of the person I'll meet at the prison, and the protocol for entering, pat downs and bag searches; it's best if I keep it simple, no pens or pencils, cameras or tape recorders. We have to be at the prison by 6 a.m. "What about Browder?" I ask, and Heather asks who I'm talking about. When I tell her he's my photographer, she says, "Remember, no cameras."

"But he's also a second listener. If I can't record anything, I'll need a second set of ears." She sighs with irritation, but curtly asks me for his first and last name.

"I'll get him added to the request, but you should know, Gabe, that none of this would have been possible without your brother telling me to help you out. He called and left a message early this morning, asking me to make sure you were approved to visit Rodney. By the way, is he okay?"

"Why?" I ask, something inside me jittery and queasy, ready to believe anything about Ike.

"Oh, well, he's out sick today is all, I guess."

"Right. I'm not in Smallwood anymore, but can you do me a favor and go check on him?"

"Gabe, I know about his drinking problem, and to be frank I don't want to get involved. Honestly though, I've been worried about him, too. I'll send a plainclothes bailiff over."

"Thank you."

"Did something happen between you? Not to pry, but Ike seemed really excited to have you visiting. Why'd you up and leave so soon?" Heather sounds like a lawyer now, almost interrogating me, but meaning well.

"He's got a problem for sure, but I don't want to tell his business, especially if he's thinking of running for office."

"But isn't that what you do, tell your family's business?" I detect some-

thing in Heather Godshalk's past that has led her to the law, maybe a lascivious uncle or the death of her father at a young age. If I were still in Smallwood, I could find out in less than half an hour, but I'm sitting in a café in La
Paz, Indiana, trying to keep Ike safe if I can.

"Thanks, Heather," I say, and it seems to impact her.

"You're right. That was an insensitive thing to say. I'll make sure the bailiff
goes to Ike's house. If you need anything once you get to the prison, let me
know."

I'm not all that hungry now as I pull the medical examiner's report from
the envelope Ike gave me, and then the other sheet, the one that states: "Dust
analysis/Riley Crime Scene/Case File: 423543."

With a mouth full of pancake, Browder asks, "Why'd you tell them my
name on the phone? Is it 'cause you haven't filled out my notes?"

"Shit," I say. "Oh, man. I forgot all about that." Browder shrugs as I continue, "But no, I was telling the killer's attorney that you would need to come
with me to the prison." Browder actually smiles now, but I have to bring his
mood down quickly. "You can't take pictures though. They don't allow that,
but we'll need to go by the Riley house before we go back to Georgia. I'll
need you to take pictures of the whole place." At this he grunts and agrees,
now forking large globs of hash browns into his mouth.

Back on the highway, Pascal gobbles down his bacon treat so fast he
seems disappointed in himself. Head now on my lap, eyes open, alert but
slowly blinking, he fades into slumber. Browder pulls his harmonica from
his pocket and shows it to me, looking for approval. "Sure," I say, "let the
hoedown begin." We drive faster now, the sun out fully, heading up US 30
toward La Porte. Fields flash by, and the landscape turns more coastal, and
I'm reminded that our science teacher back in Smallwood used to say the
entire area had been a huge swamp. It's not lost on Browder either, and he
perks up and points out the window as we slow down and make our way
over the Kankakee River. "This looks like our swamp." Soft green grasses of
varying height sway in the breeze. The trees over the dark ribbon of water
are mirrored back to their clawing branches, the Indiana sky reflected there,
too, billowy clouds easing along the stillness as if they truly did make up
the surface. We're only half an hour away from Michigan City, where Rodney Finch sits on death row. I slow down some more and let Browder take

in the sights. We cruise along the northeast shoreline of Pine Lake, the tall meadowlands and green water alive under the clouds and the sun peeking through, throwing light and shadows over all we can see, a heady mixture of shape and shade.

As we continue on State Road 35, I can feel that old sickness in my stomach, the sense that our destination is always behind us, and that by moving forward, I'm only pretending to solve the mystery, while getting farther and farther away from the visible truth.

Chapter Twenty

The hotel is called The Singing Sands because of the sound the dunes make in and around Michigan City; they creak and groan, slip and moan. The tourist brochure states that there has to be a great deal of silica in the sand to produce the dull whining sound. The grains have to be .5 mm in diameter, the humidity around 62 percent. It's early afternoon now, and I can't seem to make any real decisions, other than to sit at the table in the hotel room and read the tourism highlights. For a moment, while Browder uses the bathroom and Pascal lies on the floor asleep, I think I can hear the sand dunes groaning all around the hotel, the foundation slipping and inching incrementally toward Lake Michigan's coastline, a body of water that might as well be an ocean, the farther shore distant and highly doubtful. If we fall into the massive lake, maybe I'll find the Riley boy's body, sunken at the bottom, a treasure, the mystery finally solved. But it's only a daydream, only a distraction from the work I need to do.

I set up the desk, booting up the laptop and searching for some free Wi-Fi, which is plentiful here. The network someone has named "Hoosier Slide" allows me to surf and check e-mail. Michael has sent three; the last one delivered yesterday is bolded in the memo line and reads: ARE YOU OKAY? DID THEY COMMUTE YOUR SENTENCE?

I can't take reading anything from him, knowing that he's going to badger me about getting the new prologue for the memoir to him. Deadlines are proof that all of us have a specific date preordained to die. Instead of clicking on the two e-mails from Cindy, who is probably trying to warn me that I've been lax about entering Browder's notes on the case manager's e-file system, I type in Rodney Finch's name and begin reading through all the news clippings, most of which I've already seen. I scroll and click, squint and hunch over, going at it until my ass numbs and my back is stiff. When I come up for air, Browder is on one of the hotel room beds asleep, his long legs bent to his chest, almost in a fetal position. I'm tired, too, but I need to reread the sections of the transcript that lay out how Rodney Finch killed the Rileys. Still, I'm afraid if I try to read from the court file papers, I will slip into a comalike slumber; something about the way that paper smells, the way it feels both slick and grainy in my hands, makes me want to avoid it altogether and simply test my memory on the specifics of the crime.

I lie down, too, and fold my arms behind my head, staring up at the ceiling, like a teenager pondering a broken heart. In my head, I assemble what I know of the murders.

The night before the killings, it was reported by two clerks at Willcom's grocery store that Rodney tried to get Mrs. Riley to follow him out to his van. The two clerks witnessed Rodney pulling Mrs. Riley by the arm as the two of them stood in the center of aisle 7, frozen breads and novelty ice creams. Mrs. Riley tried to be polite at first, shaking her head and attempting to push her cart forward, but after Rodney apparently applied more pressure, both physically and verbally, Mrs. Riley scolded him. While Rodney had a driver's license and could read and write at a fifth-grade level, he rarely used much language, but when he was around Mrs. Riley, apparently his mouth was foul, proposing to do any number of things that he said she'd love. Some grocery store personnel had overheard him a few times before, and Mrs. Riley on at least two occasions told her mother about Rodney's advances. One of the clerks said Mrs. Riley dismissed her questions when she offered to phone the Smallwood Police. Mrs. Riley reportedly told her, "No, he's harmless. Just a little infatuated is all."

The next day Rodney drank alone at a bar called Baldies near the county line. The owner testified that Rodney wasn't fall-down drunk, and that he even seemed to quit a lot earlier on this night than he normally did. When Rodney left the bar, he could walk fine, and the owner testified that Rodney had said he was tired and eager to get home for bed. Two fellow drinkers at Baldies testified they'd seen Rodney leave in his battered-up van, rusted through at the wheel wells, at around 9:45 p.m.

The court records show that Rodney could not be accounted for during the next two hours. During his first interrogation by the police, Rodney said he was out driving the back roads, smoking cigarettes and drinking Mountain Dew, not booze. He stopped by an older woman's home near Calhoun.

She'd babysat him as a child, and the two had been sleeping together off and on for years. During Heather Godshalk's presentation of the defense, it was even presented that the woman, Claire Brillson, had been engaging in sexual acts with Rodney since he was eleven. She was twenty-five years his senior, and there were at least two police reports dating back to the early 1990s that dealt with the two of them fighting at her house, resulting in one instance of him calling the cops, and another of Claire doing the same.

By 11 p.m., Rodney was back on the roads, driving around aimlessly, cruising the McDonald's and then speeding out to the reservoir before circling back—almost a forty-mile loop—and parking on the road in front of the Riley home. He smoked nearly an entire pack of cigarettes and drained a two-liter bottle of Mountain Dew. It was almost 3 a.m. when he slid out of the van and walked toward the Riley home. The house was outside of Smallwood, on County Road 350 North, just about three miles from the Grant County line, where the town of Swayzee is and where Browder and I talked with the little boy with the kite, the town where the Pipe Creek Sinkhole holds the fossils of ancient plants and animals buried by the Pleistocene glaciers.

Only one vehicle passed that night, a DOT truck spreading sand on the overpasses, fearing freezing rain would make driving treacherous by morning. The DOT driver testified in court that he saw Rodney's van parked almost in the ditch and assumed it was simply broken down. He used the county CB to call it in and proceeded with his night's work. It would be that sighting that would enable police to get Rodney to confess within four hours of his arrest. His confession was coupled with all manner of DNA evidence: Mrs. Riley's skin under his nails; his semen inside her; Mr. Riley's brain matter on Rodney's coat; his own blood on seventeen-year-old Lisa Riley from where she fought back, bit him so hard on his right index finger that she almost cut straight through bone. Good for her, I think, still lying on the bed, the ceiling now out of focus, blurred from too much straining, too much of trying to see it all in my head.

Rodney's intellectual capacity was far from delayed. He'd thought out how to have a key made to the back door of the Riley house, a fact that Heather Godshalk had to know was going to severely impact her ability to paint her client as mentally retarded. Rodney waited until he knew the Rileys weren't home and called a locksmith. He pretended to be the owner of the home and shelled out nearly a hundred bucks to have a new lock-and-key set installed on the back door of the garage, an entrance he knew they didn't use very often. He told one of the police officers, "It was all rusty. I could tell they didn't go in that way." Just a week later, he used that key to let himself into the home. He also confessed that he'd been to the house four or five times when he could tell no one was home, just walking around the perimeter, looking at stuff.

The court documents state that, based on the time of the murders and Rodney's own testimony, he hung around the living room for almost an hour, sitting down on the sofa, then in a recliner. He told the agents from the Indiana Bureau of Investigation that he had almost fallen asleep in the recliner, but one of the Rileys had gotten up to use the bathroom, and the hallway light that spilled onto his face had stirred him. Rodney told the agents he was hyped-up by now, anxious and ready to get things over. He felt he had to do it.

He walked down the hall to the master suite and stood outside the door for the count of twenty or so. He pulled the .38 from his belt and made sure the safety was off, and then slowly opened the door. Rodney got down on his knees, waddled right up to the edge of the bed, and placed the gun to Mr. Riley's head. When he woke up startled, Rodney punched him in the face so hard it cracked Mr. Riley's cheekbone. Mrs. Riley woke with a start while Rodney ran to close the bedroom door. He flipped on the light switch as well and unbuckled his pants. The court papers state: "The defendant reports that he trained the handgun on Mr. Riley's head, holding the tip of the barrel just below his right eye, as he took off his pants and proceeded to rape Mrs. Riley. The defendant told the IBI agents that he said to Mr. and Mrs. Riley, 'I'm not going to kill any of you, but if you try and stop me from doing this with your wife, I'll blow your head right off.'"

Even though she was fighting to save her family's lives, Mrs. Riley's instincts took over for a few moments, and she scratched long, fairly deep abrasions into Rodney's neck, three red burns, but he hit her in the face and told her he'd put a hole through her husband's head if she fought anymore. Afterward, Rodney reported that he didn't know what he was going to do next, and for several long, drawn-out minutes he paced the Rileys' bedroom, listening as Mr. Riley held his wife and tried to convince Rodney to just leave, that they wouldn't call the police. But it didn't work.

Rodney first took aim at Mr. Riley, then brought the gun back down to his side, but Mrs. Riley's crying, according to Rodney, irritated him, so he quickly brought the gun up point-blank to Mr. Riley's forehead and shot him once. Mrs. Riley tried not to scream, but it came out anyway, which must've woken her daughter. Rodney shot Mrs. Riley in the back of the head as she tried to run down the hall, and then he grabbed seventeen-year-old Lisa as she, too, ran from her room, screaming when she saw her mother on the floor. Rodney immediately threw the girl to the ground and jumped on top of her. Lisa kicked and punched and delivered the bite on Rodney's index finger before she, too, was shot at close range in the neck and again in the stomach.

The court documents make no mention of the Riley boy. His name, his murder, his disappearance, none of it is contained within the reports. When Heather Godshalk tried to enter the missing boy into evidence, it was struck down, and the prosecutor simply said he didn't know anything about a missing boy, that Rodney Finch was being prosecuted for the murders of the three Riley family members. Essentially, with his confession, and his DNA, the trial came down to simply trying to keep him out of the death chamber, but Heather lost the bid to give Rodney Finch only a life sentence.

I get back up off the bed and walk to the desk. I pull out the crime-scene photos and look for the one of Mrs. Riley. In the photo, you can't see the white dust that was later found; only matted hair, clotted with maroon. Rodney had also shot her through her right forearm, and in the photo it looks entirely fake, the bullet wound perfectly round, and only a bit of blood the size of a quarter surrounding the black gunshot. I take the papers from the envelope and unfold them. The analysis on the dust found in Mrs. Riley's hair and on the doorknob on the front of the house is confusing. There's a list of digits that string from margin to margin, and a graph with red, green, and blue equations, which I'm sure have nothing to do with calculus but remind me of taking the class in college nonetheless. Stapled to the second sheet is the business card of a man who apparently works at Science Crime Laboratories in Indianapolis. Ike has simply written on the bottom of the card: "Call him."

Outside the hotel room window, the sky is clear and blue. We are in an outpost once again. Waiting like always, and I can't help but think it's not just for the chance to meet Rodney Finch in person. It seems I've structured my life to live like this, first the swamp and the group home, and now in Smallwood, in an enclave up in Ike's attic, watching from afar, timing my actions. Standing at the window, I can smell my father, his clothes, the fragrance of spicy cologne and breath mints, the old wool coats ripe with mothballs, his leather billfold, the stale scent of a few five-dollar bills, the copper of his counted-out pennies, and the whiskey in his soda can. The smells are so strong and real to me that I have to turn from the window and inspect the room. If he came strolling out from the bathroom with a rolled-up newspaper in his hand and his sleeves cuffed at the elbow, hands red from hot water, it wouldn't seem unbelievable, not with the scent of his ghost in this hotel room as tangible as footfalls or a bellowing voice.

That's why I'm startled when I happen to look over at Browder, who is sleepy-eyed and sitting straight up in the bed, legs out before him, looking dazed and maybe even a little cranky. "Where are we?" he asks.

I rub Pascal's ears. "In the hotel room. You've been asleep awhile. Are you hungry?" He nods, and we quietly put on our shoes—and since it's getting a little later, and the wind off the lake will be cold—we each zip up jackets. We ride the elevator down in silence, and I'm experienced enough to know that a potential serious emotional funk could set in. My body is tired and my mind is fragile, and the energy it takes to step off the dingy elevator feels monumental. Pascal trots alongside us, and his leash feels clammy in my hand, as if it's the leather that's perspiring.

We find a steak house with a bar, and Browder inspects the menu in the window and then nods. It halfway seems that my emerging depression is contagious. Inside the restaurant the sports channels take over no fewer than ten screens: baseball and the NBA, flashes of color and spinning bodies, limbs in constant movement. Browder and I stare dumbly at this, too, as we order and sip sodas. We've been out to eat too much on this trip, too many processed meats and soft drinks with ice pellets. Who wouldn't be a little depressed? Still, we can see the sky from our booth, and the paling blue does seem to lift my spirits some.

Browder gnaws on a double-decker Monterey Jack Angus burger, while I try to choke down a blackened salmon salad. "You going to call Ike?" asks Browder, his skin a bit more sallow, as if by leaving Smallwood I've taken the spirit out of him, somehow managed to dampen his naturally good effect. The chatter and blasting wide-screens make it difficult to hear, but I get his gist and nod.

"Sure. I'll call him tomorrow," I tell him. "Listen, Browder, if we don't get anywhere by then, if we don't get to visit the prison, we'll just head back down to Georgia."

He stops chewing. "I don't want to."

"Why? You could see all the guys again."

"I want to stay with you."

"Well, I'm coming, too. I don't mean I'd send you back alone. Of course I'd come."

"Maybe we could be roommates," he says, and that expression of his, the way he's timid and a little scared and all of it showing in his eyes, nearly makes me lose my breath.

"Maybe," I say, and he cheers up, chews more and then asks if he can have a milk shake.

I untie Pascal from the bike rack out in front of the restaurant and give him a hunk of my salmon. The sun is starting to set, and it's beautiful. A swirl of pink and lemon encases the center of the horizon, where a robin's-egg blue seems just that fragile. There's a sidewalk that leads down to the waterfront, and Pascal nearly drags me toward a little flock of mallards waddling along a worn dirt patch. They explode toward the sky when Pascal barks, and for just a little while this scene seems worth the trip, but once they've flown away, and the chill picks up, I can feel my phone is about to fully ring, the early vibrations leading to a trill tone. I want to chuck the thing into the lake.

"Hello?"

"Gabe, it's Heather Godshalk."

"Yes," I say.

"I've got some bad news for you."

"What is it, Heather? Rodney has changed his mind, right?"

"No. Ike was taken to the hospital for alcohol poisoning. He's going to be fine though. The bailiff found him on the garage floor. Anyway, he's stable, and I've got someone calling Susana. He'll be in there for a few days. Again, he's fine, but I wanted you to know."

I tell her thank you and hang up. The visit to the prison is first thing in the morning, and I'm glad for it. I can't think of returning to Smallwood, even for a poisoned brother. Shame runs you out of town and tails you forever, doing it all from the safety of its limitless boundaries.

Chapter Twenty-One

It's still dark outside when we climb into the truck. Really early mornings have always made me feel sick to my stomach.

I hate it, but Pascal will have to stay at a kennel while we visit with Rodney Finch. Death row doesn't allow pets. As I try to follow the MapQuest directions under the aid of the truck's dome light, Browder fidgets and looks around as if he thinks we're about to run into the killer as we drive. I have to pull off onto a side street to keep from getting rear-ended, the dark morning hosting a rambling herd of commuters, all of whom seem to prefer using their bright lights. I hold the page of directions up close to the dome light and squint. I say the names of the streets out loud. The American Kennel Kamp is supposed to be only three blocks from the hotel, en route to the prison. More than anything, I don't want to be late. "What's the name of that street?" I say to myself, but Browder thinks I'm asking him.

"I don't know," he says, and his voice is trembling a little. I think I hear him sniffling some.

"Hey, are you okay?" The blinding headlights of Michigan City's commuters flash over us as we sit idling at the curb.

Browder shrugs, peers out the window. I assume he's just grumpy from getting up so early. I focus my attention back to the directions and finally figure out I've taken a wrong turn. Clear now about where I'm to go, I ease back into traffic and take two rights before arriving in front of the kennel. I'm pleased that it looks as nice as on the Web site.

"Sit still and I'll be right back." Browder just hangs his head, apparently asleep.

Pascal and I jog toward the front entrance, clean glass doors that open up into a waiting area that smells of bleach. There's an interior play course as big as a high school gymnasium, and dogs of all sizes scale obstacle courses made of bright colors. Along the walls are drinking spigots activated when the pooch puts his tongue to it. Employees of the business are called Pet Daycare Technicians, all wearing matching pink uniforms. They work the area, engaging the little fellas that are first-timers or that might just be shy. A woman greets me from behind the counter, sounding as if she's about to sit me down in a restaurant booth. I'm offered extra services like a pet massage, organic snacks, and a tea tree oil treatment for Pascal's paws. But judging by how he's pulling to get in with the rest of the dogs, I don't think he'll notice that I'm gone or that he's not getting the royal treatment. I watch as he's taken from me and led into an area where, the woman says, the new dogs get acclimated. Through the glass I see Pascal sit, shake hands, and take a treat from a man with a goatee, wearing a tight pink T-shirt that reads: "Sit, Shake, Play!" Then Pascal begins romping with another Lab, and it's as if he's known the dog all his life.

I check on Browder one more time as we drive to the prison, but he ignores me, and I decide to give him some space. The sun is up now, peeking around flat industrial complexes and turning the sky a pale peach. Pigeons flutter along the sidewalks and around bus stops. The weather for our day on death row looks as though it couldn't be better, the landscape forming under the increasing sunlight: narrow streets, train tracks crisscrossing coastal flats.

At the gate to the prison, I show my ID and give them the confirmation number Heather Godshalk made me repeat on the phone. The guard pokes at a computer terminal. "You're not in here," he says, shrugs.

I offer to call Ms. Godshalk. "His attorney set it up," I say. The guard enters more information, makes phone calls as we idle, the truck rattling, gas fumes as potent as perfume. He takes my ID again, phone clutched to his ear. He asks now for my social security card. Another ten minutes slowly tick by, and finally he hands me the documents. The guard inside the gate hut points at Browder. "What's wrong with him?" I tell him that he's fine, just a little grumpy from waking up early. The guard looks at me for the count of three and raises his eyebrows a little.

"He's tired from our road trip," I say, hoping to sound manlier, more professional. The guard hands me back my license and raises the crossing arm. Still, there are two other vehicle stations to pass through. I say to Browder, "Wow, Brow, you should see the razor wire. Looks like real silver, like dangerous necklaces. It'd make a great pic." He has his head pushed against the door window. His back is slumped, and his left hand lies next to his leg, pale fingers stretched out straight. He makes a grumbling sound. "Really, you should look. They've got some real pretty German shepherds. Maybe we could've brought Pascal after all."

Finally, a series of guards directs us toward a visitor parking lot; it makes me think of an outdoor concert. After we park, an enormous guard with a broad chest opens my door and nods, waits for me to step outside the truck. He starts to go around and open Browder's door, but I tell him I'll get it. The guard looks at me blankly, his stiff crew cut glittering in the early sunshine as if it, too, were made of steel, razor sharp, capable when necessary of inflicting gruesome harm. I think for a moment that I can smell the lake, the fish and decay. Once, when Dad and I and Ike were driving around on the day after Christmas, Dad checking on customers, seeing if they liked their HomeBeam presents, he told us about a group of people that had once been told Lake Michigan was actually the ocean. They were poor, elderly people from Chicago on a trip from their church. They'd never been out of their three-block neighborhood. On their return, they told everyone about the ocean, and not a soul had the heart to tell them otherwise.

Together, the three of us walk toward the sturdy brick entrance of the prison. I have to keep stopping and waiting on Browder, who I'm afraid isn't just sleepy; something is wrong. The mammoth guard spits once, and excuses himself, opens the door for us and leads us to the first of several screening stations. As I remove my jacket, Browder just stands there. The guard looks at me, then back at Browder. I walk over to my friend and ask if he's okay. "Do you need to sit down, or use the rest room? What's wrong?" For a pause of several seconds, Browder doesn't move, then he looks up at me with tears in his eyes.

"I don't wanna go in there," he says, pointing up for some reason. "I'm scared. I just want to be outside taking pictures." He sobs a little, then steps back from me.

"It'll be fine, Browder. I promise. You can sit next to me. There'll be guards there, too, and Rodney Finch won't even be able to touch us. He'll be cuffed and have on leg irons, and he'll be sitting behind a big thick wall." Browder steps back some more and shakes his head no.

The large guard says, "If he doesn't want to go in, let's not force it." It seems to me he's picked up on Browder's disability. "We can't have any type of distractions."

"Okay," I say, thinking maybe this is too much. Browder is tired and worn out from my family, the trip, all that has changed. "What do you suggest?"

"How about this," says the guard, and something about him seems suddenly intimate. "He can stay with me down here in the control office. I've got to sit there and observe the monitors. He can sit with me." The guard smiles, then adds, "My partner hates this place, too."

"Thank you," I say. "Thanks a lot."

The last screening I go through is intense. I'm patted down three times, by three different guards, none of whom seems to know how to speak. The smell of pine cleaner is so strong, it feels like I'm damaging my lungs by breathing. After I put my shoes and belt back on, I'm led to a tiny waiting room. For the first time since I've been inside the prison, it's quiet. There are no metal doors clanking or radios crackling, no monotone brutal voices or buzzing doors. I sit in a chair in an empty room and listen to the clock tick. It's only around 9 a.m., but it feels like we've been here for an entire day; my senses are out of whack, and I half expect the lights to dim, and the air to cool, as the power surges to accommodate someone in the electric chair. But that's impossible, since Indiana uses the lethal injection. I think of Truman Capote chatting with Perry inside his cell, the two of them admiring charcoal drawings and whispering about how no one really understands them. Without a pen or paper, wallet or keys, I feel naked, bared, brought down to the essential use of my memory and speech, my ears and eyes. I'm nervous, stomach empty and dull. My tongue tastes bitter, and I can't remember if I just had the hiccups or if I was thinking about having them. Either way, I don't have them now. Time passes, the white room receding as I simply sit and stare. I think of Ike of course, and Wendy, and it's hard to imagine ever getting back to Smallwood without being in a casket.

Finally, a man in a suit walks into the room carrying a clipboard, a handgun at his side. He pulls up a chair and smiles. For a guy working death row, he seems calm and happy.

"So, we're here to do an interview for a book, they tell me." He's chewing gum, but his morning coffee is beating out the spearmint.

"Yes. My brother's the county clerk in Smallwood, which is close to Fort Wayne." Even I don't know why I've said this, but the man doesn't seem to notice.

"I see," he says, checking off boxes, chomping gum. He hands me the form, and I sign it. "We'll get Mr. Finch out and into the secure visitation unit in a few minutes. Would you like some water?" His Midwestern courtesy hasn't died on death row. I nod yes.

"Okay, then. Let's get you into the next room, and I'll bring you a bottle. Just a few tips first though. One, these guys will just about say anything if it means getting some attention. Rodney's been fairly cooperative as of late, but you never know. Just take everything with a grain of salt. I'm sure he'll tell you we're torturing him. Two, don't give out any personal information, phone numbers, e-mail addresses, that sort of thing. They get to the point in here where they can remember everything, and lastly, you have thirty minutes, no more. If you want to leave earlier than that, just ring the guard on the phone, push # 7. Any questions?"

"No. Thank you." He nods and turns away.

I follow the man out the door and down a small hallway. I'm surprised to see a bulletin board edged with red construction paper, with employees of the month listed and their photos pinned next to a summary of their years of service. We stop by a break room and he opens a refrigerator, grabs a bottle of water and hands it to me. "There you go, Mr. Burke." I didn't imagine people working on death row would be so cordial. We enter a dull teal room with shiny tile. The man directs me toward a series of booths with phones, the thick clear glass showing some smudges. "Just have a seat at one of those, and we'll bring Mr. Finch in." I watch him walk back out the door we just came through, and then his shoes tapping the floor grow fainter and fainter until the room is still and silent; this time there's not even a clock. I sit before the glass booth and feel stupid. I pick up the phone and press the cold receiver against my ear, hang it up again. My lips feel chapped, but there's nothing I can apply. I sit back in the chair and stretch, realizing I've been tightening every muscle since the day began. I imagine Pascal running around the gym, jumping through hoops and drinking water profusely; I wonder if Browder is okay. I see Ike in my head, lying poisoned on the garage floor, and I can't help but wonder if those pictures he's kept stowed away made it back inside the safe before the bailiff found him. The image of Wendy running away from me is so vivid, I believe I'm at a drive-in, watching the home movies of the dysfunctional Burke family.

The sound of a door banging open brings me back to the moment, and before I can even swallow hard, Rodney Finch is shuffling before me, the guard pulling out the chair for him. Rodney uses his cuffed hand to expertly lift the phone off the hook, tucking the receiver between his ear and the top of his shoulder. I don't pick up immediately, and he smiles just a bit and mouths something. I reach for the receiver.

"Hello," I say.

"Hi," says Rodney. "You the guy that's writing a book about me?"

"No, that wouldn't be accurate. I'm writing a book about the Rileys and how you murdered them."

"Same thing." Rodney looks much older now, swollen in the face, the dark circles under his eyes the color of a field mouse. He could be any guy, and he reminds me of a man that changes oil at the Quick Lube.

"No it's not." I feel something like contempt for the guy. "You're of little consequence actually. The book will be about the Rileys and Smallwood. You'll be a minor player."

"But there wouldn't be a story if it weren't for me. I killed them. People always want to know why someone killed somebody." I tend to believe Heather Godshalk now, that Rodney's low IQ was only test related. He sounds pretty smart to me.

"Fair enough," I tell him, wanting to make the most of my thirty minutes. I scoot closer on the chair and try to make eye contact with him. "Who helped you with the murders, Rodney?"

He doesn't look surprised by the question, but he does ignore me. "Will there be a picture of me in the book? My aunt has a good one of me fishing on Coon's Lake before I ended up here. I can get it from her if you want."

"We'll just use your arrest photo, Rodney." I try again, "But tell me about that night. Who helped you kill the Rileys? I know you know where the Riley boy's body is. Tell me so the family can give him a proper burial."

"But I want a picture of me in that book with that big fish I caught. Its mouth looked like a dinosaur's, teeth and stuff like that. It was a pike."

"I heard you like dinosaurs. If you help me, I'll make sure you get a subscription for a dinosaur magazine. I'll work it out with the warden."

Rodney smiles so broadly, you'd think he'd just learned he was a father. "Okay. I'll help you. What do you want to know?"

"Like I said before, tell me who helped you that night. Did the person have white dust on them? Was there some kind of powder or something involved?"

Rodney's smile fades. "You're not gonna get me that magazine in the mail. I don't know nothing about white dust. I don't know nothing about any of it." He looks like a child trying to pout his way out of a situation.

"Sure you do, Rodney. Just tell me who was there with you. The other person had to be the one who took the Riley boy. Wes Riley was gay, you know. Did the other man that helped you say anything about hating gay people?"

"I want that magazine, mister," says Rodney, looking more at me. "You tell the warden I want it or I'll be a problem again."

"Nope, I can only get it for you if you tell me who helped you. Where'd the dust come from?"

Rodney's lip begins to quiver, and his seal-like eyes turn glassy. "I wish I hadn't of done it."

"I know. But you can make it all right if you tell me where the Riley boy is."

"I want that magazine. You get it started and then I'll tell you."

"That's not the deal, Rodney."

He starts to put the phone back on the hook, but I tap the glass, motion for him to listen to me. "Why can't you just tell me where the body is? Tell me that. You don't have to tell me who helped you."

"I don't know."

"Then I can't get you the dinosaur magazine."

"Okay," says Rodney, resigned. "You know they got a dinosaur cemetery in Swayzee. There's lots of bones there. Some are from a million years ago. They say there are human ones there, too."

"Rodney, are you telling me that's where the Riley boy's remains are? Is that what you're saying?"

He removes the receiver slowly from his shoulder and uses his cuffed hands to gingerly put it back in the cradle, as if it might be made of eggshell. Rodney smiles wickedly at me through the glass, and while I can no longer hear him, I can clearly read his lips when he mouths: "Boom, boom, boom, boom."

Four gun blasts instead of just three.

Chapter Twenty-Two

We return to the same hotel, The Singing Sands. Browder is asleep now, but the entire drive back to the hotel, he couldn't stop talking about how cool the muscled guard, Richard Ribbons, was. Browder had commented on the photos that were on the man's desk. "He's got a silly one where him and another man are getting married!" Richard had bought Browder lunch and, more importantly, allowed Browder to play his harmonica, which I'd thought he'd left in the truck.

In the hotel room, I have to get very close to the large window to get a signal, but finally the phone at Kate's house rings.

"Hello."

"Hey, Kate. How's Ike? Is he still in the hospital?" There's a long pause, and then the sound of gum being chewed. "Wendy?"

The receiver rustles, and I clearly hear my daughter say, "It's him."

"Hello, Gabe."

"Kate, how's Ike?" For the first time since I've been back, I think I'd like to sit my daughter down and have a strict conversation, preach about respect and forgiveness, but I know I don't have the right.

"He's fine," says Kate, sighing. "But Susana's a mess. Allen Godshalk from the *Plain Dealer* was at the courthouse asking all kinds of questions."

"Godshalk? That's the last name of the attorney that defended Rodney Finch."

"So, it's Smallwood. Everyone is related to somebody in town."

"What's next? Will they release him soon?"

"No, well, yes, I guess." Kate pauses, and I don't talk either, the line sort of clicking with the feeble connection of a landline to a cell. "Gabe, he's probably going to be ordered to undergo substance-abuse treatment. They have a program at the hospital. He'll likely need to detox."

"Well, that's probably a good thing." I can picture that box of Dad's secret photos, the burden Ike must've felt having those things right there in his house.

"Where are you? Did you go back to Georgia?"

"No, I'm in Hoosier Land. I visited Rodney Finch today on death row."

"And? Did you crack the case wide open?"

"Almost. Just a few more minutes with the guy and I'd have had a map drawn of where the Riley boy's body is located." Kate laughs, then gets serious again.

"You know, you should make an effort to see Ike. If he goes through treatment, you could be a big help to him. You're the only other person who could talk about your father's sickness, and his suicide. Ike will need you. You owe it to him."

"Thanks for the insight, Kate, but spending time at Smallwood General in detox and therapy doesn't sound like something I'd want to do." I'm pissed off some, but she has a point. Still, I'm tired and wired and ready to get off the phone.

"You're not supposed to want to do it, Gabe. Nobody wants to be embarrassed in their hometown, but that's just the way it—" Kate stops. "Never mind."

"Can I talk with Wendy?"

"You'd have more luck getting that map from Rodney Finch."

When I hang up the phone, I peer out the window at the lights dotting the darkness, some twinkling, others blinking, a few red and blue ones easing across the night sky. Pascal's so tired from his daytime romping that he fell asleep as soon as we got into the hotel. He's right next to where I'm standing, and I have to step over him to sit down at the desk. I fish out the dust-analysis papers and the card Ike gave me. It's late, and I know there won't be an answer at Science Crime Laboratories, but I call anyway. The phone rings and rings, then trips over to voice mail.

"Dr. Shelpenfry, this is Gabe Burke. My brother, Ike, who is the county clerk in Smallwood, told me to call you about the dust sample from the Riley case. It was found in Mrs. Riley's hair sample from the DNA files. I think you're the one who analyzed it, and I was hoping to talk to you about it. I'm writing a book on the case. Anyway, I'll try you again tomorrow. Thanks."

I open the laptop and pull up Word, finding the file marked "New Prologue—Leaving Smallwood." I begin reading it, and something cold and dark runs through me, as if I'm the one who's had the lethal injection. The words almost have an odor to them, and I smell burnt rubber and gasoline. I read on until I reach the end. The hotel room is dark except for the light on the desk. The idea that Ike paid to have the word *pervert* sandblasted from our father's tombstone haunts me again, and I imagine my brother's shaky hand as he forked over the cash or scribbled out a check, money to protect a dead man's reputation, our family's, too.

For a while, I read about the limestone quarry in Swayzee, finding several Web sites about the fossils discovered there. There's nothing in the news archives about human bones ever being found, and as I rummage through the court documents, especially the section that spells out Rodney's activities on the night of the murders, there's no mention of Swayzee at all. I'm wiped out and about to fall asleep, but I check my e-mail to find three new ones from Michael my agent, and some from Cindy. All four of hers are labeled *"Urgent!"* I click on the most recent.

> Hey, Gabe, I talked with Browder's case manager today, and she says you haven't put in any of his case notes online. You have to get it done pronto or she says she'll file a complaint. I don't know what that means, but just do it, okay?
> P.S. How's the book coming along?

I log off and close the computer. Browder's case manager in Georgia is the least of my concerns, but I tell myself I'll e-mail Cindy back tomorrow. Browder's asleep, slightly snoring in the other queen. When I crawl into bed, it's almost 1 a.m. Pascal perks up and slowly stands, then waddles to my bedside, tail wagging. He puts his paws up on the mattress first, then waits for the okay. With a grunt he climbs on the bed and lies down parallel to my legs, his head at my hip, perfect to pet as I fall asleep and forget about the entire state of Indiana.

We are ten miles outside of Smallwood, and I imagine our route being tracked as if in a cartoon, a red line coursing all over the state, stopping, starting again, retracing the same routes, not lost, but to the uninformed viewer it would certainly look that way. Browder is happy-go-lucky again. "We going back to Ike's, then?"

"Kind of. He's in the hospital." Browder's eyes widen, and he shakes his head in disbelief. "But he's going to be fine," I add. "I thought we could stop in on our way to Indianapolis."

"What's in Indy-nap-olis?"

"A scientist. A man who can look at dirt and dust under a microscope and tell where it's from."

"Wow," says Browder, smiling. "Can I get a picture of him doing it?"

"Sure, if it's okay with him."

Outside, there's a spring storm amassing along the horizon. Gray roiling clouds birth others like swollen Molly fish, dropping their offspring into the haze. It's hard not to watch out the truck window as clouds heavy with rain seem to float along like small *Hindenburgs*, their underbellies ripe and distended, about to burst. I flip on the radio, and there's a tornado warning for Smallwood and the surrounding areas. Fat raindrops smack the windshield, and it seems electricity is pulsing all around us. It's only been a little over a week since that ice storm hit, but now it looks as though spring has truly taken over. The wind picks up, and the grass in the ditches lies down and doesn't get back up. I can feel the truck fighting the wind shear as we cross over into the city limits. It's a Saturday, and as I make the turns toward Ike's house, there are still kids playing outside, hair full of static, moms peering out kitchen windows, watching the skies, waiting for the town's alarm system to ring out before calling their children in. With the windows down, the rain smells so fresh and cleansing, I want to get out and dance in it, wash myself, allow the water to rinse away my dirt.

Browder and I run to the door, and instead of ringing the doorbell, I knock loudly. Susana is before us, wearing a floral dress. She doesn't have on makeup, and her eyes are tired. She falls into my arms and sobs. Browder pats her on the shoulder and snaps a photo. Susana pops up her head and smiles, then kisses him on the cheek. "Come in. The kids are at my parents'. I'll fix you some lunch."

"Thanks, Susana, but we have to get to Indy. I just wanted to stop by and see how things are going with him." Her face falls some, but she still motions us inside the house. In the kitchen, she prepares glasses of ice and Coke for us, and Browder slurps his loudly.

"Can't you just stop by and see him for a little bit before you go?" Thunder rattles the house, and two rapid-fire bolts of lightning follow, illuminating the kitchen. Susana turns on the lights, as the storm has darkened the midday, giving the house the feel of depression, loneliness, and cold despair.

"Yes," I say reluctantly as I get up from the island. "When are visiting hours?"

"Right now. He's not in the regular hospital, you know. He's in the Substance Abuse wing. He'll have to stay for four weeks. But I guess the good thing is he wants to participate." She tears up again. I think of the garage and those pictures.

"I left a notebook in the garage. I'll go get it," I say, feeling flushed, ashamed, as I lie to her.

"Don't bother, Gabe. The pictures have been destroyed. Ike burned most of them after we left. When the bailiff found him, the garage was full of smoke. He thought Ike was trying to hurt himself."

"Was he?"

"I don't know. He won't talk about it right now. We've had one family session, and he's been in individual therapy a few times. He's in the phase he calls 'Face it.'" She grins a little as Browder wolfs down some Oreo cookies from a package on the counter. I hug her again, and she sobs. Susana tells me, "Browder and I will hang out together and look at his pictures while you go see Ike." She closes her eyes and mouths "thank you," as if she might be in a confessional.

When I turn to leave, she says, "I'll call over there and let them know you're coming. If not, they'll tell you they cannot divulge whether or not he is there. I'll tell them to add you to the visitation list." I nod.

I drive so slowly toward the hospital that it probably appears my truck is running on empty, or that the downpour has flooded my engine. The parking lot is as nondescript as the squat brick building attached to the rear of the hospital, no signs at all on the facade. Of course, anyone who's ever been in recovery would know what the place is. Once I'm inside the waiting area, a male nurse asks to see my ID. I'm wet from the rain, and some of it falls onto the floor in quick drips. He has me sign on a clipboard, then tells me, "Your brother's in group right now. You can wait for him in his room. I'll send him right down as soon as it's over." I follow the guy to what will be Ike's room for the next month. It's bare bones, but I find a tiny washcloth and try to dry my hair.

I sit down in a chair next to the bed and wait. There's another bed in the room, but it looks unoccupied, tightly made, nothing on the bedside stand to indicate a roommate for Ike. On his table, there's a vase of flowers from the courthouse and a photo of Susana and the kids, sunlight in their eyes, a placid lake behind them, most likely taken at the reservoir. On his bed are a bundle of socks and two pairs of khaki pants, and some boxers folded neatly in a stack. His shaving kit and toothbrush have been placed on the sink with care. It does indeed look as though Ike has accepted his fate; still, I'm nervous to see him, frightened I guess, because in some ways he's started his own book, and I'm fearful that he's going to narrate something even more awful than I have. It's a hypocritical thought, but lying to myself would be silly at this point. Even with the fear though, I'm hopeful, eager to travel to Indy to meet with Dr. Shelpenfry, discuss the Riley dust. My mind drifts and comes back, thinking of how little I've actually gotten done since arriving in Smallwood. Other than reading court files and visiting Rodney on death row, I'm hard pressed to see how I can create a true crime book in two months, meeting the deadline.

The storm outside has started to recede, and that old sound of distant thunder rumbling like train cars is soothing. I close my eyes and just listen. I'm tired and could fall asleep right in the chair. The room, and this treatment center, remind me of the therapy we had after Dad's suicide. It wasn't required, but Mom's pastor asked that we come along with her. A counselor who wore a necktie with piano keys told us we were all at a new, heightened risk of suicide attempts simply because our father had done it. I couldn't help but think the guy would've made a great HomeBeam salesman.

I've drifted off to sleep, and when Ike enters the room, I first smell his cologne, then I open my eyes, sit up straighter, swallow. He moves toward the bed and sits down, doesn't speak. He looks exhausted, and thinner. His lips are a little dry, and the red laced into the whites of his eyes gives him the look of a much older man.

"Nice digs," I tell him.

He works hard at a smile. "It's such a lovely place. What a nice surprise. Bring your alibis."

"What?" I say, thinking they've got him medicated.

"You can check out anytime you like, but you can never leave."

"Are you okay, Ike?"

"Sorry. I thought you'd recognize the lyrics. You know, 'Hotel California'?" I'm relieved he's not hallucinating from the alcohol withdrawal, but he still seems disconnected, maybe on a sedative.

"Oh, right," I say, nodding. "How are they treating you here?"

"Like a mayoral candidate that's fallen from grace."

"Well, that seems pretty specific, a whole regimen just for you." I smile, and he acknowledges it. He lies back on the bed though and brings his legs to his chest, rolls onto his side so he can make eye contact with me. Ike lies there in a fetal position, and I admire his strength to accept his vulnerability.

"Did you talk with the forensic scientist that examined the Riley dust?" he asks, forcing his face toward serenity, focusing, sometimes allowing his eyes to shut for extended moments.

"On my way to do that now. Browder and I are driving to Indy today. The good Dr. Shelpenfry can see me this afternoon."

"That's good. Although I wouldn't get your hopes up. The first round of testing didn't shed much light on anything."

"Right, but apparently he's got some new method. He did a test that can identify within a statistical certainty where the material originated from."

"Still, remember it's most likely just part of the trip, not the destination." Ike closes his eyes fully now, and I can hear him humming to himself.

"Rodney Finch more or less told me that the Riley boy's bones would be found in the Pipe Creek Sinkhole near Swayzee. He made four gun blasts instead of the three he made when he confessed." Ike opens his eyes slowly. His expression doesn't change, but he looks even more tired than before.

"That's just because he has a fascination with dinosaurs. He once told Heather Godshalk that he ate the boy, just like a T. rex." Ike rolls his eyes and allows a smirk to move his chapped lips.

"Ike," I say, scooting my chair right up next to his bed, focusing on my brother, his knowledge. "Then you tell me, where is the Riley boy's body? Where could it be? It's not like there's a mob in Smallwood. Bodies just don't disappear."

"Happens every day, everywhere, Gabe. Bodies do vanish. People think that when there's a murder, eventually the body will turn up. I bet we've got at least ten cases over the last decade, just in our county alone, that list victims as missing persons, but in every one of those, the family members know the person was killed, and sometimes they even know who the likely murderer is. But you know what they say." Ike has to be on a drug, maybe Valium by the way his speech seems to be drifting along on little puffs of gaseous clouds. He's on the verge of slipping into a deep sleep.

"No, what do they say?"

"Dead men tell no tales. Dead men tell no lies." He looks at me and raises his eyebrows. "Dead men don't read books," he mumbles. "We're the mystery, brother," and he falls completely asleep.

"Ike? Ike, talk to me just a bit more," I say, standing up now, shaking his shoulder, but it's no use. He's out cold, and as I pull a blanket over him, I can see that little boy from back when we were kids. Brothers are men's other halves, competing with each other, fighting not to, always testing, the first to push and push back, the last to give up. That's why I wish my brother were coming along with me as I leave his room and quietly turn off the light, the storm outside returning, the thunder now coming back around, rumbling closer and closer, as if the whole thing were starting over again.

Chapter Twenty-Three

Dr. Shelpenfry's office building is off Thirty-Eighth Street, in an out-dated and nearly empty industrial park from the 1990s. The love seat is mauve, and the glass tables with their gold trim seem to hover over the Wedgwood blue carpet, giving the waiting area the feel of a small ship out to sea. Browder is using a swatch of white cloth to clean the lens of his camera as we wait to see the dust scientist. The woman behind the desk is the doctor's wife, has to be; she wears the same last name on her white lab coat. And there's the framed photo of her and the man I assume to be Dr. Shelpenfry, the two of them standing arm in arm near the Egyptian pyramids, wearing dark shades and sporting sleeveless flak jackets, tightly cinched fanny packs, and knee-length walking shorts. Many other photographs show the couple surrounded by friends and family, at weddings and beaches, dinner tables and Colts and Pacers sporting events.

The storm didn't follow us from Smallwood to Indianapolis. Instead, the sun's out, but the time trials at the Indy 500 racetrack are in session, and even this far away the cars sound like distant rumbling thunder, and I have to re-mind myself there's not a storm here, that I'm not still in Smallwood.

"I can take a picture of him looking in his microscope?"

"Yep," I tell Browder. "Listen, while we're waiting, will you run out to the truck and check on Pascal? There are some treats in the glove compartment. Will you give him a few?" I hand the keys to Browder, and he beams with pride.

"I'll be right back," he tells me, handing me his precious camera. When he slips out the door to the parking lot, the Nikon feels strange in my hands, as if it might x-ray my soul. I realize I'm holding it out in front of me, stiff and stupid, but I can't help it. Browder bounds back inside after a few minutes and gives me a thumbs-up.

"He was sleeping, but I gave him four treats." I hand his camera back.

Mrs. Dr. Shelpenfry smiles, then looks behind her at a bulletin board. The office is quiet, and other than the fact that we're a little early, I can't see the reason for the wait.

"You ever been?" asks Mrs. Dr. Shelpenfry from behind her cubicle; I can only see her round head floating above the wall.

"Excuse me?"

"To the race? Have you ever been?" The roaring sounds of Indy cars now seem even closer.

"Oh yes. A few times, back in college. I don't know how they do it though."

She nods that detached noggin. "He'll be right out. He's on a teleconference with detectives in France." She smiles, clearly proud of her husband.

"Wow, that's impressive."

"Uh-huh, they've got a serial killer working the Bastille area again. There was the Beast of Bastille back in the 1990s that slit the throats of young women. He killed eight. They think this new one is a copycat killer. But he apparently is leaving behind very tiny, tiny dust balls on his victims. They're so little, you'd just think they were wool fibers or something, but George has analyzed them, and they're actually made up of a minuscule amount of potter's earth and cotton, as if you wiped your hands on your pants after, say, working in a greenhouse. You might think you'd cleaned yourself up, but these things still cling to you. They're about the size of a half grain of sand."

All of her talk has piqued our interest, and I stand up and walk to her counter, lean on it, while Browder asks if he can take her picture. She tells him sure and winks at me. "Our new daughter-in-law has a child with Down syndrome from a previous marriage." Browder snaps three quick photos before Dr. George Shelpenfry appears alongside his wife, who remains seated. "I was just telling Mr. Burke here about our new family," she tells him. He nods and smiles, extends his hand. I can tell now that the Shelpenfrys are good people. He introduces himself to Browder and agrees to have his photo taken as well.

He leads us down a narrow hallway to a large room that serves as both his office and the area where he analyzes material. An entire wall of microscopes and centrifuges, beakers and test tubes, laptops and computerized gadgets with glowing red digits divides the lab from the more mundane side, where stacks of manila folders and file cabinets sit dutifully near a large walnut desk. Posters mounted on the wall include one of the movie *Top Gun*, signed, and two of *Ghostbusters*, along with a series of old advertisements for cigarettes, one portraying a detective who's supposed to look like Sherlock Holmes, smoking a Chesterfield, two magnifying glasses floating aimlessly in front of him.

"Please, sit down," says our doctor. He remains standing and leans back against an onyx-topped table, the kind in high school biology class. A window is open, and the roar of the Indy cars as drivers compete for the pole position is louder back here. Dr. Shelpenfry makes no effort to close the window, just speaks up. "So, in your message you indicated you were writing a book about the Riley murders, is that correct?"

"Yes," I say, feeling a bit like we're in a courtroom.

"Mmm-huh." The doctor shuffles through a stack of papers behind him, puts on his glasses. "Very interesting," he says, reading. "The material found in her hair was unusually dated; that is, it was from what would be considered fossilized materials."

I feel like I can't breathe. Could it really be this easy? As far as I know, there's only one dinosaur pit being excavated in north-central Indiana. "Do you mean to say that the dust came from the Pipe Creek Sinkhole in Swayzee?" I sound as earnest as Browder in wanting to take the doctor's photo.

"Well, no, not exactly. Actually no, I'm not saying that at all. Certainly the fossilized dust could originate from a location similar to that, but you have to understand that, in terms of raw material, this dust could just as easily come from a limestone pit in Bloomington. I'd need months more of analysis to determine within a statistical certainty exactly where this dust came from. For instance, it's just as likely that someone who had been working with gravel at one of the local nurseries around Smallwood could have had traces of dust on them and transferred that to Mrs. Riley. The analysis as it stands now couldn't pinpoint whether the dust was from Pipe Creek, your local Home Depot, or a limestone pit." The doctor closes the file and looks directly at me. "Why? Why do you ask about Pipe Creek?"

"The killer, Rodney Finch, he as much as said the body of the Riley boy was buried at Pipe Creek, that there have been human bones found there."

"To my knowledge, there haven't even been ancient *Homo sapiens* bones found at Pipe Creek." I must look dejected, because he offers up some hope. "Listen, I'll have some time come fall to really delve back into this one," he says, pointing over his shoulder to the file. "If you want to come for another visit then, I'll be able to provide much more in the way of ruling out possible obtainment sites. In the meantime, I've got a sample from Pipe Creek. I can compare the dust collected from the woman's body to it."

"Great," I say, feeling more positive.

"But of course, that alone will take nine weeks."

Browder stands up, clutching the camera. "Can I take it now?" he asks the doctor. For the next ten minutes Dr. Shelpenfry allows Browder to shoot photos of him bent over a microscope, mixing a blue liquid in a beaker, and finally making a muscleman pose, which Browder calls "doing the wrestler man." The doctor looks completely comfortable hamming it up for the camera, which makes me admire him even more.

The three of us walk back out front to the Mrs., who's chewing gum and listening to the time trials on the radio. "You mustn't get frustrated, Mr. Burke," the doctor tells me. "These things are not resolved easily. Just last month we finally were able to link the sand granules found in the home of a murdered man in Wichita to a worker at a cement-mixing outfit in Kansas City. The case had stalled for over a decade even though everyone knew the men had been bloody enemies, but with the new evidence linking the man to the crime scene, the DA got a confession. You can't allow your thinking to become like our culture, everything fixed and tidied up by the end of thirty minutes, just before the commercials come on."

The Mrs. nods, and the doctor and I shake hands; Browder hugs them both. Suddenly, I really don't know what I was thinking here, and the realization strikes me hard, makes my face actually redden with embarrassment, the heat indicting me before the Shelpenfrys, as I mop my brow with a shirt-sleeve. I'm supposed to write the book with the evidence I have, leave the missing Riley boy up to law enforcement, but I had wanted my trip back home to mean something, redeem me, wash away all the shame, and deliver me a new man to my family, especially my daughter. It was silly to think I could do anything more than write words about what had already happened; I've never been able to impact the present, solve the future. There's a sinking cramp in my stomach, and I feel sweaty all over, colder.

The Shelpenfrys are benevolent as they usher us to the door and out into the mottled sunlight of the parking lot, the doctor patting Browder's back and the Mrs. telling me about the best little Italian restaurant in the city. The nearby Speedway is quiet now, and it's funny to look up in the sky and see off in the distance the storm from Smallwood making its way to Indy. I climb into the truck, and much fuss is made over Pascal. As I begin to back up, Dr. Shelpenfry says, "Remember, these things get resolved with patience. It's all about time."

I reverse the pickup into the street and wave back at the couple standing in the parking lot, arms around each other's back, smiling. I glance at them again in the rearview mirror, and they appear smaller. Like any family, if you stay in it long enough, the mystery will reveal itself.

We can't find the Italian restaurant and instead end up once again at a Cracker Barrel just off the 465 bypass. The Indianapolis skyline is barely visible against the thunderstorm looming heavy and nearly charcoal in the background. The rain hasn't started, but the air outside is laced with electricity, fast-food wrappers tumbling over the lot, little swirls of dust and grit whipping around the rocking chairs on the restaurant's porch. Browder is famished and eats without chewing much. My spirits are so low, I can't even nibble on the chicken sandwich I ordered.

"We're going back to Georgia, Browder. Once we're done here, we'll start out for home, but we don't have to hurry. We can visit Mammoth Cave in Kentucky and the Country Music Hall of Fame in Nashville. We could even hang out in Savannah for a day or two."

"What about Ike in the hospital?" says Browder, mouth full of mashed potatoes. He takes a big gulp of Coke and licks his lips.

"He'll be okay. Susana and the kids will make sure he's all right." I can feel my throat tighten, but Browder nods.

"Where am I gonna live when we get back to Georgia?" He looks at me with clear, dark eyes, his face pale in comparison.

"I don't know, Browder, but we'll figure something out." The dishes clink, and silverware scratches plates as the restaurant talks to me, the sounds breaking my heart. I feel I've failed, lost time, given up, backed down, screwed them over, accomplished little, and turned my back, twice.

Inside the truck again, I will myself not to watch as the Indiana landscape rushes by on Interstate 65: flat fields, red barns, and gray clouds, the worst of the storm still swirling over Indy. I stare straight ahead and press the gas pedal toward the floor, maneuvering in and out of lanes, the engine nearly squealing as I focus on getting out of the state. I don't answer the phone when I see it's a call from south Georgia, Cindy being the only person who would call, telling me Browder's case manager is putting a warrant out for my arrest, signing papers that will label me as some sort of kidnapper. I push on, now tailgating some, even to my own dismay, honking at those cars that refuse to get out of my way. Browder notices. "You okay?" he asks, and I only nod and fix my eyes tighter on the other vehicles in front. I can feel him watching me

as Pascal licks my hand, moans for me a little. I'm scared, and so are my dog
and my friend.

The sun is setting over the Ohio River, and if Browder were taking photos
any faster, the damn Nikon would snap and smoke, fizzle. The paddle wheel
on the *Belle of Louisville* riverboat is his subject matter now, his flash blinding
the other tourists. I watch the murky water churn below us, the wide deep
river speaking to me, calling out for something I can't quite decipher. My
mind whirls, and for some reason I see Dad's perverted headstone floating
on the water as a throng of bats dip and dive, gobbling up pests, living off the
death they create. The edges of the river seem impossible, distant and false. I
could dive in and let Browder photograph it, but something murmurs in my
ear, and I step away from the railing, take hold of Browder and lead him to
the buffet line. We eat, and I drink four beers, pale ale from Bluegrass Brewing. In a few hours, our little excursion on the riverboat will end, and I hate
to think of sleeping in the hotel downtown, but that's the plan. Tomorrow,
I tell myself, will be better. We'll be farther away, and I can begin thinking
through where we'll live. Of course, it doesn't need to be back in Georgia,
near our swamp, but it's like sitting in the same chair in a classroom; it's not
assigned, but you feel more secure when you're in it. For the next two hours,
Browder eats and I drink, and by the time we dock, I'm struggling to walk a
straight line.

As we file off the *Belle*, three young women with dates rumble behind us,
clearly wanting to pass us and get to the bars on Fourth Street. My vision is a
little wacky, fuzzy, and I stumble some, then fall back a little, grabbing on to
the chute rail and inadvertently falling into one of the girls, hands briefly on
her chest. I regain my balance, though her beau, wearing a blue suit jacket,
pushes me as I try to stand up. "Fucking perv!" he says, and for the life of
me I can't stop laughing, laughing right into his face, until he seems to scare
some, and the group rushes off ahead of us. One of them yells back at me,
"Loser!" Hanging on to the deboarding chute, I reach for Browder, who tells
me, "You're gonna get sick like Ike did."

Pascal greets us at the door of our Days Inn hotel room, and I stagger
directly to the phone and order two cheeseburgers just for him from room
service. When I tell the order taker the name is Pascal Burke, Browder laughs
out loud. Then he says, "Can I have one, too?" I can't believe he could eat
more after the buffet on the *Belle*, but I say into the phone, "Make that four

cheeseburgers and a six-pack of whatever you have handy."

Once the food arrives, my drunkenness needs two quick beers, guzzled down, or I'll fall asleep with a headache. We switch on the television as Pascal eats chunks of bun, meat, and cheese from Browder's hand; in the other, Browder clutches his own burger, and the sound of the two of them eating brings a quick smile to my face. It fades almost immediately as I flip past channels of obese people crying in some competition, and at least ten programs aimed at watching celebrities, voyeurism at its most impersonal. I hand the channel changer over to Browder, and he gladly takes it, aims for the television, and begins running through the same channels I just did.

"I'm going to take a shower," I tell him, grabbing my backpack and another beer. Once inside the bathroom, I actually catch myself leaning up against the closed door as if a killer were trying to get in. I unzip the backpack and rummage through it, find the memoir. I hold the book out in front of me and look at that title: *Leaving Smallwood.* The early acrid taste of vomit surges in my throat, but I swallow hard, down another half of a beer.

I sit down on the commode and open the book, looking for the short section near the end, in the chapter called "This Is How You Turn Your Back."

> The truck feels like a horse; it gallops or slows, trots and advances not so much under my physical command, as it does through my thoughts, the mental energy I'm giving this escape. Dad had grown up, worked and lived, and served time within a radius of no more than one hundred miles, and I can feel them incrementally shedding off me as the truck engine races, churning the wheels against this Indiana tarmac, this solid surface that deserves to be traveled. There are a hundred places from here to Bloomington where I can pull off, turn around, head back toward home, but the animal I'm riding in won't allow it, and for that I'm grateful, grateful that I have no control over what I'm doing.

In the morning, I find that I've somehow managed to climb into the tub to sleep. At first, I think the pile of confetti—and there's a huge mound of it on my chest and crotch—is from something Pascal has torn up, but then my pounding head recalls how, before I passed out, I'd sat in the tub and ripped each page from the book, tearing it into tiny pieces like a voided check, even chewing some of the pages up and using them as spitballs. They cling on the shower stall, as if a wasp were building a home. I crawl out of the tub, head so woozy it feels like the medulla is made of quivering plasma and sick light, but with a dead weight right in the center, a core of ache. I can barely whisk off the remaining pieces of torn pages that litter my clothes. In the hotel room, Pascal is awake, but Browder is curled up in the bed. My dog needs to go out; he thumps his tail and laps at my face when I bend to leash him, and it's all I can do to keep from puking. I shield my eyes in the parking lot and let Pascal sniff and do his business. When he wants to run back toward the hotel doors, galloping and tugging on his leash, I feel bad that I can't muster up the will to play with him.

Breakfast goes down sourly, the eggs and biscuits, like the *Belle* on the Ohio, roiling in the eddy, heavy over the deep, dark murk. We pack up and load everything into the truck. Browder pats my back. "You gonna be okay?" I nod, pat his back, too. "I won't take any pictures," he says. "I won't bug you." I get a quick hug. "No harmonica either," he adds, and we start out for the interstate, ready to leave Kentucky for Tennessee.

The storm from yesterday has cleared, and the bright sunlight bounces off the vehicles in front of us. I scrounge around the interior of the truck but can't find my sunglasses. The coffee in the holder is lukewarm when I bring it to my lips, and the first swallow almost comes right back up. I roll my window down all the way and let the fresh air blast over us. Pascal yaps loudly once, and Browder rubs the boy's ears. The traffic is lighter as we drive more slowly toward another state line. Three hours on Interstate 65 to Nashville seems both inconsequential and staggeringly impossible. I can't imagine what we'll do when we get back, and it dawns on me that neither Browder nor I have a home. His is closed down, and my apartment is likely rented out by now. We're orphans on the highway, lost-and-found items zooming along toward what? Our swamp? Maybe that's all we can shoot for, the swamp and the campground. We could camp for a couple of weeks, then I'd have to find a place to write the Riley book, but even that thought seems ridiculous now. Sooner or later I'll have to tell Michael the agent that I can't allow the memoir to be reissued. The thoughts make me even sicker to my stomach, and before I can really understand what's happening, my body is convulsing, and I aim the truck toward the next exit, but I can't make it and swerve onto the shoulder. The truck's tires crunch gravel as it slows, and I leap out. I lean on the tailgate and vomit until a car honks, Pascal barks, and my friend Browder plays a low improvised tune on his harmonica, something he just couldn't resist.

I stand up from bending almost completely over the tailgate. The sunshine and breeze seem to lift my spirits, and even though I can smell the stink of my own vomit, there's a scent of late spring in the air: flowers and warmth, the mown grass in the median where DOT workers mulch. My cell phone rings, and I don't even look, just hit the green button and put the thing to my ear. I can hear Susana nearly begging me to help. Kate is on the line, too, along with Mom. Dick hacks a booming cough in the background. I tell them to take me off speakerphone; I can't hear. Traffic rushing by blows hard against me, the truck, slightly rocking it. Browder and Pascal stare through the back window, both of them giving me concerned smiles. I shove a finger in my ear and listen to just Susana now.

She says Ike snuck into the hospital pharmacy and nabbed a bottle of hydrocodone and took them all. When they finally found him, he was out, pulse almost nil, slipping from this world into the next, his skin losing color, cooling. He hid under his bed. "Can you believe that, that he hid under the bed?" his wife asks me, her voice hoarse. Susana tells me this time to hurry. "Please come home. Your brother needs you."

I creep along the side of the truck as if it were the railing on the *Belle*, careful not to slip, fall overboard. When I'm back inside the truck, Browder says, "Told you you'd get sick like Ike."

"You sure were right," I tell him as I carefully back up on the shoulder and wait until the lane is clear, punch the gas pedal, and merge into southbound traffic. Once again, I push the truck to high speeds, but after we've traveled twenty miles or so, I slow, and slow some more, looking at the median for a worn place, where tire tracks already exist, created by others who've answered this same sort of call. We ease into the hollow of the grassy median, and it feels safe here, hidden, the other travelers zooming past us in both directions. All I have to do is give the truck some gas and point it toward where I came from. It's the easiest thing in the world to do, if you're not afraid to change course this late in the trip.

Chapter Twenty-Four

The meeting room is cold, air-conditioning blowing down on us all as we sit nervously in a semicircle, the moms and dads, daughters and sons, the siblings, and frightened friends, the loose singles. Some look like movie extras, too hip, eyebrows raised, thinking of a million other places they'd rather be than here. People twiddle their fingers, scratch at elbows and cheeks, give in to their anxious ticks, their mouths dry, audibly so when they whisper to the person in the seat next to them. They are trapped, trying to accept that the twelve steps to recovery can't be done alone. In fact, in Smallwood, Indiana, it can't even be done in privacy; the nameless facade and supposed secretive detox unit are useless ploys for anonymity. Since I got back two days ago, no fewer than a dozen people have stopped me on the street to tell me how sorry they were to hear about Ike's "situation." Our Midwestern euphemisms. Even Becca stopped by our booth at the wing café and told me to call her if we needed anything. "We can always miss our ballroom class if you guys need us to."

This group session is called "Co-Recovery for Family." I'm here to help Ike admit his life has become unmanageable. It's the first of many of these, and while they were able to pump his stomach and keep him alive, Ike's only been in individual therapy since the attempted suicide. Susana has seen him, but no one else. I'm staying at their house, and the kids ask about their father's treatment as if it were one of their school functions. "So we've got Dad's session tomorrow after school? I'll have to miss track, but I'll do a makeup with Coach Weidler."

I wish I were with Browder, who is out to eat with Dick and Mom, all the way up to Shipshewana—Amish Country. Other than his case manager threatening to call adult protective services in Indiana, not much came from all the notes I was supposed to log but didn't. Cindy took the time to create them for us. She left a voice mail saying, "Don't worry. I put the notes into the online system. Three weeks' worth. If you're asked, Browder and you are working on his social skills through photography, travel, and meeting new people. That should do it."

The clock ticks like it's defective, off beat and way too slow. People glance up at it, then at their cell phones. At least two of the older men in attendance make loud sighs, unaccustomed to waiting, but they check their silver wrist-watches. In the seats next to me, on my left and right, are brothers of a guy they call Randall. I've asked them twice if they'd like to switch seats with me so they can sit next to each other, but they act as if I'm suggesting space travel.

Finally, two counselors walk in, iPads in hand, and saunter to the front of the sterile room. If I could leap through the cinder block walls, I would, bust-ing out of the place.

"Okay, folks, thanks for being here today. As you know, your loved ones are in the very early stages of their sobriety, and this is a critical part of them starting off on the right foot. I realize some of you might be tired or skeptical of your loved one's ability to get clean, but let's try to give this our best ef-fort. In a few minutes, the eleven individuals in treatment here will enter the room and for the first time lay claim to their alcoholism. Today's session will be short, about an hour, and from this point forward you'll need to decide how much time and effort you'll give this process. Most of the patients in here now will be discharged in a month, which doesn't mean they'll be fixed. You've signed confidentiality forms. Please take those seriously, ethically and legally."

With that, the man motions for the younger woman counselor to bring in our clowns. The whole atmosphere does have a circus quality to it, not that it's insincere, but parading people in before their ashamed loved ones seems like something Barnum & Bailey might have tinkered with.

A door at the side of the room slowly creeps open, and the female coun-selor leans through the crack and speaks to the people waiting outside, which now gives me the impression of a child's school play. There's even nervous laughter, and for some reason I think it's a bit rehearsed. I can't imagine how Ike is handling it all, and I wonder how many of the people in this room will know Ike, know about our father and family, my book. It's a small town, but looking around the room a fourth time at the faces in the semicircle, I don't recognize anyone, except maybe a guy about my age, balding, a tattoo of a horse on his forearm, and a nose ring. He's too old to be sporting these things, but he looks familiar, maybe someone I went to school with or met during Dad's HomeBeam Wares sales jaunts.

The door opens fully now, and some in my group don't even bother to look up, having been through it all before, doubtful that this time will be any different. The room holds a collection of cologne and perfume smells, the Pine-Sol and warmed-up food from the cafeteria, the overriding stink of burnt microwave popcorn. It's enough to turn my stomach a little, since I'm nervous to catch that first glimpse of my brother, broken and beaten, at the end of his rope.

The first few people are your stereotypical drunks and addicts or both, their heads hung low, young, no older than twenty-five, long hair on the men, bobbed on the women. They are followed by a man and a woman holding hands and wearing matching IU basketball sweatshirts. Next, a line of gray-haired older men, all of whom have the sunburned faces of farmers or the wrinkled expressions of factory men. At the end of the line, two people straggle behind, one of them a heavyset woman with almost yellow hair and Ike, who is clear-eyed and healthier-looking than I would have thought for a guy who tried to off himself. He's wearing sweats though, and a T-shirt, slippers on his feet. He shuffles to his chair and smiles at someone across from him, someone like me from the outside. So he does know people who are here. For a while, it looks as though he won't scan the circle of folding chairs to see if I'm in attendance, but then, slowly, as if he's organizing files by memory, he trains his eyes on me, waves, and looks a little embarrassed. My heart aches, and I think I might break down right off the bat. I'd expected some tears, but not this, not my brother looking as vulnerable as a twelve-year-old, unsure of himself.

The male counselor begins again, telling the assembled group that each person will take their turn, tell their story, and admit they are powerless against their disease. Everyone is to remain quiet and listen, and no judging via sighing, rolling eyes, coughing, or the like.

First up is the woman with yellow hair. She stands, pulls down her gray sweat shirt, and begins talking. "I'm Denise. I'm an alcoholic."

"Welcome, Denise," mutters the group back to her. She nods and smiles, the look of utter loneliness in her brown eyes.

"I started drinking when I was ten. My uncle began molesting me at eight years old. My mom and dad were alcoholics, and I managed to raise a family as a functioning alcoholic. When I stopped drinking and smoking the first time, I gained almost eighty pounds, and my husband of thirty years left me and got married to a thirty-year-old girl that works in Kokomo at the parts plant." Denise stalls, seems lost. The female counselor mouths something, and Denise begins again. "Anyway, last fall I tried to kill myself in the garage with the car running. My neighbor found me though, and I've been in and out of treatment twice since then. If I don't make it this time, I'll be dead." Denise looks slightly to her left where Ike is sitting, and I can tell he's said something to her when she smiles. "I really want to get better," she says. Denise sits down, and the next person is called to witness.

I sit as still as I can, even though it feels like jittery moths are fluttering around my insides, nesting, burrowing. Two more people take their turns. One of the older men tries to explain his reasons for drinking, to which the male therapist says, "Reasons or excuses?" The older man tells him to screw himself and storms out of the room. No one comments or makes any reference to the scene.

The female counselor turns toward Ike. "Why don't you go next, Ike."

Ike stands up and looks around a bit, nods, and licks his lips. He's clean-shaven, hair combed. At first, it seems he won't be able to open his mouth, but then he looks over at me directly and holds my gaze.

"My name's Ike. I'm an alcoholic." They chant back to let him know he's welcome. "I started drinking seriously around age twenty-two, kind of late, I guess, considering the stories I've heard today." He smiles, and a couple of the others grin knowingly. "It started with just drinks after work to unwind, then my dad was arrested for being a peeping tom, and I guess I just started drinking to cope with the embarrassment."

My face burns red, and I can't look away from my brother. His lip is quivering now, and he's trying hard to keep it in. "My brother is here, and he wrote a memoir about our family. Maybe some of you were bored enough to read it." More laughter from the group. I feel the sting of not being the one in control of revealing our family's shame. Good for Ike. "Anyway, I've been hating him for a long time for doing that, and I guess also hating him for leaving town." Ike's tears drip from his eyes, and Denise reaches out her hand and holds his. From across the room, I can't see all that clearly now, tears thick in my eyes. Ike sucks in snot and air, sounding like a car wash vacuum sucking up pennies. I stand and start to walk toward him, but before I'm halfway across the floor, the male counselor stops me with his voice, as if talking to a pet.

"No. No. We don't allow reconciliation this early in the process. We're only addressing the first stage here. There'll be plenty of time for you and your brother to make amends as his treatment progresses. You both will have to process many more emotions before getting to forgive." Frozen in mid-step, I look to the counselor like a good dog. Anywhere else and this would be a humiliating experience, but here, I have to confess, it feels part of the norm, and I do as I'm told and return to my chair.

"Thank you, Ike," says the female counselor to my brother. "You may sit down now."

For the remainder of the session, we listen to everyone else's spiel of use and abuse. One of the older men, with a walrus mustache and wearing, unbelievably, a pince-nez, complete with a chain and ear hook, bellows like a sailor. His story is brief but poignant. "I'm a drunk, have been since the seventies. I'll die a drunk. The thing is, my only child is getting married next month, and I'd like to be sober for it. After that, I don't care what happens to me."

When he sits back down, even the counselors are at a loss of how to move the group forward, but eventually, after some mumbling between them, the female counselor speaks. "You all have ten minutes to visit with your focus person." The man with the walrus mustache sits alone, until another loner, a younger man with a goatee like a big furry cone, approaches and sits down with him.

I walk over to Ike, and we pull two chairs together near one of the concrete posts that hold up the place.

"Thanks for coming," says Ike, and the sight of his pathetic little slippers makes it hard for me to enunciate.

"No problem. Smallwood in the late spring is a lovely place."

"Right," says Ike.

"I was being serious."

"Oh," he says, running his hand through his hair. His eyes are bleary, but he appears more honestly alert than ever. "So how'd the dust analysis turn out? You gonna solve the Riley boy's disappearance and write a best seller about it?"

"Not likely. It'll take nine weeks to process the material enough to see where the dust really came from." Ike nods. "But I'm working on a newspaper piece, something that might get published if the dust analysis is useful."

"How's Brow doing? I heard he and Susana are at it again with photography."

"Good. We're right back up in the attic like stowaways."

"Listen," says Ike, hunching over in his chair, leaning toward me. "It's going to be a rough go here for a while. I need you to make sure the kids and Susana are okay. I mean, I know you're there, but I need to know you're really looking out for them. Can you give me your word?"

"Words are all I've got. And yes, you have my word. I'll look out for them."

Ike leans back, suddenly looks tired as he surveys the room. "Maybe these people will vote for me," he says, and grins.

"Not a bad constituency if you ask me."

"You know, there'll be a couple sessions of family therapy, too. I'd like for you to be here for that. I know it's a lot to ask, but if I don't deal with . . ."

"I'll be here."

"It'll include the kids and Susana, Mom and probably Dick. I've asked Susana to invite Kate and Wendy, too." Ike sees me flinch. "I know you'd rather not get Wendy involved, but I've had a lot of time to think, and maybe this is just what we needed, what you and Wendy needed."

"What's that?"

"An excuse to be angry."

"Oh, I think she's got that all covered. I'm her excuse."

"I meant for you to be angry, too. Writing a book is one thing, but really letting yourself feel the hatred he's left us with is another."

"I don't have any hatred for him."

Ike stands up, just as they are telling us to file out of the room, visiting time is over. "Bullshit," he says calmly to me and pats my face. "You ruined your own life because of him. I'd think that would make a guy pretty pissed off." Ike's hand gently pats my face one more time, then he turns and shuffles away, back to his bed, his room. Back to his stay.

Chapter Twenty-Five

As the spring turns warmer, edging into full summer, I spend my days at detox and my nights writing the newspaper feature. The story will be timely, says the editor at the *Indianapolis Star*. Along with new DNA evidence exonerating people on death row, the courts and the public alike are interested in microanalysis, and Dr. Shelpenfry is among the top forensic researchers working in the field. In fact, the editor wants me to use the Riley case to profile Dr. Shelpenfry, not the other way around, but either way, the case will get new attention, maybe even get picked up by the New York Times News Service, something my agent Michael calls "simultaneous tipping points." He was understanding about my not wanting the reprint of the memoir, but told me I might end up regretting it. Still, he believes in me, he says, adding that as a writer I'll have to finally find out what I'm willing to do. Now, after two weeks of the same daily schedule, me showing up at the detox center, sometimes with Susana, other times alone, we have a preconference for our family therapy session.

Mom has indeed brought along Dick, who nods and shakes hands and towers over us all. The male counselor from the group sessions makes us wait in a conference room. Susana is there, too, and just when I think it's the counselor finally entering the room, the door opens and Kate walks in. She goes directly to Susana and hugs her, and they stay in the embrace for longer than Dick or Mom or I can ignore. It's touching that after all these years, they've truly become sisters. Kate hugs Mom, shakes Dick's hand, and gives me a tight hug and kiss. She, too, sits down at the conference table, and we make small talk that is so painful, I think my ears will bleed. Browder is at home, Susana tells me, watching a mob-movie marathon on cable, snapping photos of himself in a fedora she bought him at a flea market on the way home from one of their reservoir trips.

I'm interrupted in the middle of a story about the time Browder insisted on talking in a high-pitched Joe Pesci voice for two weeks straight. The male counselor comes in and smiles. "Hello, everyone. Ike will join us in a few minutes. I wanted to lay out what to expect tomorrow during your family therapy." He seems to check something off on a clipboard. "How about we go around the room and say who we are and how we are involved in Ike's life."

Mom looks at me as if someone had asked her a *Jeopardy!* question about sixteenth-century poet John Donne. "He wants us to introduce ourselves," I say to her. She's not used to therapy speak, and Dick looks scared he'll mess up right off the bat. I decide to introduce all three of us. "I'm Gabe. We've met in group. I'm Ike's brother, and this is our mom and her friend Dick."

"I assume they have voices themselves?" asks the therapist, without a trace of arrogance, sounding more factual and inquisitive than anything.

Still, I really want to flip him off, but I nod. "Right, I just thought I could expedite things." The counselor makes a note.

Kate introduces herself, and Susana smiles at the counselor and gives a tiny wave and then clutches her shoulders as if she's cold. He tells her it's okay, and I realize they've likely had long, drawn-out sessions about our family.

"Okay, folks. Tomorrow will be an hour-long session. The goal for these family therapies is to start Ike and all of you down a path of structured insight. For two weeks now, Ike has been engaged in finding out what has driven him to drink and act on his character flaws. He's found out a great deal about himself, I must say." I force myself not to speak up and ask the therapist who's speaking for whom now. He continues. "But let me ask him to come in. He's prepared something, and as is customary, this is the patient's opportunity to set the stage for what will be the most grueling part of the treatment. Please listen and don't interrupt."

He stands up and goes to the door, opens it a crack, mumbles, waits, and looks back at us as if he's about to perform the big magician's reveal. Some of us pick cuticles and pretend to polish smudges from the conference room tabletop. Ike enters and smiles at all of us. He immediately looks to his wife, mouths what I think is "I love you." I'm uncomfortable on multiple levels.

Like a schoolboy giving a book report, Ike clears his voice and reads from a sheet of lined yellow paper.

"Thank you all for being here today and for supporting me in my sobriety. I know it can come as a shock to hear me like this. After years of me being sarcastic, deflective, and sometimes cruel, I realize now that I'm sober and feeling a wave of emotions. I might appear to be overly engaged, maybe even sappy. I'm sorry for that. And it's okay to be uncomfortable in this process. I was and still am somewhat uncomfortable. My goal is to try to live honestly though, and treat each of you with love, patience, forgiveness, and respect, of course hoping you'll be able to do the same with me. Since the children of this family are old enough to participate in the treatment, I hope that," Ike now looks up to Kate and me, "you Kate, and you Gabe, will allow Wendy to be a part of this. Susana and I've urged our kids to be involved. If I've found out anything, it's that my alcoholism isn't just mine. It's part of a family dynamic that we've all allowed to take root without attention. As Burkes we are often defensive, secretive, scared, and angry. This may sound strange coming from me, but I truly wish Dad were still alive. I have a lot of questions for him, information I'd like to know, and I think finally, at least on some level, I could start the process of forgiving him. I'd also like to understand more about his parents, since they died before we were old enough to really know them. I think they, too, probably had addictions or serious mental issues or both." Ike is nearly out of breath, and Mom seems like she's holding hers.

"Anyway, thank you again for being patient with me. I love you." Ike sits down, and the therapist takes over once again.

"Any questions for Ike?" My mouth is dry and I do feel strange, what with Ike so freely talking about himself, his love, our family, but I have to endure, make room.

I think Dick is the most amazed by the fact that he's the one to speak up first. "That's nice what you said there, Ike. I sure hope this place and what you guys do here will help. I've become pretty attached to your mother, and I think all of us could use a good airing out. People make mistakes." He hugs Mom, who appears not only to be holding her breath, but also to be seized in a permanent slouched position. Still, she manages a weak, tired grin.

Kate and Susana take turns talking, giving Ike encouragement, tempered with doses of reality, phrases like "it won't happen overnight" and "we're all in this together." I don't disagree, and at times it's hard to tell the two of them apart by just their voices and what they are saying. Finally, it's clear that I'm supposed to offer up something, too, but I'm drawing a blank. When the therapist asks if I have anything to say, I shake my head no.

"Gabe, if I may," says the therapist, "I would offer you a bit of insight. You were quick to speak for others when we started, and it's clear to me that your role in this family is to control what is known about them. Your book is a clear example of that need. I'm not judging that, but I think if you're going to be of assistance to Ike, you might want to think your role over." This time, I can't resist a hand gesture, and when I do slowly flip him the bird, Ike frowns, and Mom is the one to smile, letting out a nice big healthy breath in the process.

"I'm sorry," I say, and Ike smiles, while the therapist writes something else down.

The desk in the attic has started to wobble. I try hard to focus, write an introductory paragraph about the dust analysis, leaving room to insert the findings, space too for explaining them. I try to make the logical case regarding an additional killer by laying out facts, the missing body being the strongest evidence. Susana is out with the kids, a dinner to help explain tomorrow, how the family therapy works, and what to expect. Kate assured me after the meeting with the therapist that she'd talk with Wendy. I offered to help, but we both smiled at the suggestion. Kate told me, "Just get ready, Gabe. Your daughter has her own way with words. They don't spill out onto a page much, but her mind is fast and her mouth can be faster. Then again, she might just decide to sit there like a mouse. I prefer when she talks."

I close the laptop and turn around in the chair. "You wanna get outta here?" I ask Browder. He nods with glee and grabs his camera. Pascal jumps up and turns a circle, barks.

The open road. As the day cools, the air feels luxurious, the wind blowing into the truck, smelling of clover. My arm is warmed, hanging outside the window. We have the radio turned up, Tom Petty blaring. The fields now have taller corn in them, green and sturdy. An orange horizon burns behind barns that look like toys, the ripeness of the land giving me hope. I can take everything I deserve tomorrow. I can write an investigative newspaper article that will make a difference, reopen the Riley case.

"Is it like a swamp though?" asks Browder as the song finishes and some commercial comes on for a monster truck bash in Indy. I turn the volume down. Pascal stares straight ahead as if he can't take his eyes from the road or we'll wreck.

"Kind of, I guess. It's big, but there's no water. Thirty thousand years ago there was water, but now it's just mined for limestone. Remember the boy with the kite? Well, it's in that town. We passed through it before."

"So it has bones?"

"Right, dust and bones. Everything's ancient."

"It's all older than dirt," says Browder, and we laugh, park the truck, and hop out, Pascal twirling, more energetic and bright-eyed than he's been since we first arrived in Indiana.

We walk along a worn path, white dust puffing up around our feet, and I wonder if this is the dust. Lately, all my mind seems to cling to is that word: DUST. It's as if the powdery white substance has actually entered my head, covering my brain.

There's a large placard at the entrance, and we stop and look. Pictures of strange fish and segmented rhinos are displayed on the exhibit, with impossible dates, 1.6 million years ago. Browder snaps a photo as Pascal pees on the posts. The sign reads: "In the Silurian Period, what is now Indiana and the interior of North America was located south of the equator and enjoyed warm tropical weather."

Things percolate through limestone, coal seams form, and entire continents drift over the massive blue waters. Swamps and forests emerge, reefs climb toward an ever-distant surface, and the primordial muck gives way to life. After I finish reading the sign, everything seems so small and insignificant, yet so necessary. If enormous ferns hadn't been abundant in swamps and left their carbon behind, we'd never have had the coal deposits that we use today to rumble through the world. Rodney Finch would never have had a vehicle to drive to the Rileys' and murder them all. Without fuel, what would our dad have been? I turn to follow Pascal and Browder, my mind mired in the details of being alive in this specific place, this specific time.

As we descend a fallow escarpment, a warm wind engulfs us, and a firm sense of peace comes over me. Life has been all around us for all time, and there's a comfort in knowing that maybe the best parts of all of us live on, leave traces, perhaps even create what follows. I help Browder, escort him, his bad leg dragging, kicking up dust.

At the base of the sinkhole, where we stand along a fenced-off area, a deep trench as serious as a canyon, Browder asks me for the binoculars. I take them from around my neck and hand them to him. He looks out over the gravel and rocks, the sod hanging along a precarious ridge. He scans and scans, stops and does it all over again, the wind shuddering the leaves of a lone white sycamore at our side. The sun slips down the sky, and it grows dimmer as I pet Pascal and listen to the crickets. Finally, Browder hands the binoculars back to me, his eyes widened, face full of anticipation. "There's so much out there to see," he says. We stand there together before the massive opening in the earth, the warmth pulsing around us, and I want to be able to see it, too. Browder smiles at me, the last of the sunshine glistening in his eyes, dancing off his hair, as he gives me the thumbs-up. I put my arm around him, and we walk with Pascal up the steep incline toward the truck. Maybe looking and watching can lead to seeing. Maybe you can return without making things worse. I pray for these things to be true, as Browder plays a six-note blues riff. I ask him how he's managed it. "Your family taught me. Susana, I mean." He plays the six notes over and over, and by the time we're back to the truck, it's dusk. When I start the engine, the three of us together in a seat, more than anything, I hope that tomorrow I'll be worthy of the call home.

A NOTE TO PARENTS

When your children are ready to "step into reading," giving them the right books is as crucial as giving them the right food to eat. **Step into Reading Books** present exciting stories and information reinforced with lively, colorful illustrations that make learning to read fun, satisfying, and worthwhile. They are priced so that acquiring an entire library of them is affordable. And they are beginning readers with a difference—they're written on five levels.

Early Step into Reading Books are designed for brand-new readers, with large type and only one or two lines of very simple text per page. **Step 1 Books** feature the same easy-to-read type as the Early Step into Reading Books, but with more words per page. **Step 2 Books** are both longer and slightly more difficult, while **Step 3 Books** introduce readers to paragraphs and fully developed plot lines. **Step 4 Books** offer exciting nonfiction for the increasingly independent reader.

The grade levels assigned to the five steps—preschool through kindergarten for the Early Books, preschool through grade 1 for Step 1, grades 1 through 3 for Step 2, grades 2 through 3 for Step 3, and grades 2 through 4 for Step 4—are intended only as guides. Some children move through all five steps very rapidly; others climb the steps over a period of several years. Either way, these books will help your child "step into reading" in style!

For my brother-in-law,
Doug,
who introduced me to Bruno
–F.W.

To Mom and Dad
–B.S.

www.randomhouse.com/kids

Library of Congress Cataloging-in-Publication Data
Wolff, Ferida. Watch out for bears! / by Ferida Wolff ; illustrated by Brad Sneed.
p. cm. — (Step into reading. A step 2 book)
SUMMARY: Henry and Bruno the bear become friends and they share Henry's honey, Henry's house, and
a camping trip. ISBN 0-679-88761-X (pbk.). — ISBN 0-679-98761-4 (lib. bdg.) [1. Bears–Fiction.
2. Friendship — Fiction.] I. Sneed, Brad, ill. II. Title. III. Series: Step into reading. Step 2 book.
PZ7.W82124Wat 1999 [E]–dc21 97-21419

Printed in the United States of America 10 9 8 7 6 5 4 3 2 1

STEP INTO READING is a registered trademark of Random House, Inc.

Step into Reading®

Watch Out for BEARS!

The Adventures of Henry and Bruno

By Ferida Wolff • Illustrated by Brad Sneed

A Step 2 Book

Random House 🏠 New York

Chapter 1
Honey for Bruno

Henry loved honey.

He put honey on his waffles.

He put honey on his pancakes.

He put honey on his toast.

When his honey jar was empty,

he went to town to get more.

The road to town
was long and bumpy.
Henry said,
"If I had bees,
I wouldn't have to go to town."

So he set up a hive in the meadow
near his garden.
"Now I will have honey
whenever I want it," he said.

One day
Henry saw something move
in the meadow.
It was big and dark.
Each day the big, dark something
came a little closer.
Henry *knew* it was a bear—
a big, hairy bear.

Henry was worried about his honey.

All day long he kept watch.

Once, he heard something

in the bushes.

Once, he saw something

by the woodpile.

Henry grabbed a broomstick.

"No bear is going to get

this honey!" he said.

Henry slept on the porch

instead of in his bed.

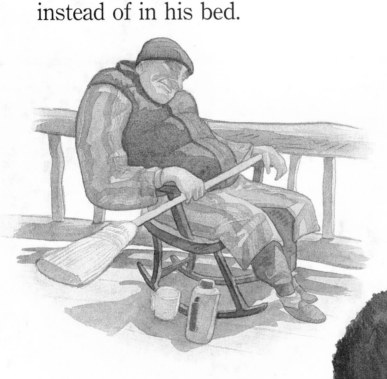

In the morning

the bear wasn't in the bushes.

It wasn't by the woodpile.

It was face to face with Henry!

Henry picked up the broomstick.

"There's no need for that,"

said the bear.

"Who are you?" asked Henry.

"I'm Bruno. Pleased to meet you,"

said the bear.

Henry remembered his honey.

He rushed over to the hive.

"I didn't take your honey,"

said Bruno.

"What kind of bear

do you think I am?"

"A honey-loving bear,"

said Henry.

"That's true," said Bruno.

"But I wouldn't touch a drop

of that honey without being asked."

Bruno smiled and said,

"Are you asking?"

"No," said Henry.

Bruno moved closer to the hive.

"Honey tastes better

on waffles, anyway," Bruno said.

"It's good on toast, too."

Henry began to get hungry.

Bruno wiggled the hive a little.

The bees buzzed.

One angry bee came out.

"Leave that hive alone,"

said Henry.

"Whatever you say," said Bruno.

He bumped the hive

as he turned away.

Many angry bees came out.

They swarmed around Henry.

"*Shoo,*" said Henry.

He waved his broomstick.

The broomstick smacked

against the hive.

"Oh, no!" Henry cried.

"There goes my honey."

Bruno stretched out his arm.

He caught the hive

in his big, hairy paw.

"You saved my honey," said Henry.

"So I did," said Bruno.

"Well, I guess I'll be going,"

Bruno said.

"Hey, Bruno. I'm asking,"

said Henry.

"How do you like your pancakes?"

Bruno followed Henry inside.

"With honey on top," said Bruno.

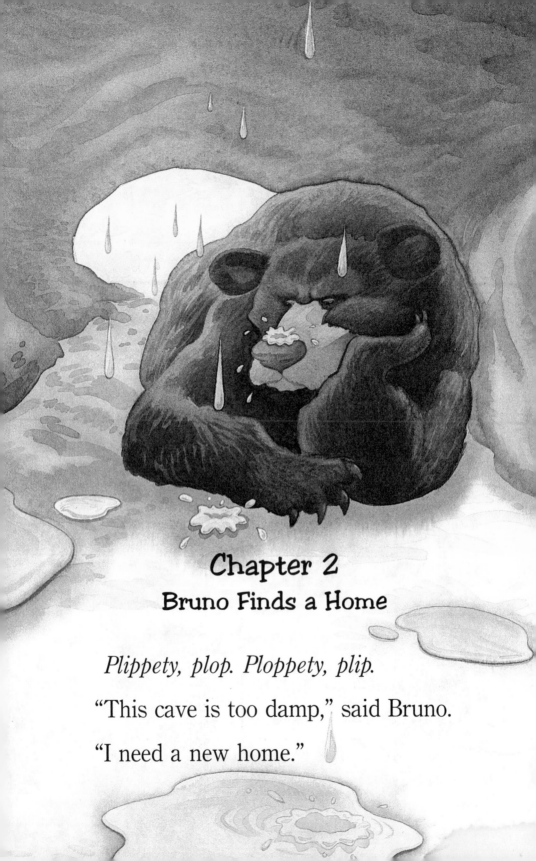

Chapter 2
Bruno Finds a Home

Plippety, plop. Ploppety, plip.

"This cave is too damp," said Bruno.

"I need a new home."

He tramped up the hill.

Henry was weeding his garden.

"What's new, Bruno?" he said.

"My cave leaks," said Bruno.

"I have to move."

Henry brushed off his hands.

"I'll help you find a new home,"
he said.

In the forest they noticed
a hollow tree trunk.
"How about this, Bruno?"
asked Henry.
Bruno squeezed into the tree.
He couldn't sit down.
He couldn't turn around.
"No good," he said.
"I need a big house
like yours, Henry."

They discovered a cave.

"This cave is big," said Henry.

Bruno went into the cave

and came running out.

"Bats," he said.

"I can't live in a dirty bat cave.

I want a clean house

like yours, Henry."

Deeper in the forest
they found an old cabin.
"It's too plain," said Bruno.
"I want a house with a front porch
like yours, Henry."

Bruno sat on an old log and sighed.

"I wonder if I will *ever* find

   the right place to live."

"Let's see," Henry said.

"You want a big, clean, dry house

   with a porch."

"Yes," said Bruno.

"Then I know just the place,"

   said Henry.

They walked through the forest
until they came to a meadow.

They walked through the meadow
until they came to a garden.

They walked through the garden
until they came to a house.

"This is *your* house, Henry,"

said Bruno.

"Yes," said Henry.

"My house is dry.

It is clean.

It has a front porch.

And it is big—

big enough for two."

"Would you like to come

live with me, Bruno?"

Bruno gave Henry a bear hug.

"Your house *does* have everything

I want," he said.

"And it has one thing more."

"What is that?" asked Henry.

"Your house has a friend,"

said Bruno.

Chapter 3
Watch Out for Bears

Henry was almost all packed.

"Where are you going, Henry?"

Bruno asked.

"Camping," said Henry.

"You mean you'll sleep

and eat outdoors?"

"Yes," said Henry.

"And you'll swim and catch fish?"

"Right," Henry said.

"I used to do that," said Bruno.

"I think I'll go along
  for old times' sake."

Off they went into the forest.

Bruno knew the best trails

from his cave bear days.

They hiked and ate gorp—

*g*ood *o*ld *r*aisins and *p*eanuts.

After a while they came

to a stream.

"Let's camp here," said Henry.

They set up the tent.

Then they ate lunch.

Bruno patted his full tummy.

"I love camping," he said.

Henry put the rest of the food
into a canvas bag.
He tied a rope to each end.
"Tie that rope to a branch, Bruno,"
said Henry.

"I'll tie this rope here."
The bag hung high in the air.
"Why did we do that, Henry?"
Bruno asked.

"We have to watch out for bears,"
said Henry.
"A bear might eat our food
if we leave it on the ground."
Bruno agreed.
He didn't want *any* old bear
eating their food.

"Want to swim?" asked Henry.

Bruno raced Henry into the water.

They played water tag.

They floated on their backs

and pretended to be whales.

"Hey, look at all the fish,"

Henry said.

"I'll get my fishing rod."

"Don't bother," said Bruno.

"I will teach you to fish

like a bear."

He scooped a fish from the water.

Henry tried it Bruno's way,

but all he got was wet.

Bruno scooped out more fish.

"You caught the fish,

so I'll make dinner," said Henry.

The fish were delicious!

Bruno thought about the bag of food.

"Do you think that bag is
sturdy enough, Henry?" he said.

"Bears are strong, you know."

"The bag is strong, too,"
said Henry.

Soon the stars came out.

Henry pointed to the North Star.

Bruno found the Great Bear.

Henry stretched.

"I'm ready for bed," he said.

"Me too," said Bruno.

Henry fell asleep right away.

But Bruno was wide awake.

Every sound made him think
of bears.

Was their food safe?

He had to check.

Bruno lowered the bag.

He looked inside.

Everything was there.

The chocolate energy bars smelled

good through their wrappers.

He ate one before he tied the bag

to the tree again.

But Bruno still couldn't sleep.

What if a bear was there now?

He shuffled past Henry

for another look.

No bears.

But all that food made Bruno's

stomach growl.

"Maybe I'll just have a little snack,"
he thought.

Bruno had a sandwich and juice.

He ate the last apple

and the rest of the gorp.

Bruno's stomach was full.

His eyelids felt heavy.

Bruno had no trouble

falling asleep in the tent now.

Henry awoke with the sun.

"Bruno, get up," Henry said.

"It's time for breakfast."

There were only empty boxes

and torn wrappers in the bag.

"What happened?" Henry said.

Bruno poked his sleepy head out.

"Bad news, Henry," he said.

"A bear ate our food, after all."

Bruno went back to sleep.

Henry began to clean up.

"Next time I will only watch out

for *one* bear," said Henry.